HOW TO LOSE A CLIENT

How to Lose a Client

A Kate Williams Mystery

Becky A. Bartness

iUniverse, Inc.

New York   Bloomington

How to Lose a Client
Subtitle: A Kate Williams Mystery

This is a work of fiction. All of the characters, names, incidents, organizations, and dialogue in this novel are either the products of the author's imagination or are used fictitiously.

iUniverse books may be ordered through booksellers or by contacting:

iUniverse
1663 Liberty Drive
Bloomington, IN 47403
www.iuniverse.com
1-800-Authors (1-800-288-4677)

ISBN: 978-1-4401-7748-4 (sc)
ISBN: 978-1-4401-9116-9 (ebook)

Printed in the United States of America

iUniverse rev. date: 11/24/2009

CHAPTER ONE

▼

I watched as the men from Snappy Signage twisted in the first screw holding the new sign above the door. It read CAITLIN WILLIAMS, ATTORNEY AT LAW, and it looked good. I am the Caitlin Williams to whom the sign refers, although everyone calls me Kate, and that's generally how I introduce myself. I'd practiced criminal law in Chicago for fourteen years before moving to Phoenix. An enlightening experience with human smuggling and murder at a dude ranch in southern Arizona prompted my decision to move. "Human smuggling" and "murder" are seldom used in the same sentence with "enlightening," but in my case, the events at the dude ranch reminded me that life is short—and for some people, it's very short, so if I wanted to do something other than work nonstop, I'd better get busy diversifying my day planner entries. I returned to Arizona and gave up my visitor status, becoming a full-time resident of Phoenix with every intention of semiretiring, which in lawyer talk means I wanted to cut back from eighty to sixty hours of work a week.

Initially, I took a job as a prosecutor in the county attorney's office. Unfortunately, things didn't work out as well as I'd hoped. I set in motion events that resulted in the arrest of my boss, the county attorney, and his second in command, as well as the sheriff and several members of the sheriff's department. After the dust settled, I decided I wasn't prosecutorial material. It was time for me to move on.

I toyed with the idea of joining an established group practice, but my friend Joyce, who was a partner in a local firm with three hundred-plus attorneys, reminded me of my first job as an associate at a well-known Chicago law firm … and my difficulty complying with the petty demands of bureaucracy, as well as my complete inability to play firm politics, all of which were well-documented in my personnel file, which, to this day, that firm uses as a training tool along the lines of a not-to-do list. Looking back on it, you could say my previous law firm experience was comparable to that of a French Resistance fighter in World War II, if you substituted alternating periods of verbal hostility and passive aggression for all the bombing and shooting.

Finding a job outside the legal profession was another possibility, but I am self-aware enough to realize that my only job skill is to argue about everything, which is a difficult talent to put to use outside the law or politics, and I had *no* interest in politics. I could stretch the truth and maybe omit part of the facts, but outright lying? Not me.

So I started my own practice, specializing, of course, in criminal defense, and found a three-bedroom 1920s bungalow in downtown Phoenix to serve as my office. The bungalow is one of those houses in the middle of a high-rise office district that makes you wonder how it survived the onslaught of commercial development: Was the owner a holdout valuing the ancestral home over profit? Was there a toxic waste dump in the cellar? Was it the site of an infamous murder, and no one wanted to deal with the negative karma? I couldn't find any records showing that a murder occurred in my little bungalow; it didn't have a cellar; and I could afford the price, so I bought it, the last of these reasons being the clincher.

Converting the residence into office space was more complicated. I hired the World's Slowest Contractor, a.k.a. Stu Nepalitano, and after three months of sporadic construction, he had only finished the reception area and waiting room.

My office used to be the master bedroom, and it has its own bathroom, which doesn't sound so bad, except the bathroom consists of a toilet, a rust-stained sink, and a shower so small you need to step outside the stall to turn around. The World's Slowest Contractor removed the old bathroom door and hadn't gotten around to replacing it, so I put up a shower curtain as a temporary fix, but whenever someone opens my office door, a draft blows the curtain sideways, so it's useless for privacy purposes. The best thing Stu has to recommend him is that he's cheap, and when he finally does get something done, the results are usually pretty good. I say *usually* because there have been a few notable exceptions.

The other two bedrooms are used as offices by M.J. Polowski, my paralegal, and Marcus John Martinez-O'Reilly Ramirez, my investigator, whom everyone calls "Sam," for a reason nobody has yet to explain to my satisfaction. Both M.J. and Sam had worked for me at the county attorney's office and accepted my invitation to join me in private practice, despite my promise of low pay and long hours. M.J. is in her midforties and sports various piercings and tattoos. Her fashion choices are difficult to categorize, but she's partial to tight short skirts, T-shirts emblazoned with the names of rock bands or pictures of skulls or both, and Doc Martens. Her hair color is seasonal. Today it was platinum blond with red stripes because it was getting close to Christmas.

Sam is tall, thin, and sartorially elegant. He favors Armani shirts and suits, Hermes ties, and Gucci shoes. Sam recently expanded his wardrobe to include several pairs of expensive high heels after meeting Cal, a cross-dressing neighbor of mine. Sam only wears his heels inside the office because he says he doesn't want to go to the bother of altering all his trousers to "pump length." Therefore, the heels have yet to make a public appearance. I have a suspicion Sam will eventually bag his trousers in favor of skirts and dresses. I have no problem with that. I figure Sam's taste in women's clothes will be as good, if not better, than his taste in men's clothes, and although he and I are not exactly the same size, we're close enough that I could borrow some of his blouses and jackets.

The final member of my staff is Beth Portucci, secretary-receptionist-administrator extraordinaire. Beth also came over from the county attorney's office. She'd been secretary to five consecutive county attorneys, all of whom were difficult to work for because of various personality quirks ranging from pathological paranoia to messianic delusions. Stan Rantwist, my ex-boss, was the proverbial straw that broke the camel's back. She ended up tackling him, holding him down in a hammerlock, and then repeatedly slamming his head into the floor. Since he was just about to shoot me at the time, the authorities let it slide.

Beth's mother was Italian, and her dad was Kenyan. She looks and sounds like a sweet middle-aged grandmother, but she is tough as hell. Most importantly, she makes great cookies, and cookies are one of my passions. The small kitchen in the back of our office was equipped with an ancient but operable oven, and whenever Beth was irritated with life, baking cookies was her coping strategy. I worried a little that during the past month, Beth had produced a couple of dozen cookies per day, but the benefits outweighed my concerns.

Now all I had to do was find some clients. My friend Joyce had already referred a few cases to me, but I needed to find a way to attract a steady flow of work. Attorneys are by no means a scarce resource in Phoenix, and it's tough for someone new in town to compete against long-established, well-known firms. It sounds mean, but sometimes I wished some of the top, older practitioners in town would retire or die off and give the rest of us a chance.

Snappy Signage finished screwing the sign in place, and M.J., Sam, and Beth joined me outside to check out the results.

Beth commented, "Looks good. Looks professional. Like we know what we're doing."

"We *do* know what we're doing," I retorted.

Beth looked at M.J. and Sam and rolled her eyes. "Geez. A bit sensitive today, aren't you? I meant it as a joke. Tell you what. Why don't you take the rest of the day off and have some fun? Starting up a law firm is hard, and on top of that, you've been supervising the redo of this place nonstop. Get away from here for a while. God knows Stu's not going to be doing much of anything today, it being a workday for him and all, so you won't miss a thing."

"Yes," Sam chimed in. "Take some time off. I know! Get your roots touched up."

I had to admit that my hair color did need some help. I'd noticed it this morning in my bathroom mirror. My natural dark blond (okay, brown) color had grown out a good two inches. Still, I rationalized that if only Sam had noticed, it couldn't be that bad. Sam was, after all, a perfectionist when it came to hair and fashion.

"Yeah," agreed M.J. "You look like a Yorkshire terrier."

This from a woman whose coiffure looked like a peppermint bonbon (which, sadly, was likely the look she was going for).

"Fine," I said. "I know when I'm not wanted. I'll get out of your lives for the afternoon." By this time, I actually thought it was a good idea, but I saw no reason to pass up an opportunity to lay a guilt trip on my staff. "But if Stu comes by, do not, repeat, do *not* let him paint *anything* without my prior approval," I added sternly.

The latter caution related to an unfortunate incident about a week ago. While I was attending a court hearing, Stu decided to paint the waiting room walls black. Seemingly, he reasoned that since judges wore black, black was a "lawyer color"; ergo, black walls would bring a serious, professional tone to the office. Instead, they made the waiting room look like a satanic temple, which, lawyer-like or not, was disturbing.

I went into my office and called my usual colorist, Michele, to see if she had any room for my roots that afternoon. While she did not, she said if I came over right away, she could get me in with another colorist who was, she assured me, as good as she. I grabbed my purse, trotted out to the driveway—waving good-bye to my staff on the way—and got into my little Honda hybrid. The Honda was a far cry from the Porsche I'd driven in Chicago, but I was self-righteously proud of my eco-friendly little car.

Even though Stranded, my hair salon, was only about a mile away, I drove over the speed limit as long as traffic allowed because Phoenix traffic is unpredictable, especially at this time of year, when all the snowbirds headed to Arizona for the winter. Sure enough, as soon as I pulled off the side street and onto Camelback Road, I got stuck behind a huge sedan with Minnesota plates. From behind, only the driver's knuckles, clutching a steering wheel the size of a ship's wheel, were visible. The traffic coming from behind sped around us in a constant flow and prevented me from pulling into the adjacent lane to pass. By the time I pulled into the parking lot of Stranded, my blood pressure was elevated to the point where an aneurysm was a real possibility

Michele met me at the door and hurriedly introduced me to Christopher, a short Hispanic man with a blond-tipped Mohawk. In retrospect, the blond tips should have clued me in on Christopher's liberal views regarding hair color.

Christopher led me to his station. Once I was seated, he stepped back and stared at me critically, with one eyebrow raised.

"Sweetie, you let your roots go way too long," he said.

Tell me something I don't know, I thought. Since his statement was true and invited no comment, I said nothing in response.

"Do you want to go with the same color … or try something new?" he asked.

I don't know what got into me. Maybe because I had been working too hard, I was suffering a temporary bout of insanity. Regardless of the reason, I said something I would come to regret: "Perhaps something new. Any suggestions?"

"Auburn," he answered without hesitation. "All the fashionistas in New York and LA are going auburn. It would look fabulous on you with your skin tone."

"Do you mean, like, red?"

"Gawd, no. Calling auburn *red* is like calling a lady a whore."

I did not find this analogy at all enlightening.

"What the hell did you just say?" a voice boomed from two chairs down.

I looked over and identified the speaker as an attractive black woman. Michele was styling her hair.

"Geez, Tuwanda. Don't take it personally. I was just trying to illustrate a point."

"Well, take your point somewhere else before I whack it off," Tuwanda spat back.

Christopher sighed. "Gawd, you're touchy. No disrespect intended. I have no problem with what you do for a living, even if I don't have any use for your firm's services, if you get my drift."

Tuwanda waved her finger like a metronome at him and made a clucking noise. "I dunno, Christopher. You just might. We're startin' an all-male division. Tangerine already leased a place and hired a manager. It has a kinda Mardi Gras theme. She's figured out a promotion where you get a set of gold plastic beads after each visit, and when you get ten of 'em, you get a free—uh—massage. There's gonna be a grand-opening party tonight with champagne and them little cocktail weenies and a cake shaped like a ..." Tuwanda glanced at me and said, "Like a, um, tower. Don't tell me you're not interested in *that*."

I was sure she'd substituted the words "massage" and "tower" for more descriptive phrases, which was understandable. For all she knew, I could be an undercover cop, although I couldn't imagine an officer willing to dye his or her hair a different color for the sake of an investigation. No sane person would take such a risk for a mere job, unlike me, who was insane enough to do it on a mere whim.

Christopher had already started slathering hair dye on my hair, although I wasn't sure we had settled the auburn issue yet. He stopped in mid-slather, though, when he heard about the men's division.

"Omigod! Can I get an invite to the party? Please, please, please, *please*. I promise I'll do your hair for free for the next year. I just *have* to be at that party."

"Calm down. You're splatterin' dye goo all over the place. I think I got an extra invite in my purse." She dug around in a Louis Vuitton handbag I'd seen in advertised in *Vogue*, and had lusted after ever since. "Yeah, here it is," she said, holding up a purple envelope. She reached over the woman in the chair next to her and handed the envelope to Chris. "But I don' want you goin' *near* my hair, little man."

Yet another hint as to Christopher's lack of professional competence that flew right over my head.

"Can customers of your new business wear costumes?" he asked excitedly. "I think costumes add so much to the experience."

"Hell, you pay the money, you can wear any damn costume you want. Just some advice, though: I wouldn't wear nothin' too complicated, 'cause Tangerine's gonna start a new billin' system. No more flat rates. She's gonna bill time like lawyers do. You know, like when you call to tell your lawyer what time your arraignment is, which takes maybe five seconds, and he charges you for fifteen minutes. Even if you leave a message on his damn voice mail, he charges you for fifteen minutes just to listen, and sometimes he plays it over and over, and charges you each time. Seems like a profitable way to do things, an' Tangerine thinks we oughta do the same. Lord knows she's paid a lot of attorney fees, so she figgers maybe we can make the same billin' system work for our company. Plus it's more professional-like, you know?"

In addition to Tuwanda and me, there were four customers in the shop. None of them seemed to find this conversation particularly startling or even interesting. Three were engaged in small talk with their stylists (about movies, restaurants, boyfriends), and the fourth was reading a *People* magazine while talking on her cell phone to someone named Peggy about the latest travails of Britney Spears.

I, on the other hand, thought the conversation between Christopher and Tuwanda was offbeat for the beauty parlor milieu. Still, when I heard Tuwanda say that she "paid a lot of attorney fees," offbeat or not, I sensed a business development opportunity.

"Who's Tangerine?" I asked.

Tuwanda leaned over the cell phone lady sitting between us and patted my leg. "You're new here, ain'tcha, sweetie." It was more of a statement than a question, but I answered her anyway.

"I moved to Phoenix about six months ago. Who's Tangerine?" I repeated.

"You ain't a cop, are you?" asked Tuwanda. I shook my head no. Tuwanda sat back and addressed the rest of the shop's patrons. "Anybody here know this woman? Can anyone vouch for her?"

Obviously Tuwanda considered my denial mere evidence of the truth, and poor evidence at that. She wanted corroboration. Wise woman.

Michele spoke up. "She's an attorney. Used to be with the prosecutor's office, but now she's doing defense stuff."

Tuwanda looked at me suspiciously. "You recovered from being a *persecutor*?"

"Hell, yeah," Michele continued on my behalf. "She's the one Rantwist tried to shoot 'cause she outed him as a lying asshole."

"That was you?" asked Tuwanda. Her tone had suddenly turned respectful, if not downright awe-filled.

"That was me," I answered humbly. "And yes, I've gotten over the *prosecutor* thing. I left the county attorney's office and opened my own practice about three months ago."

"You any good?"

"I practiced criminal defense law in Chicago for fourteen years before coming to Phoenix. I did pretty well."

"Since you're only open a few months, you givin' any introductory discounts?"

I could see where this was going. "No," I replied. "Who's Tangerine?"

Tuwanda leaned over cell phone woman again. "Tangerine is only the best, and I mean the *best*, professional ho manager in town. She's got fifty or so of us workin' for her. We got a health insurance plan and everythin.'"

"What's the difference between a *professional* ho and a regular ho?" I asked.

"A marriage license," she said, slapping her thigh and laughing uproariously.

I smiled politely, even though I wasn't sure I got the joke.

Tuwanda's laughter tapered off, and she wiped her eyes. "Seriously, though, professionals got performance standards. We got *rules*."

"I see," I said seriously. "In the legal field, we have to pass a bar examination. Do you have something along those lines?"

Tuwanda studied my face as if to make sure I wasn't making fun of her. Seemingly satisfied that I was not, she said, "Tangerine checks your references, sends you to a doctor to get everythin' checked out, and interviews you for, like, an hour before she hires you."

References? I thought.

"An' rules; we got lotsa rules. No drugs, no booze, dress nice, and wrappers on every weenie, no exceptions. You even look at a weenie, it's gotta have a wrapper on. Tangerine gives us 'valuations every three months, and if you get two bad 'valuations, you are *out*, girl."

"Impressive," I said, and I meant it. I'd represented more than a few call girls in Chicago, and while some were sophisticated businesswomen, they worked alone. "If Tangerine is so well known, though, how does she keep from being arrested?"

"'Cause she's got insurance," Tuwanda smirked. "Lots of it."

Tuwanda didn't have to explain further; obviously Tangerine had a little black book with the names of many important people in it, which is often an important piece of protection in the prostitution racket.

"'Sides, lotsa cops figure she does the community a service by runnin' a good, clean operation. I mean, people's gonna do *it* no matter what the law says; there's a reason we're the oldest profession, you know. But that guy Rantwist wasn't one of them enlightened types. Tangerine hated him. She had to spend lotsa money on bail and attorneys for us while he was around."

Michele, who'd managed to work on Tuwanda's hair without missing a beat, despite Tuwanda's constantly shifting position, spritzed Tuwanda's impressive hairdo with hairspray and pronounced it done.

Tuwanda patted her hair and formed her mouth into a moue. "Looks real good. Thanks, Michele."

"Same time next week?" asked Michele, pocketing the substantial tip Tuwanda handed her.

"Yes, *ma'am*, an' next time I need somethin' real sturdy, maybe a updo or somethin'. The Home and Garden Show is at the Civic Center next week, and that's always a busy time for us. Somethin' 'bout appliances and floor coverin' excites a man."

Tuwanda stopped by my chair on her way out. "Say, you got a business card I can have? Tangerine'll be real impressed I met you. Like I said, she hated Rantwist, and you're why he ain't around to hate no more."

I pulled a card from my pocket and handed it to her. Attorneys in private practice always have a stack of business cards within easy reach. You never know when a client development opportunity might present itself.

"It was nice talking to you, Tuwanda," I said. "Maybe we'll run into each other again."

"I'd like that. No offense, though, but I don't wanna ever hafta see you in your professional capacity, if you get what I mean."

I understood. I was used to hearing that.

Not long after Tuwanda left, Christopher ordered me over to the hair wash station, where he rinsed out the hair dye, and then vigorously worked shampoo through my hair. The shampooing part actually felt kind of good—like a head and neck massage. So I was fairly relaxed by the time the drying and styling process started. The tension began to rebuild in my neck, though, as my hair color emerged under the dryer's blast. I thought auburn was dark brown with subtle reddish highlights. My hair was red. Fire engine red. Lucille Ball red.

I pointed the problem out to Christopher. "It's red, dammit."

"Of course it's red, sweetie. That's what you decided."

"I did not! Change it back."

"I can't, sweetie. I've got another appointment in five minutes. You'll have to reschedule. But I need to warn you: red is an *extremely* difficult color to change. You really should have thought things through more carefully."

"You said auburn, not red," I sputtered.

"You say potāto, I say potăto. Red is red."

"No, it's more like I say *auburn*, and you say *red*."

Michele intervened, which was fortunate because the debate was going nowhere, and I was close to resorting to physical dispute resolution measures.

"Enough, you two. Christopher, remember that the customer is *always* right. Kate, if you don't like how your color turned out, Christopher will change it at no charge."

"He's not coming near my hair ever again," I growled.

"If I move some stuff around, I can get you in tomorrow afternoon at two," said Michele soothingly. "Can you make it then?"

"I'll be here at two. Believe me. Nothing and no one will stop me. And you … you … you get no tip!" My last comment was directed at Christopher, who responded by handing his hair dryer to Michele and stomping off in a huff. I could hear him in the back muttering. I thought him say something about temperamental redheads.

CHAPTER TWO

▼

I drove home, trying hard not to catch a glimpse of my red tresses in the rearview mirror. I reminded myself repeatedly that after two o'clock tomorrow, my hair color would be back to normal. I would just need to stay away from mirrors and all other reflective surfaces until then.

I parked my car in the covered garage and took the elevator to my floor, quietly praying that I would not run into anyone I knew. My guardian angel must have finally been paying attention after napping all afternoon, because I didn't see a soul. As I unlocked the door to my condo, I heard Ralph's welcoming bark. Ralph is a large dog I adopted while I was at the southern Arizona dude ranch. The ranch employees assured me that Ralph was a purebred, but no one seemed to be able to put his finger on what the pure breed was. When I'd first met Ralph, he'd been living off whatever leftovers the kitchen staff sporadically fed him. After living with me for a year, thanks to a good food supply and city living, Ralph had put on a few pounds and now tipped the scales at close to 150 pounds.

I opened the door and braced myself for the welcoming ceremonies, which usually consisted of Ralph running to the door and joyously hurling himself at my legs. Today, however, Ralph pulled back in mid-hurl, skidded to a stop a few feet in front of me, and then scrambled backward, his nails slipping on the tile in his haste. My first thought was that he was sick or injured. Seriously alarmed, I dropped my briefcase and hurried over to him. Ralph responded by increasing his backward momentum. Even after his backside hit the wall, he still tried frantically to push himself away on the not altogether far-fetched chance the wall would collapse under his weight and allow for further backing. He flinched when I raised my hand to stroke the top of his head.

"Ralphie boy," I said in my *good dog!* voice. What's the matter? Are you okay?"

Ralph had been staring at me distrustfully, but after hearing my voice, a look of recognition slowly crept into his eyes. He wagged his tail uncertainly. The more I talked to him, the more the tail wagging increased in coverage and cadence, with the unfortunate result that he knocked over a small carved wooden table, one of the few pieces of furniture I'd brought with me from Chicago. Finally, he jumped to his feet and completed the "joyous hurling" part of the welcoming ceremony.

It dawned on me what had happened. Ralph hadn't recognized me at first because of my red hair. I had the only dog on the planet that differentiated among humans based on hair color.

I caught sight of myself in the hall mirror. Ralph had a point. I looked like Lucille Ball. It wouldn't surprise me if I found Fred and Ethel sitting in my kitchen drinking coffee.

I turned the mirror around so it faceed the wall and repeated what had become my mantra: "By two o clock tomorrow, this will all be over."

I changed into jeans, a sweatshirt, and tennis shoes, and then filled a beer tumbler with wine. The amount held by a wineglass was not adequate to produce the numbing effect called for under the circumstances.

Hiding in my condo until tomorrow afternoon was not an option. I had to go to work in the morning, and, more immediately, Ralph needed to be walked. For the purpose of taking Ralph out for his evening dump, I figured I could cover my red head with a hat or scarf. How to handle work was a tougher problem. I put off thinking about it until I was in a more creative mood.

I went to the hall closet and dragged a box of winter accessories left over from my Chicago days down from the top shelf. I opened the flaps of the box and dumped the contents on the floor. I rummaged through the pile while Ralph excitedly sniffed lingering Chicago smells. I pulled out a ski mask, but quickly dismissed it as an option. No one in Phoenix wears a ski mask except to rob a bank. Next I pulled out a pair of earmuffs; no good. My ears weren't the problem. Then I pulled out a stretchy cap with a New York Giants logo on it. I couldn't remember where or why I got it. I had never been to a Giant's game, and, to be honest, I'm not sure whether it's a baseball or a basketball team.

I gathered my hair into a ponytail on top of my head, and then donned the cap on and pulled it as far down as it would go. I turned the hall mirror around to check how I looked. I immediately turned the mirror to the wall again. The cap was definitely not flattering, but it was still better than the hair underneath it.

I chugged the rest of my wine and grabbed Ralph's leash off the couch. Ralph was already waiting for me at the door.

I was once more alone on the elevator and didn't meet anyone on the way to the front sidewalk, so my luck was holding. I hustled Ralph toward the entrance of an older housing subdivision down the block. The area had big, soft grassy lawns, which, according to Ralph's sensibilities, were the equivalent of soft quilted toilet paper. We were only a couple of houses into the subdivision when he created one of his fecal masterpieces. Since it was winter, Phoenix's hot summer wind wasn't around to dry and blow away the poop (one of the only benefits of one-hundred-degree-plus dry heat), so I had dutifully brought along an empty plastic grocery bag, which I now flourished for the benefit of any onlookers. I pretended to scoop up the poop, and then I threw the empty bag into a garbage can. No way was I touching that steaming pile.

Normally I take Ralph for a longer walk, but the hat was itchy and I wanted to take it off, so we headed back to my building. We were almost to the elevator when someone called out my name.

"Kate? Is that you, dear?"

I didn't need to look to identify the speaker. Macy Gendler's strong Brooklyn accent is unmistakable. Macy's condo is across the hall from mine. She's in her seventies and was a real estate agent in Brooklyn for years before retiring in Phoenix. At just under five feet tall, she barely comes up to my shoulder. I am only about five foot seven, but I always feel like a giant around Macy. Ralph looks like a wooly mammoth next to her.

Plastering a grin on my face, I swiveled my head around and said, "Hi, Macy," in what I hoped was a neighborly tone. I genuinely like Macy, but this wasn't the best time for a conversation.

"It *is* you, dear. I wasn't sure. With the hat, you look like one of them rappers."

"I decided to take Ralph out for a walk and my head was cold, so I grabbed the first one I could find." Since it was about seventy degrees out, this was a patently stupid thing to say, but it was all I could think of on short notice. I should have planned ahead and figured out a better story before I left my apartment since at some point I was bound to run into someone I knew.

"It ain't that cold out," said Macy, pointing out the obvious flaw in my explanation. "Maybe you're coming down with somethin'. I got some soup I made yesterday. You want I should bring it over?"

"Thanks, Macy, but no need. I'm fine. I think I'm just a little run-down."

Just then, Bryan Turner emerged from the parking garage. He spotted us and headed over. Bryan was absolutely the last person I wanted to see in my present condition.

I'd met Bryan when I worked for the county attorney. He was a sheriff's deputy then, and he helped me investigate the odd and, as it turned out, illegal activities going on in the sheriff's department and the county attorney's office. The sheriff resigned as a result of the investigation, which was probably a good idea since it's hard, not to mention incongruous, to run a sheriff's office from prison. Bryan was second in command when the sheriff "retired," and he was appointed as interim sheriff until the county could hold another election for the office. Bryan and I were more or less a couple now, but our relationship was still too new to bear the strain of red hair.

"Hey, Kate! I thought I'd drop by on the off chance you were home, and here you are. Hi, Macy."

I waved weakly.

"This is a new look for you," he said. "What's with the hat?"

"I told her she looked like one of them rappers," chimed in Macy.

I was getting irritated. Was I so predictable that the addition of a hat to my wardrobe was cause for major comment?

'It's just a hat," I snapped. "The way you two are acting, you'd think I was wearing a four-foot feathered headdress with pinwheels."

That's when Cal Jenkins, my cross-dressing ex-FBI neighbor, emerged from the garage. (Cal claims cross-dressing is a habit he picked up at the FBI when he worked as an undercover agent. Now retired, he still liked to go "undercover" and patrol the neighborhood to ensure the safety of the local citizens. I guessed he wasn't coming back from patrol now since he was in his civilian clothes: a black jogging suit and black sneakers).

"Kate, Macy, Bryan, good to see you!" he boomed.

Macy blushed and fluttered her fingers in greeting. Cal is also in his seventies and is in great shape for his age—for any age, for that matter. He jogs a couple of miles every day and watches his diet. Macy has the hots for him

"Hi, Cal," we chorused with varying degrees of enthusiasm.

"Kate, what's up with the hat?" asked Cal.

"That does it," I sputtered. "It's a hat. A simple friggin' hat. I suggest you people find something more interesting in your lives to pursue than the whys and wherefores of my clothing choices."

I stomped to the elevator with Ralph in tow and punched the "up" button.

Behind me, I heard Cal say to the others, "Did I say something wrong, or did I walk into the middle of another conversation and get hit with collateral fire?"

Bryan said something I couldn't hear, which made me even angrier because I was sure he wasn't saying anything in my defense. Men always stick together when confronted by what they deem irrational female behavior.

The elevator arrived, and as soon as the doors opened, Ralph and I stepped in. I simultaneously banged the button for my floor and the "close door" button. Bryan still managed to slip in before the doors shut.

"Why are you so testy?" he asked.

I was about to snap out a witty retort, but Bryan looked so adorable with his wavy blond hair and midnight blue eyes that I suddenly wanted to keep on friendly—very friendly— terms with him. Besides, I couldn't think of a retort that was particularly witty.

"Wait until we get to my condo," I sighed. "I'll show you then."

Bryan looked apprehensive as I opened my condo door. He was no doubt imagining all the terrible things he might see inside. He stepped in and glanced around, and then did a quick search of the premises in cop mode. He was back in the foyer before I'd finished unhooking Ralph's leash. Once free, Ralph sat on the floor next to him and leaned against his leg as if to say, It'll be okay, buddy. I'm here for you.

"Everything looks fine to me," said Bryan, patting Ralph's head. "It's a little messy, but that's not unusual."

I narrowed my eyes at him. "You're no Felix Unger yourself. I found a stack of old pizza boxes under your bed the last time we were at your apartment."

"You never know when you might need a box for Christmas or birthday presents," he said defensively.

"Some words of advice: do not give anyone you care about a gift wrapped in a pizza box. For crying out loud, the lids had melted cheese and grease on them.

Bryan shook his head and laughed. "Truce. Let's admit it; neither one of us is a type A when it comes to housecleaning. We save our perfectionist tendencies for work." Bryan delivered this last sentiment with mock humility, but it was pretty much true. While our personal lives were disorganized and unfocused, we were both conscientious workaholics when it came to our professions.

"Back to the issue at hand. What is it you want to show me?" he asked.

I pulled off my hat, operating under the theory that it wouldn't be so bad if I got it over with quickly—kind of like ripping off a Band-Aid so it doesn't hurt so much, which doesn't work either.

Bryan didn't cringe or cry out in shock and revulsion, which is what I had expected. In fact, he made absolutely no noise whatsoever. He didn't even seem to be breathing, and his face was turning bright red.

"You're trying not to laugh," I accused.

Bryan pressed his lips together tightly and shook his head no.

"You are too! Just go ahead and laugh. Get it out of your system. I don't care." Of course, I *did* care, but I was damned if I'd let him know that.

Bryan's breath came out in a whoosh, and he started to laugh. It was not polite laughter. It was a series of boisterous guffaws with intermittent gasps for breath. Eventually, probably realizing I was not joining in on the hilarity, he got himself under control and wiped his eyes on his sleeve.

"Are you through?" I asked darkly.

"I have to be honest with you; I don't think I am. Maybe I should go into another room."

"Please."

Bryan covered his mouth with both hands and rushed into the powder room off the foyer. He closed the door behind him, but I could still hear him laughing inside.

My hair looked a little weird, but not *that* weird. It deserved no more that a brief expression of strong emotion, after which I expected murmured comforting words once I explained my traumatic experience at the hands of Christopher the Destroyer.

I turned the hall mirror around to see if I had somehow underestimated the dramatic impact of my appearance. I had. My new hair color was as outrageous as I remembered, but the rubber band had worked loose, and my freshly dyed hair follicles, completely jazzed by static electricity from the hat, stuck out in all directions, moving agitatedly. I looked like a giant red sea anemone. I went into the bathroom off my bedroom and did what I could with mousse and water to calm and return order to my deranged locks. When I emerged, Bryan was sitting on the living room couch waiting for me. He was smiling, but otherwise held his emotions in check.

"Do you want to talk about it?" he asked solicitously.

I sat down next to him and told him about Christopher's felonious assault. I reassured him, and me, that everything would be back to normal after my appointment with Michele at two tomorrow afternoon.

"Actually," he said, nuzzling my ear, "this could be interesting. Maybe you could pretend to be Lucy, and I could pretend to be Ricky, and ..." He went on to describe an innovative Latin-themed scenario, which he revised when I told him I did not have a set of bongos, but it still sounded good.

About an hour later, my hair was an even bigger mess than it was during its static-inspired performance of the Electric Slide, but neither of us were complaining.

I went to the kitchen and came back with a couple of glasses of Chardonnay. I handed one to Bryan and sat down next to him again. We snuggled companionably and sipped our wine.

"Have you ever heard of someone called Tangerine?" I asked lazily.

Bryan did a spit-take with his wine. "What are you implying?" he asked, sounding genuinely offended.

I smiled at him teasingly. "I take it, then, that you have heard of her?"

"Every law enforcement officer in town knows who Tangerine is. Maybe I should be asking how you know of her."

"I met one of her employees, a woman named Tuwanda, at the hairdresser's today."

"What kind of beauty shop did you go to? You make friends with a hooker, and some nut job with poor communication skills dyes your hair red."

I laughed. "Tuwanda was actually quite nice, but if she was here right now, she'd slap you upside the head for calling her a hooker. She is, as she explained to me, a 'professional ho.'"

I briefly described my conversation with Tuwanda, but left out the part about Tangerine's new man-ho division. It was bad enough that Tangerine was involved in traditional prostitution.

I wasn't sure how the law-and-order side of Bryan would handle the news that she was expanding into new territory, while the card-carrying ACLU member bleeding-heart liberal defense attorney side of me, which is pretty much the only side I have, was in favor of Tangerine's egalitarian approach to her service industry.

"So," I said, once I concluded the condensed version of my conversation with Tuwanda, "are you one of the 'enlightened' law enforcement guys Tuwanda mentioned? The ones who look the other way when Tangerine conducts her business?"

Bryan sighed and chugged the remainder of his wine. "Tangerine is most definitely breaking the law. But she runs a clean operation, and reported cases of AIDS and STDs have gone way down in the county since she started her operation. So, as long as she doesn't branch out into other areas of crime, we pretty muchleave her alone. We bust a few of her employees from time to time for misdemeanor solicitation when things get too out of hand, but that doesn't happen often. That's the way it's worked ... except for when Rantwist was county attorney.

"Rantwist came down hard on Tangerine and her ladies in the name of God-fearing people everywhere. Once, at a press conference, he called her a 'pus-filled boil oozing sin and damnation.' Tangerine is used to being called a lot of things, but this time she took especial offense because the image evoked was bad for business. Would-be customers are turned off by associations between infected boils and sex for hire. After Rantwist left office because it was discovered that he in fact was the pus-filled boil oozing sin and damnation, things returned to the way they were pre-Rantwist. In fact, Tangerine cooperated with us on a couple of cases and gave us some good information."

"You've met her?" I asked.

"Once, about a month ago. She helped us bust a drug ring operated by one of the South Phoenix gangs. She's one of the most organized people I've ever met. If she'd chosen a different direction, she'd be the head of a *Fortune* 500 company by now. By the way, I heard she needs a new lawyer. Apparently, the guy who used to represent her got a life and retired."

Now, this was good stuff. I smelled opportunity. I was sure every other criminal law attorney in town had already swooped down on Tangerine, dropping firm resumes like leaflets in a mall parking lot. But if she hadn't hired anyone yet, maybe I still had a chance.

I wanted to find out more about Tangerine, but other matters had distracted Bryan. It soon became too difficult to talk through all the kissing, and then I completely lost track of the conversation as our activities became even more intimate.

Bryan left around ten o'clock, and I went to bed soon after. I slept fitfully and dreamed that Bozo the Clown was chasing me with a bowl of red hair dye, insisting he was my soul mate.

CHAPTER THREE

▼

I paused under my newly installed business sign to plan the explanation I would give to my staff. It's a good thing I did because when I went inside, Beth, Sam, and M.J. were in the reception area, drinking coffee and talking.

At least I don't have to call a meeting, I thought. My plan had been to call everyone into my office and handle the problem in one neat disclosure. That way, I wouldn't have to repeat the story throughout the day as each staff member discovered my hair color change.

The three of them looked up at the sound of the door opening. Sam sucked in his breath and bit his lower lip. Beth, who had been saying something to M.J. when I entered, stopped in midsentence, and her lips formed an O. A stunned silence ensued. M.J. was the first to recover.

"Gawd! You look *great*! I *love* your hair!" She reached her hand out to touch it. She probably wanted to see if the color would come off on her fingers. If only it would.

Clearly, I had underestimated the more grotesque aspects of my hair. If M.J., she of the seasonal hair colors, liked it, it must really be bad.

Sam, no doubt prompted by sheer amazement at M.J.'s comment, blurted, "How can you say that? She looks like Lucille Ball, and I don't mean that in a good way."

I had to ask. "How does one go about looking like Lucille Ball in a *good* way?"

Sam blushed. "I meet with some of my friends for cocktails every week. We take turns hosting, and we all dress up for the occasion. One of our guys likes to dress like Lucy. He's got this great little fifties-style dress and pumps and ..."

"Your point, I take it, is that I look worse than a drag queen in a red wig?"

"That sums it up," Sam said lamely.

Beth was starting to revive, so I jumped in before she could add her two cents' worth. "The hairdresser made a mistake. That's all. I'm going in at two this afternoon to undo the color. After-two-it-will-all-be-back-to-normal," I chanted. All I was missing was a yoga mat and a prayer bowl.

"Geez, I don't know if your hairdresser mentioned this, but red is a hard color to get out," said M.J.

I remembered Christopher saying something like that, and it made me nervous to hear it again.

"M.J., what are you talking about? You don't seem to have any problems changing your hair color. You go from white to purple to green to red and back again, with no shades in between," Sam pointed out.

"Yeah, but I don't use permanent color. I use the stuff that washes out after a couple of shampoos. I have a friend who went red with the permanent kind, and she had to wait for her hair to grow out to get rid of the red."

"If that's true, the guy who did this to me will pay," I said with feeling. "I will sue him, and once the judge and jury get a load of Exhibit A here, they'll award punitive damages in the millions." I pounded the wall agitatedly to emphasize the depth of my feeling, and a dusting of ceiling plaster fell on my head. Now I probably looked like Lucy in a snowstorm.

After taking a couple of deep breaths to collect myself, I continued more calmly. "Let's get off the subject of my hair and do something productive to help pay the bills around here. Beth, do I have any appointments today?"

"Only one: a new client by the name of Katherine Paar. She called this morning and will be coming in at eleven o'clock."

"Did she say what she wanted to talk to me about?"

"She said she needed ongoing legal representation," said Beth, reading from her notes.

M.J. snorted. "Ongoing representation from a criminal defense law firm? What is she—a kleptomaniac who plans ahead?"

"Henry the Eighth had a wife named Catherine Paar," interjected Sam, obviously feeling the conversation had gone on too long without him.

"What does that have to do with anything?" retorted M.J. "You're just trying to show off."

"I don't think an intelligent observation constitutes showing off," countered Sam.

"Enough," I said. "Go do something productive. M.J., don't you have some legal research to do on the Boyle case, and Sam, aren't you supposed to be interviewing witnesses?"

"I'll get to work on it, although with what I get paid around here, I don't know why I bother to show up every day," grumbled M.J. as she ambled off toward her office.

"Yes, ma'am," said Sam, saluting me.

As he strode off purposefully, I remarked, "By the way, I like your new shoes. Manolo Blahnik?"

"Louboutin," he said over his shoulder before disappearing into his office.

Beth peered at me over her reading glasses. "That boy's got expensive taste. You payin' him a lot of money?"

"No. I get the feeling Sam has a sugar daddy, though. Remember last week when he got all those roses?"

"I sure do. I've never seen that many flowers in a room without a casket. I read the card. It said, 'All my love, Boots.'"

"Boots?" I asked, raising an eyebrow. "Boots sounds like a cat's name."

Beth shrugged. "Somebody gives me that many roses, he can call himself Bin Laden for all I care."

Beth passed me a stack of files. "You might want to look at the Jailey file first. The motions in there all need to be reviewed and filed by the end of today. I gotta say, though, that a guy with a name like that has *no* chance of getting out of jail time. The karma's too obvious."

I took the files into my office and worked on them until Beth came in at eleven o'clock on the dot to tell me Katherine Paar had arrived for her appointment. I asked Beth to show her in, and she returned a few seconds later, followed by a plump older woman with a kind expression. After extending offers of coffee or water, both of which Ms. Paar politely declined, Beth left, closing the door softly behind her.

I stood, extended my hand, and introduced myself. "Please have a seat, Katherine, "I said, gesturing to the comfy cushioned client chair facing my desk. I had purchased the chair consistent with the theory that anyone coming to an attorney for advice on a criminal matter needed all the comfort he or she could get.

Katherine sat down daintily and carefully arranged her skirt to cover her knees. Her appearance was not typical of most clients in my practice, who tend to be on the south side of thirty and dress according to the latest street style. This usually means baggy jeans and tight T-shirts, or short, tight dresses. Katherine looked like Aunt Bee on *The Andy Griffith Show,* right down to her graying brown hair pulled back into a neat bun, flowered polyester dress, and brown Hush Puppies.

"May I place this on your desk?" she asked in her matching Aunt Bee voice, nodding to the large brief case she was carrying.

"Of course," I said, pushing aside stacks of files and papers to make room.

She glanced distastefully at my messy desktop, took a Kleenex out of her purse, and then wiped the area I had cleared. A couple of spots required extra scrubbing. Appearing to conclude that this portion of the desk was cootie-free, she carefully centered her briefcase in the cleaned space, punched a code into the lock, and opened it. I was almost disappointed when she removed two neat black binders with multicolored index tabs. I had expected something magical and exotic after that buildup. Kind of like in *Mary Poppins* when Julie Andrews pulled all sorts of unexpected objects out of her valise, including a hat stand and an umbrella.

"I will assume for purposes of this conversation that everything I tell you is covered by attorney-client privilege. Am I correct in this assumption?"

I nodded vigorously and launched into an explanation of the ethical obligation of all attorneys to hold clients', and even prospective clients', disclosures confidential. She cut me off with a wave of her hand in a way that indicated she knew all about the attorney-client privilege and had needed reassurance, not elucidation.

She handed one of the binders to me. "If you turn to page one," she said, "you will find the index."

I dutifully turned to the index and read the list of section headings, starting with "Introduction and Mission Statement," followed by "Employee Biographies" and a list of names.

I wondered if Katherine mistakenly thought I was a corporate or employment law lawyer.

"Please turn to page two now," she asked politely. "I will wait and give you a chance to read it."

Page two was the Introduction and Mission Statement, which read as follows:

> *Pole Polishers, Inc. (the "Company") was incorporated in 1995 under the laws of the State of Delaware. Katherine Paar is the sole shareholder and CEO of the Company. The Company's principal place of business is 6969 E. Bunker Road in Phoenix, Arizona. Pole Polishers began with one*

employee in 1995 and now employs over thirty service agents (whom the Company refers to as "Care Bares") and five administrative assistants. The Company is known for the creativity and quality of its services, as well as the hygiene of its operations. Company employment is conditioned upon employee compliance with ongoing training requirements, and training materials are continuously updated to reflect market trends and improvedl safety requirements.

As part of its menu of service, in addition to individual sessions, the Company offers sessions for groups of fifty or less, as well as educational seminars.

The Company motto is "Trust us to blow it every time."

I figured the company motto was a play on words of some sort. Maybe the company provided building demolition services. The company name was odd, but the sweet little old lady in front of me probably didn't realize it could have a different meaning, although every junior high school kid in America would spot the double entendre immediately.

"What kind of services does your company provide?" I asked.

Katherine patted a stray hair back into place. "My Care Bares provide a unique blend of physical therapy and spiritual enlightenment. Most of our clients experience a great release of ... stress ... as a result of our services."

"Oh. Kind of like yoga?"

"Like yoga, the therapies we offer involve a number of positions, but we primarily focus on our clients' erogenous zones."

I was starting to get the picture. "Who referred you to me?"

"One of my employees met you yesterday when she was getting her hair done. You gave her your card. The timing was excellent because our current counsel recently retired from the practice of law."

"You're Tangerine?" I blurted in disbelief. I'd pictured Tangerine as someone who looked, well, like the opposite of this woman.

"Yes. People call me Tangerine because I love tangerines." As if to prove the point, she dug around in her dress pocket and produced a small tangerine, which she proceeded to peel in record time. She deposited the peel in a plastic Ziploc bag she pulled out of her pocket.

"I compost," she offered by way of explanation when I eyed the bag. "Would you care for a section?" she offered. I declined, after which she popped the entire tangerine into her mouth and chewed with such obviously sensual pleasure that I was tempted to excuse myself from the room to give her some privacy.

Once Katherine, a.k.a. Tangerine, finished chewing, she wiped a small drop of juice from her chin with a flowered cloth handkerchief and picked up her copy of the black notebook, which had fallen on the floor during her citrus rapture.

She reopened her notebook and asked that I turn to page three of my copy.

Page three was the beginning of Employee Biographies. The first biography was that of Tuwanda Banks. No doubt this was the same Tuwanda I'd met at Stranded. I mean, how many people could there be named Tuwanda?

"The biographies of all of my current Care Bares are in this section. Basic information such as date and place of birth, home address, telephone numbers, e-mail addresses, names and contact information for family members, and criminal records are included.

"From time to time a Care Bare will be arrested while carrying out her employment duties, and I need an attorney willing to be on call in the event of such an arrest. Should you agree to be that attorney, I will pay you a retainer of one hundred thousand dollars by direct deposit into your firm's trust account."

Wow. I quickly did the math and figured out that one hundred thousand dollars added to my existing account balance would make a grand total of ... one hundred thousand dollars.

The inner me danced around ecstatically. The outer me maintained a neutral expression, as though retainers of this size were common in my practice. "I see. How many hours per week do you estimate I would need to allocate for representation of the ... er ... Care Bares?"

"Let's take Tuwanda as an example. If you turn to page four, you will see her criminal record. In the past three years, Tuwanda has been arrested once a week on average. That result is skewed, however, by her atypically high number of arrests while Mr. Rantwist was in office. If you ignore the seventy-nine arrests in that six-month period, she averages one or two arrests every calendar quarter. The other Care Bares in your notebook have a similar pattern of arrests."

A caseload like that would be no problem for me to handle.

"My billing rate is two hundred dollars per hour, and I bill my paralegal and investigator at seventy-five dollars per hour each," I said in my most businesslike voice.

"That's acceptable. Please have your office e-mail a retainer agreement to me. I will print it out, sign it, and have the signed agreement hand delivered to you." Katherine hesitated a moment, then continued. "I will also need you to keep certain private documents for me. I assume that will not be a problem."

I thought of my limited storage space. "Are they bulky?"

Katherine opened her briefcase and pulled something out of the side pocket. "They are stored on this," she said, handing me a black plastic object about two and a half inches long and one inch wide, to which a nylon cord was attached.

Admittedly, I am somewhat of a Luddite, but even I knew it was a thumb drive, which is a data storage device capable of holding large amounts of information. The information is accessed by sliding the drive into a slot on the side of a laptop or in the CPU of a desktop.

"I think I can find room for this," I said, smiling.

"Good," said Katherine crisply. "I will leave it with you, then. When I send you the signed retainer agreement, I will send a letter of instruction concerning the disposition of the information contained on the thumb drive in the event I am ... not available to give you verbal instructions. Until that time, do not tell anyone about it or do anything with it unless you receive instructions from me in person."

Katherine packed her notebook, snapped her briefcase shut, and then stood, making it clear that, at least as far as she was concerned, our meeting was over. I stood as well and fought back the urge to salute. The authority emanating from this businesslike woman impressed me. I could see how she became successful in her business and, as Bryan pointed out, would likely be just as successful in any other business she chose to go into.

We shook hands, and Katherine collected her briefcase and purse. As she exited my office, she said over her shoulder, "Your hair color does not suit you, dear. You might consider changing it."

She was gone before I could say, "After two o'clock today I will be blond again." To avoid having to continually repeat myself, maybe I should have explanatory cards printed and hand them out to everyone I ran into until my hair color was back to normal.

Stu had not installed our new fireproof safe yet, so I put the cord holding Katherine's thumb drive around my neck and shoved the small plastic rectangle under my sweater. It created an unattractive lump, kind of like a third, smaller breast, but keeping it on me was the best I could do for the time being.

Besides, everyone would be too busy looking at the mess on my head to notice the extra boob.

I glanced at my watch. It was eleven forty-five and I was ready for lunch. I didn't want to go out, though, and take the chance I might run into someone I knew, or even someone I didn't know. Besides, I needed to work on Katherine's retainer agreement. I hit the intercom button on my desk, and then, remembering that Stu hadn't hooked it up the yet, walked out to Beth's desk. Beth was frowning in concentration over a crossword puzzle. She recently read an article that claimed working crossword puzzles was a good way to keep the mind agile and hold Alzheimer's at bay. Beth had an inordinate fear of getting Alzheimer's, even though no one she knew, much less anyone in her family, had ever suffered from the disease, so she had been doing crossword puzzles in her spare time ever since.

"I hate to interrupt your daily mental calisthenics, but are you going out for lunch today?" I asked.

Without looking up, Beth shook her head and pointed to a brown lunch bag sitting on her desk.

I went over and knocked on M.J.'s door.

"Wait until I get dressed and get all these naked guys out of here before you come in!" she shouted.

I opened her door. "Very professional. What if it was a client instead of me?"

M.J., who had been sitting at her desk marking up a document, sat back in her chair and looked up at me sardonically. "We represent criminals, for God's sake. They'd probably be impressed."

"*Alleged* criminals," I corrected. "Are you going out for lunch today?"

"Yeah. Me and Sam are going over to Paco's Classy Tacos. You want us to pick something up for you?"

"If you could bring a couple of tacos back for me, that would be great." I forbore from pointing out that the term "classy taco" was an oxymoron.

I dug into my pocket and handed her a twenty-dollar bill. I knew from experience not to expect change. "I need to stay in to work on a retainer agreement for Katherine Paar. She's going to pay us a substantial retainer to represent her company and the company's employees." I couldn't keep the joy out of my voice.

"Cool!" said M.J.

"What's cool?" I turned around to see Sam standing behind me. I repeated what I'd said.

"What does her company do that it needs a criminal defense attorney on retainer?" asked Sam.

"Well, her trade name is Tangerine, and ..." I started to say.

"*Tangerine?*" chorused M.J., Sam, and Beth, the last of whom had obviously been listening at her desk to our conversation.

"You've all heard of her too?" I groaned. "Where do I find these things out? Is there a Web site I can go to? Or a visitors guide?"

"You weren't working for the county attorney yet when the whole Tangerine thing hit," said Sam. "Rantwist cracked down on her ... what do you call them?"

"Care Bares," provided M.J.

"That's it, Care Bares ... in a big way. He made a public stink about them, so, to save face, the sheriff more or less *had* to start arresting them. As soon as one got arrested, Tangerine would post bail and she was back at the job, and then the sheriff's guys would go and arrest her again. It got crazy. It was like a revolving door at the jail. The charges kept getting more serious as all the priors piled up and the bail kept getting bigger, but Tangerine just kept posting and the sheriff kept arresting. Finally, the sheriff must have told Rantwist to back off because his deputies didn't have time to do anything except arrest Care Bares, and it was getting to be a big joke."

"How come Tangerine never got arrested during all this?" I asked.

"Word is, she's got a list of clients hidden somewhere, and the list has some powerful people's names on it," contributed Beth.

Tuwanda had implied the same thing.

I thought about the thumb drive hanging around my neck; could this be Katherine's "little black book"? I dismissed the possibility. I couldn't see why Katherine would trust anyone to keep something that important for her. She would likely just put the information in a safe deposit box somewhere. Still, I didn't mention the thumb drive to my staff, even though I assumed they were not included in Tangerine's directive to keep quiet about the device, in that the protection afforded by the attorney-client privilege extends to information shared by an attorney with his or her staff. I simply figured the fewer people that knew about it, the better.

"Regardless of any influence Tangerine might have in political and law enforcement circles, it seems her Care Bares are still in need of legal representation from time to time," I said, "and our job is to provide it."

"Too bad Rantwist's not in office anymore," said M.J. wistfully.

"*What?*" Beth, Sam, and I yelped simultaneously.

"I mean if Rantwist was still in office we'd have *a lot* of business," M.J. said defensively.

"Not worth it," Beth pronounced with feeling.

I nodded in agreement. Rantwist was now the guest of the federal penitentiary system, which was the best place for him as far as I was concerned.

"Why don't we meet tomorrow morning around ten to discuss how we're going to handle Tangerine's cases? We can decide who does what when a case comes in. If we get it down to a system, it'll be easy."

M.J., Beth, and Sam enthusiastically agreed.

"Now all of you; go out and get some lunch," I ordered with mock seriousness. "And M.J., don't forget to pick something up for me."

M.J. held out her hand.

"I already gave you twenty dollars," I pointed out.

"Oh, yeah. I forgot."

Like heck she did.

I went back into my office and started to draft a retainer agreement for Tangerine's—I mean Katherine's—signature. Most of the language was boilerplate, so it was mostly a matter of cutting and pasting. I was midway through when a knock sounded at the door. It was too early for M.J. to be back, and besides, she never knocked. Beth only knocked for appearance when she was escorting a client to my office, and if that were the case, she would have called me first to give me a heads-up. I narrowed the possibilities down to Stu.

"Come in," I called out.

The door opened and someone who wasn't Stu stepped in and stood just inside the doorway. He stared shyly down at the baseball cap he clutched in front of him, and seemed exceptionally nervous.

He was short and thin, and looked to be in his late thirties. His hair hung to his shoulders in greasy light brown stands. He wore a light blue, long-sleeved work shirt and gray pants. Both the shirt and the pants had the same design: stained. Even though he was standing at least five feet away, I could tell he needed a shower.

I made a mental note to talk to Beth about screening walk-ins more carefully.

"May I help you?" I asked politely, but with a cold, formal edge to my voice.

The man cleared his throat. From the sound of it, there was a lot to clear out.

"You probably don't remember me, ma'am," he said in a barely audible, high voice.

I looked at him more closely. There was something familiar about him.

"Who are you?" I asked suspiciously. Recognizing a familiar face in my line of business sometimes isn't a good thing.

"My name's Larkin, ma'am. Larry Larkin."

Now I remembered. Larry Larkin was one of many defendants caught in Rantwist's dragnet during his infamous crusade against evil. Larkin had exposed himself during rush hour in downtown Phoenix to the delight of bored drivers who appreciated the diversion from the bumper-to-bumper traffic. Rantwist's office charged him with a second-degree felony, even though by statute, exhibitionism was at most a Class 1 misdemeanor, and my discovery of this charging discrepancy launched me on the investigation that eventually resulted in Rantwist's arrest. I had seen Larkin's mug shot in the file plenty of times, but I had never met him face to face until now.

"Ah, Mr. Larkin. Of course," I said, staring nervously at his baseball cap and praying Mr. Happy was packed and stowed.

Larry lifted his head and smiled shyly, giving me a good view of his few remaining teeth. "I heard it was you, ma'am, who was responsible for me getting out of jail. Thank you. I didn't never think a prosecutor would do something like that."

"Which might explain why I'm no longer a prosecutor," I said ruefully. "Did you just come to thank me, or did you need something else?"

Larry stared down at his cap again.

Uh oh, I thought. *This is it: the unveiling.* I shut my eyes reflexively.

"Are you okay?" Larry asked solicitously.

I forced one eye open. The cap was still in place. I relaxed. "I'm fine. I'm just a little tired," I lied. "Now, what can I do for you?"

Larry shifted his weight and stared down at his right toe. "I think I need to hire you to represent me. I may have a problem."

In my experience, people were usually pretty sure about if and why they needed an attorney. Something definitive, like an arrest, most often triggered the request. However, Larry seemed to lack conviction, no pun intended.

"Did something happen that made you *think* you might need an attorney?" I prodded.

Larry answered by reaching into his pocket and producing a waterlogged billfold for my inspection, as if this would explain everything.

"Did you steal this from someone? I asked, flipping the wallet open.

"No!" said Larry, with unexpected force. "I found it."

"Do you want me to help you find the owner?"

Larry shook his head furiously.

"Larry, I can't help you out if you don't tell me what's going on, and I have lots to do today. I don't have time to sit here and try to pull information out of you. Why don't you set up an appointment with Beth, my receptionist, and come back once you've had a chance to organize your thoughts." I figured that if our present conversation was any indication, it would be months before Larry could organize his thoughts into anything approaching cohesion.

"I found the billfold. I found it in a man's pocket."

I sighed. "So you stole the billfold from a man."

"It doesn't count as stealing. Dead people can't own things."

"The man was dead? Are you sure?"

"He was floating facedown in the canal. A pigeon was sitting on his butt. I figured anyone who let a pigeon sit on his butt had to be dead."

I let that sink in. I pictured the cross-examination in court: "Sir, please tell the jury what brought you to the conclusion that the victim was dead." "Why, he had a pigeon sitting on his butt, of course."

"Which part of the canal?" I asked. The greater Phoenix area is crisscrossed by a series of canals bringing water from the Colorado River via upland storage reservoirs to the thirsty desert.

"The part just before it runs underneath Thirty-Second Street near Camelback Road. He was kind of stuck up against the grate. At first, I thought it was just a bunch of trash and some old clothes. I thought that maybe I could use some of the clothes, so I waded in. When I got close, I saw it was a body—a man's body."

"Did you call for help?" I asked.

"Wasn't anyone around."

"And so you took his wallet?"

"First I shooed the pigeon off his butt," Larry said sanctimoniously.

"Have you told the police about the body yet?"

"Didn't need to. I left as soon as I got the wallet. When I was a couple of blocks away, I heard sirens and saw police car lights. I figured someone else must've called 'em. It occurred to me then that things didn't look so good for me. He's dead, and then I come along and laid ownership to his wallet, but the police may not believe things happened in that order. I got a record, you know. The police'll say I killed him."

"Why would they think that? They'd be more likely to think the man was drunk, fell into the canal, and drowned."

Larry seemed to give this some thought, and then he shook his head slowly. "It coulda happened that way, but I know how the cops operate. They see the bullet hole in the back of that guy's head, and they're gonna jump to the conclusion that he was shot."

"Bullet hole?" I asked weakly.

"Yeah. Right between the ears."

I sighed. "Larry, you're going to need to go to the police, explain what happened, and give them this billfold," I said, handing it back to him. "I will go with you as your counsel, but I have to tell you I don't work for free. Do you have any money?" I asked doubtfully.

Larry opened the billfold and peered into the side pocket. "I got fifty dollars," he said, pulling out a sodden wad of cash.

Maybe we could install one of those doors like they have in jewelry stores: The kind with bars where customers can't get in unless you deem them worthy of being buzzed in.

"Put the money back, Larry. I will be your attorney for the limited purpose of accompanying you to the police station so you can tell your story and return the billfold. But that's *all*. If the police take any action against you, and I doubt that they will, an attorney from the public defender's office will be appointed to represent you. Do you understand?"

Larry nodded. "Do you think I'll get a reward?"

"No," I said flatly.

I looked at my watch. It was twelve thirty. A trip to the station with Larry should take an hour at most. Then I could grab something to eat and get to Stranded in time for my two o'clock appointment. My stomach growled in protest of my priorities, but I wanted to get Larry's visit to the police over with, and no way was I offering to take him to lunch first.

"Let's go," I said, standing. "We can go to the main station at Tenth Avenue and Van Buren. We'll take my car."

Not that we had choice on the issue of transportation. It was either my car or the bus, and Phoenix's public transportation system is notoriously erratic; its bus schedules are approximations at best. I looked at Larry's soiled pants and inwardly cringed. I considered spreading a newspaper on the passenger seat before he sat down, but decided that would be rude. True, Larry had burst into my office unannounced, which was not the least bit polite, so technically I was entitled to be rude under the theory of reciprocity. But we had sort of a history together. In an odd way, I felt responsible for Larry. He'd definitely gotten a raw deal from Rantwist, who'd set him up as kind of a poster boy for all that was evil in modern society. He seemed to me to be just a sweet, slightly stupid guy who likes to air his genitals in public once in a while. If exposure of private parts was the worst thing anyone did in this world, we'd be in pretty good shape.

Beth looked up from her desk in surprise when we walked through the reception area. "Where did he come from?" she asked, a bit late, I thought.

"Outside, ma'am," offered Larry politely.

Beth ignored his comment. "He must of snuck in when I was in the bathroom. Should I call the police?"

"Beth, I would like you to meet Larry Larkin. Larry, this is Beth Portucci."

Larry extended his hand, but Beth ignored it.

"I remember you," she said, looking at his crotch suspiciously, "and I ain't touchin' your hand. I *know* where it's been and what it's been doing. And don't you *dare* move that hat of yours unless your crusty ol' dingle is behind doors."

"Yes, ma'am," said Larry, letting his hand drop to his side.

"Beth, I'm going to take Larry to the downtown police station," I said.

"Hell, yes," said Beth emphatically.

"Larry has information concerning a possible homicide. I am going to accompany him to the police station as his counsel so he can give his statement, but Larry understands that once he gives his statement to the police, my representation of him is over." I looked meaningfully at Larry since the last part of my recitation was more for his benefit than Beth's.

Larry continued to smile benignly.

"Right, Larry?" I prompted.

He nodded happily.

I turned back to Beth. "I'm going to pick up some lunch and then go to Stranded after I'm through at the police station, so I probably won't be in again until tomorrow morning. If Stu shows up, don't let him do anything without talking to me first."

Beth nodded. "And you don't have to keep reminding me about Stu. Before he so much as looks at a can of paint, I'll tell him he has to call you first."

"Thanks, Beth. Oh, and when M.J. gets back, tell her she can have my tacos."

Beth nodded, but we both knew my tacos would be in M.J.'s stomach as soon as she saw my car was gone.

CHAPTER FOUR

▼

The drive to the station took only a few minutes. Larry nervously tapped his long nails on the dashboard nonstop. On every fourth tap, he thrust his head out the passenger side window and took huge gulps of air. When he saw my questioning look, he explained, "I got a hard time handling enclosed spaces. It's like everything collapses in on me and I need air."

I had my window open too. I needed air for another reason: Larry smelled like old sweat and urine. Every so often, I would stick my head out the window and take a deep breath. To onlookers, we must have looked like a couple of cocker spaniels out for a ride in the family car.

I parked at one of the pricey parking meters in front of the station (twenty-five cents for one minute; come on—who carries that kind of change?). After digging around in my purse and under the car seats, I came up with five minutes' worth of change. I told Larry we were going to have to make it quick.

After I fed the meter, we ran up the twenty-some steps to the glass front doors. A police officer wearing a name tag that read HELLO ... MY NAME IS OFFICER HARRY (an attempt at making the police officers more "user-friendly," I guessed) stood inside the door by the security desk. Officer Harry searched my purse, taking a ridiculously long time to do so, in my opinion, and after he had memorized the types and brands of my pens, lipsticks, and mascara, and scrutinized the store receipts in my billfold, he asked me to walk through the weapons detector. The machine beeped as I passed through. Officer Harry unsnapped his holster and placed his hand on top of his gun. I'm sure he would have called the head of the Arizona branch of Homeland Security if anyone knew it was; the position never seemed to be filled by the same person for more than a day..

I mentally smacked my forehead. "My keys," I said. "I have car keys in my coat pocket."

"Which one?" he asked suspiciously.

I pointed to my right pocket. He reached in slowly and pulled out my keys, which were attached to a huge metal key ring that looked like one-half of a pair of handcuffs. Beth had given it to me in response to my constant complaints about having such a hard time finding my keys in the chaotic interior of my purse. The key chain manacle solved the problem— not because it made my keys easier to find, but because it wouldn't fit in my purse. I therefore had to carry it in my pocket. Since the key chain was new, I had forgotten about this arrangement.

I went through the weapons detector again, and although this time I had nothing on me that could set it off, in my heightened state of paranoia, I believed it to be overly judgmental and capable of jumping to unsubstantiated conclusions. I breathed a sigh of relief when it didn't make a sound.

Officer Harry waved Larry through, and the weapons detector didn't react. Larry looked smug.

I collected my purse and keys and we took the elevator to the third floor, where the detectives' offices were. We disembarked and approached a dour-faced police officer sitting behind the reception desk.

"Hello," I greeted him politely. "I am Kate Williams, and this is my client, Larry Larkin." The officer ignored my extended hand and stared stonily at me.

"Are you an attorney?" he asked, in the same tone one might use when asking, Do you have a deadly, contagious disease?

"Yes," I said, smiling brightly as I withdrew my hand. "My client has some important information concerning a body found earlier today in a canal."

The officer checked a sheet on his desk. "The body on Thirty-Second Street, the body on Central and Hatcher, or the body on Seventy-Fifth Avenue?"

"The body on Thirty-Second Street," I answered briskly, although I was taken aback by the range of choices.

He checked his sheet again. "Detective Webber. I'll see if he's in."

Larry and I waited while the officer punched a couple of buttons on the intercom and said "Webber" in a loud voice. Apparently, he didn't get that the purpose of intercom systems is to cut down on the need for yelling.

After a short pause, we heard a voice answer. "What is it, Bramer, goddamnit?"

Nice office manners, I thought.

"Some attorney's here with her client, saying the client's got some information on the Thirty-Second Street floater. You wanna talk to them?"

"No, but it's part of this crappy job, so I have to. I'll be out in a minute."

I had to give Webber high grades for honesty.

A few seconds later, a door behind Officer Bramer opened, and a man I assumed was Officer Webber entered and walked over to us. He was of medium height, with thinning brown hair and pale blue eyes. His navy blue suit was rumpled, and his striped tie hung crookedly over a slight paunch. His thin lips were pressed into a tight frown.

"Detective Webber," he said, holding out his hand. I shook it and introduced myself and Larry. He started to extend his hand to Larry, but after giving him a quick once-over, he seemed to think better of it. He shoved it into his pocket instead.

I started to explain why Larry and I were there, but Webber held up his hand to silence me. "Let's go back to my office, where we'll have more privacy."

Since Bramer was the only other person in the room, I figured the comment was aimed at him. Bramer must have thought so too because he frowned and glared at Webber.

Larry and I followed Webber through a labyrinth of cubicles and offices to a small office with a view of the alley and a huge Dumpster with "cops suck" spray-painted in red on the side. Still, it was a corner office, and that meant Webber was high in the pecking order. Webber sat behind a metal desk and pointed to a couple of chairs in front of him.

I sat down, but Larry nervously moved near the window and continued to stand.

"Larry has a problem with enclosed spaces," I explained.

"Why do I get the feeling that's not Larry's only problem," muttered Webber, who then continued to address me and ignore Larry. "What can your guy tell me about the body in the canal?"

"Go ahead and tell the detective, Larry," I said.

"Can I tape this?" asked Webber, pulling a handheld recorder out of his drawer.

"My client will not go on record until we have discussed the terms of his cooperation."

Webber lifted an eyebrow. "Well, then, let's hear what he has to say, and I'll tell *you* what terms, if any, will apply."

"Can I open the window?" asked Larry, a touch of hysteria in his voice.

"Be my guest, said Webber magnanimously. "I'm warning you, though, we're downwind from the Dumpster, and trash pickup isn't until tomorrow."

Larry pulled the window open, leaned his head out, and took a deep breath of garbage-scented air, after which he seemed to relax and look a lot happier.

Larry pretty much recited the same story he'd told me. At first, he left out the part about taking the man's billfold, but I gently reminded him to tell the detective everything. Larry concluded by handing the soggy billfold to Webber.

Webber flipped it open, looked at the driver's license inside, and grunted. "Mr. Larkin, is this the guy you found in the canal?" he asked, removing the license and sliding it to the edge of his desk where Larry could see it.

"Yeah, I guess it could be. Hard to tell for sure 'cause most of his face was in the water and the back of his head was blowed off. I remember, though, that he had somethin' written on the part of his face that wasn't covered by the water."

"What did the writing say?" asked Webber with interest.

"It was starting to wash off pretty bad, but it looked like it said "tag." Maybe instructions to the intake guy at the coroner's office or somethin'. Pretty thoughtful if it was."

"Had you ever seen this man before today?" asked Webber.

Larry energetically shook his head no.

I leaned over and looked at the license as well, seeing a swarthy-faced man with thick, wavy black hair and a mustache. The name on the license was Richard Goldman. Neither the face nor the name was familiar to me.

"Did you see anyone else in the area around the time you found him?"

"Nope."

"Did you see any vehicles in the area?"

"I saw a white Mercedes, one of them big ones, comin' down Thirty-Second Street when I first got there. I hid 'til it passed before checking out the stuff in the canal. I didn't see no other cars, but I did hear the sirens after I left."

Webber turned to me. "I'd like your client to make an official statement. What assurances were you referring to earlier?"

"Mr. Larkin has a prior record, and he is concerned about future charges. We would like assurances that Mr. Larkin won't be charged with anything in connection with his removal of the wallet."

Webber smiled thinly. "What are his priors?"

"An arrest for felony assault and battery. The charges were later reduced to a misdemeanor charge of exhibitionism."

"And an arrest for public nuisance," Larry added helpfully.

"Did the arrests relate to similar activities?"

Larry nodded.

I sighed. "I wasn't aware of the arrest for public nuisance, but in any event, neither arrest involved dishonesty or endangerment of people or property."

"I'm guessing Mr. Larkin's penis shares his distaste for enclosed spaces," said Webber. "Look, I need to cite your client for theft. If I don't, defense counsel will make a big deal out of us letting him off the hook in exchange for his testimony. The bigger problem, though, is that, unless I miss my guess, nature boy here does not have a permanent address, and if I let him go, I'll never find him again."

We both looked at Larry, who nodded in confirmation.

"That being the case, I need some way of making sure your client will appear in court to answer the charge of theft. The easiest way for me to do that is to take him into custody."

"Coincidently, putting him in jail to make sure he shows up in court on the theft charges also ensures he'll be around to testify in the canal case," I said grimly. "You and I both know this theft could in no way justify more than a day of jail time."

At the mention of jail, Larry started to climb out of the window.

"Sit, Larry," I commanded. Larry obediently sat on the floor underneath the window. "My client will give you his statement provided you do not take him into custody on a theft charge."

Webber looked at me speculatively. "If I release him into your custody, will you make sure he shows up in court when he's supposed to?"

I looked over at Larry, who stared back at me in supplication.

"I'm an attorney, not a social worker," I groused under my breath.

I knew the police had no legal recourse against me if I failed to keep Larry in my line of sight; Webber hadn't formally arrested Larry, so technically he couldn't release him into my custody. He was just being a prick when he said that stuff about custody. If Larry bolted, the only consequence to me would be, at most, that I would feel bad. Larry would be the one in trouble, not me.

"Sure," I said. My stomach growled hopefully; it knew food would come once the Larry matter was concluded.

Webber shifted his gaze to my stomach. "That reminds me," said Webber. "One of the guys in the office ordered pizza for lunch. I'm going to go grab a slice. You two can stay here and work on Larry's written statement. I'll be back in a few."

Webber had a sadistic streak a mile wide.

After he left, I wrote Larry's statement on a legal pad, stopping to ask questions every so often to refresh my memory of what he'd said earlier. I read the statement aloud when I was finished, and Larry gave a confirmatory nod when I asked him if what I had written was correct. I showed Larry where to sign and held the pad while he affixed a large X at the bottom of the page, a process requiring that I go over and squat on the floor next to him since he wouldn't leave the window.

A few minutes later, Detective Webber returned, holding a half a slice of pizza on a napkin. He sat down, and I handed him the statement, my eyes fixed on the pizza, which looked great.

Webber nodded from time to time as he read the statement, but he frowned when he got to the signature on the bottom.

"What's this?" he asked curtly.

"That is my client's signature."

"I'll need you to sign a statement verifying that your client signed this document," he said, shoving the legal pad across the desk to me.

I'd been expecting this. I wrote a verification clause and signed it while the detective chomped noisily on his pizza. I figured he was exaggerating the process of mastication for my benefit. Either that or he had the manners of a pig. I guessed it could be both.

"By the way," he said, through a mouthful of cheese, "our office just confirmed the ID on the body your guy found. He's one of yours."

"What do you mean by one of mine?" I asked, without pausing in my writing.

"He is, or was, an attorney. Guy by the name of Richard Goldman. He practiced criminal law, like you. He got a name around here because he represented a local madam named Tangerine. Not too long ago, he was in court just about every day, all day, defending the madam's girls. The guy did pretty good money-wise. Drove a Bentley."

My head was bent over the legal pad, so I don't think Webber saw my shocked expression. I remember Tangerine saying that her previous lawyer retired rather suddenly, but I hadn't thought much of it at the time. Lawyers frequently leave their practices because of the sudden onset of sanity. Most of them did not end up with bullets in their brains, however. The fact that Goldman had didn't bode well. I tried to calm myself by rationalizing that there was no reason to believe Goldman's death was related in any way to his representation of Tangerine. Criminal law attorneys make many enemies during their careers: unhappy clients who blame their counsel (not the facts and, God forbid, not anything they did) when they end up in jail, or victims angry that the defense attorney got the bad guy off. Someone was going to be pissed no matter what the verdict was.

I finished writing and then stood, motioning to Larry that we were leaving.

"It's been lovely," I said sarcastically.

"I'm sure it has," said Webber, equally sarcastically. Holding his hand up with his palm facing me, he added, "I would shake your hand, but I've got pizza sauce on my fingers."

Asshole, I thought. I tried to comfort myself with the thought that lunch was in my near future.

Officer Bramer was eating a large slice of pepperoni pizza as we came back through the waiting room, and did not acknowledge us.

When we got to my car, I jerked a parking ticket out from under my windshield wiper. I threw it into the glove compartment when I got in the car was, and then detached the key from the weapon/key ring Beth had given me. I was not risking the possibility of another security check incident. As it was, I was lucky the overly conscientious Officer Harry didn't subject me to a body cavity search.

I glanced at my watch. It was already one thirty. "Larry, I'm going to drop you off in front of my office, and then you're on your own."

Larry, who had lowered his window immediately after getting into the car and had his head hanging out again, said, "You need to stay with me."

"What? What do you mean?" I asked apprehensively.

"I'm like your kid now."

"You are not," I said emphatically.

"I am too. I heard that cop say so. You got custody of me."

"He means I'm responsible to see that you show up for your court dates. That's all."

Larry vigorously shook his head no. "He said *custody*. I know what custody means. If he meant something different, he would have said something different. You're a lousy parent, by the way. You should have gotten me lunch by now."

"Stop it," I countered. "I am not your parent. I repeat: I'm going to drop you off in front of my office. That's more than you deserve after all I've done for you today."

"Do I get an allowance?"

"No!"

Larry slouched down in his seat and crossed his arms over his chest. "I'm gonna call Child Protective Services and report you for child abandonment and abuse," he said, following up with a self-righteous sniff. "People like you shouldn't be allowed to have children."

"Amen to that," I said with feeling.

I have a huge soft spot for society's outcasts, though, and Larry definitely fell into this category. In fact, he could be the poster child for society's forgotten and unwanted. I glanced at him and wondered when he'd eaten last. My ingrained Presbyterian guilt kicked in and I felt ashamed that I, a well-nourished woman with a comfortable life, was so concerned about my own lunch and getting my hair done, for God's sake, that I couldn't take time out to help this lost soul.

"Look, I'll swing into MacDonald's and buy you a hamburger before I drop you off," I said resignedly.

The lost soul grunted in disgust and said, "Yuck. You would feed a child food from MacDonald's? Do you *know* how much fat and salt is in their food, not to mention the negative effect the beef industry has on the environment?"

Talk about looking a gift horse in the mouth. But then I reasoned that Larry had every right to be a picky eater, and just because he was poor didn't mean he should lower his standards.

I dug around in my purse and produced a twenty-dollar bill. "Here," I said. 'Buy something organic."

Larry took the money without so much as a thank-you.

We were at my office, so I pulled over to the curb and stopped. "Before you get out, I need to know how to get hold of you in the event the police or prosecutor's office needs to talk to you again," I said, grabbing paper and pen from my purse to write down whatever information Larry could provide.

Larry felt around inside his pockets, produced a cell phone, powered it on, and peered intently at its screen. "You can call 602-945-2900," he said.

I messaged my left temple and sighed. "Is that your cell phone or is it Mr. Goldman's?"

"It *was* Mr. Goldman's," Larry said, "but like I said before, dead men can't own things. So I guess now it's mine."

I experienced a feeling of déjà vu. Apparently, I had to be very specific with Larry.

I held out my hand. "Give it to me, and give me everything else of Goldman's you still have."

He handed me the phone, then dug in his pocket and produced a pen, a folded, soggy piece of paper, and a set of keys. I would have to call Webber and let him know about the additional items. Maybe M.J. or Sam could deliver them to the station. I was in no mood to see Webber again today.

"How do I get hold of you?" I repeated.

Larry gave me a telephone number to call and assured me that either he or someone who could tell me where he was would answer. He also gave me the address of a shelter down on Van Buren Street, in an area largely populated by prostitutes, drug dealers, and panhandlers.

I tossed Goldman's stuff on the backseat and hit the gas as soon as Larry was out of my car and clear of the wheels. Lunch was out of the question. I was already late for my appointment, and rehabilitating my hair took priority over a murder investigation and just about everything else I could think of. I called Webber en route and was relieved when he did not answer. My call rolled over to his voice mail, and I left him a message describing the additional evidence and promising to have it delivered to the police station later in the day.

The traffic was relatively light, which was a good thing for the health and safety of Phoenix drivers because had it been otherwise, I would have bulldozed over anyone who got in my way. Stranded's parking lot was full, so I pulled into the driveway of a defunct hardware store next door, narrowly missing a man walking on the sidewalk, and screeched to a halt in a no-parking zone adjacent to a wall of oleanders separating the two properties. I threw the car into park, turned off the engine, and twisted around to grab my purse from the backseat, only to find that its contents had spilled out onto the floor. I'd probably forgotten to close it after giving Larry his lunch money.

I swore under my breath as I crammed everything back in with no regard for organization; not that I gave much regard to organization under normal circumstances, but this was an especially haphazard effort. I considered cramming Goldman's stuff in as well, but thought better of it since there was a good chance I'd never find it again in the capacious interior of my handbag. My friend Joyce claims that my purse will provide future archeologists with a challenging excavation, resulting in publication of findings that the twenty-first-century human diet consisted of mints, gum, and cough drops, and hypotheses concerning uses for the narrow cardboard cylinders containing hard-packed cotton. I decided to leave Goldman's things in my car, but hid them under the front seat in case anyone walking by got the urge to do a smash and grab. Stranded is not in a great area of town.

The oleanders swayed violently. A man burst through the foliage, which was startling but not particularly frightening. The frightening part was that he was pointing a gun at me.

My first thought was that he was a robber, although he seemed rather well dressed for that line of business; he was wearing a shiny Armani suit (probably a knockoff), a white shirt, and a red tie.

To speed things along, I tried to give him my purse. He pushed it aside and snarled "We're going to get back in your car. You drive."

He didn't want my purse, and he didn't want to steal my car. The remaining possibilities were kidnapping and/or rape, which, as far as I was concerned, were way less desirable than theft. I dropped all attempts to cooperate and swung my purse hard, knocking the gun out of his hand. Never underestimate the power of a handbag with ten pounds of pennies at the bottom.

I thrashed through the oleanders. The vegetation fought back by shredding my pantyhose and scratching my hands. I got through to the other side, made a run for Stranded, and burst through the front door. Four pairs of startled eyes turned to meet my single hysterical pair. I felt relief as the door closed behind me. The feeling evaporated when someone behind me grabbed my upper arm.

"Make an excuse to leave, and make it good, or everyone in this room dies," he whispered in my ear, shoving a hard object into my back, which I assumed was the barrel of the gun.

I scanned the room and spotted Michele standing with Christopher at the back of the shop. I smiled with forced gaiety and waved. "Hi, Michele. I just thought I'd drop in to tell you I've changed my mind. I've gotten such wonderful feedback on my hair. Everyone loves it. So I've decided to keep it this color."

Michele looked at me doubtfully, but then shrugged. "Whatever makes you happy. Call me if you change your mind and want to go back to blond, though. The offer of a free hair color change is still open."

"Thanks," I said, and then mouthed, "Help me." None of the faces turned my way gave the slightest indication that they understood. I tried again, this time exaggerating the movement of my lips. Nothing.

"Aren't you going to introduce us to the dude?" asked Christopher, eyeing with interest the guy standing in back of me.

I thought fast. Introducing him as "the guy with a gun in my back" would likely trigger—no pun intended—a negative reaction from him. "This is a friend visiting from Tucson ... Chris MacKay." Chris MacKay was a man I'd met while at the dude ranch, and with whom I'd had a brief, but intense, relationship. I silently apologized to Chris for blaspheming his name.

"Oooooh. What a coincidence. My name is Christopher. Are you a Christopher too, or is it just Chris?" Christopher smiled and wiggled his eyebrows flirtatiously (or suggestively—it was hard to know) as he continued to give Gun Guy the once over. He went on without waiting for an answer. "So are you and Kate friend friends or *friend* friends? Do you like male friends?"

I felt Gun Guy shudder.

Michele side-slapped Christopher's head. I silently applauded her, although I thought she'd waited too long. Despite my desperate circumstances, a small part of me was offended that Christopher had actually hit on a guy I was with.

"Well, we've got to go. Toodles," I said hurriedly, wiggling my fingers in the air like a sorority girl. I have no idea where the "toodles" thing came from. I'd never used that word before in my life.

My captor tugged my forearm, and we backed out of the shop. His large pinkie ring dug painfully into my skin. Michele did not offer a responsive farewell, but stared suspiciously at us. Christopher, however, waved merrily and chirped, "Toodles."

I prayed Michele would call the police, or at least my office, and raise the alarm.

Once we were outside, my escort roughly grabbed my purse cum weapon and hurriedly escorted me to my car. This time, we went around the oleanders. The plants had made their point to both of us; the fingers wrapped around my arm were scratched and bleeding.

"Get in the driver's side," he ordered.

I could tell from his tone that his patience was wearing thin.

The car was locked. "I'm going to need to get the keys out of my purse to open the door," I pointed out.

Without taking either his eyes or the gun off me, he placed my purse on the top of the car and conducted a one-handed search of its interior. A few moments later, he said, "You've got a lot of crap in here. Did you put your keys anywhere specific?"

"I just threw them in. They could be anywhere." I figured the longer it took for him to find the keys, the greater the chance someone would walk or drive by and see what was up, so I wasn't about to make his job any easier.

Out of the corner of my eye, I saw a car traveling toward us. The driver must not have seen us, though, because the car didn't slow down.

"Got 'em," the gunman announced triumphantly, as he hauled out a stash of bobby pins clipped to an elastic hair band. He tossed them on the ground and swore.

Once again, I chose to point out the obvious, even though Gun Guy's behavior indicated his mood was becoming dangerous. "That's not them."

No longer leaving the search to luck, he dumped the contents of my purse on the ground. "Find 'em," he snarled, pushing me down.

I took my time sorting through the various items, commenting every so often, "So *that's* where that was," and "I wonder if this still works."

Gun Guy waggled his weapon at me and nudged me with his foot. "Hurry up!"

I glanced again at the road and wondered why it was that every time I was in a hurry to get somewhere, the traffic in Phoenix was horrendous, but now, when I could really use a traffic jam, no one seemed to be on the road. I figured I'd stalled long enough, because Gun Guy was winding his foot up for more than a nudge. "Here they are," I announced, holding up my car keys, which were entangled in a string of neon pink party beads from last New Year's Eve.

He grabbed the keys from me, clicked the door opener, and then ordered me to get into the driver's seat. I complied, once again taking my time and daintily folding my legs into the car, after which he slammed the door shut and ran around to the passenger side. He tossed my purse into the bushes before getting in. Once seated, he slammed the door shut with unnecessary force and thrust the keys at me. "Head east on Camelback," he said.

I started the engine but hesitated and asked for clarification before shifting into drive. "I'm relatively new to the area. Is east right or left?"

"Right." He spoke through clenched teeth, and I could see the veins in his temples pulsing. I thought of suggesting that he have his blood pressure checked since he seemed entirely too excitable, but I thought better of it when I saw him tap the gun's trigger with his forefinger as if debating whether to bag the kidnapping and kill the witness. Now was not the time for flippancy.

The traffic was still disappointingly sparse, so I had no trouble pulling out onto the road. I tried to keep my speed at twenty-five miles per hour or under, which in Phoenix is the equivalent of standing still, but Gun Guy responded by reaching over with his foot and pushing down hard on the accelerator. Since my foot was under his, the situation was not only dangerous but uncomfortable, so I assured him I would keep the speed at the posted limit, which in Phoenix is still considered barely moving and invites all manner of creative hand gestures from other drivers, but is not as egregious and attention-getting as going under the limit.

I'd read somewhere that you should try to talk to your captor and "humanize" yourself, with the hope that if he sees you as a person and not as an object, he will change his plans. I certainly had nothing to lose, so I gave it a try. I started with the basics to break the ice.

"My name is Kate. What's yours?" I asked.

"I already know your name, and my name is none of your business," he answered.

So I was not a random target. Interesting. Could he be a stalker? Had he been following me for a while? I used side vision to study his face. I didn't recognize anything familiar about him.

"Have we met before?" I asked.

"No."

"How do you know me?"

"I know who you *are*. I don't know *you* ... and believe me, I don't want to know you. I hate redheads."

Looked at from a certain point of view, his antipathy toward my hair color was good news. It meant he wasn't attracted to me physically.

"Could you at least tell me why and where are you taking me?"

"None of your business. By the way, on the subject of hair, yours looks like crap. You shoulda taken that lady up on her offer and changed the color."

Gun or no gun, I came very close to letting go of the wheel and strangling him.

"Take a right on Fifty-Sixth Street," he ordered, oblivious to my murderous thoughts.

Through massive exercise of self-control, I did as I was told, and we turned off the main road into a residential subdivision ironically named "Happy Hollow." We were in the Arcadia District, a lovely older residential area with a scattering of churches and schools, irrigation-fed lawns, and lush greenery. The church I attend, Phoenix Presbyterian, is in this area. I could use sanctuary just then, but I didn't think Gun Guy was a churchgoer.

Many of the discreet ranch homes in this area, built in the 1950s, had been torn down and replaced by large, garishly appointed luxury homes as the newly rich discovered the charm of Arcadia.

"See that white house up there at the stop sign?" said my captor, pointing to a large McMansion that looked like the White House on steroids.

I nodded.

"Pull into the driveway."

I knew that whatever was going to happen, it was going to happen soon. Panic seized me, and I started to shake. Thoughts raced through my mind, foremost of which was who would take care of Ralph if anything happened to me. I pulled into the driveway and parked, but continued to clutch the steering wheel, based upon the irrational belief that as long as I stayed in my familiar little car, my home on wheels, I would be safe.

Gun Guy leaned over and grabbed the keys out of the ignition. "Get out!" he barked.

I managed to peel my hands off the wheel and step out of the car. My escort quickly walked around the back of the Honda, planted the gun in my back, and pushed me forward. "Go in the house," he said. "The door's unlocked."

I looked around to see if any of the neighbors were around. I felt a spark of hope when I saw the curtains of the house across the street move.

I figured my best strategy was to stay put. Once I was inside the white house, no one would see what happened to me. If he wanted to shoot me here in the driveway, well, let him try to explain *that* to the neighbors.

"Move, dammit."

I noticed an undercurrent of panic in his voice. "Not unless you tell me what this is all about," I countered.

I heard him punch numbers into a cell phone. "She won't move until I tell her what's going on."

I couldn't make out the other person's response, but a few seconds later, a man came out of the front door and strode over purposefully. He stopped in front of me and thrust his face within inches of mine.

"You know where something is that we need. You tell us where it is, and once we get it, you can drive away in your little piece of shit car free as a bird."

"It's a hybrid," I said defensively.

The new guy was shorter than I, maybe about five-six. He was wearing a business suit, white shirt, and a tie. An impressive beer belly hung over the waist of his pants and strained against the lower buttons of his shirt. His facial features were obscured by a Ronald Reagan mask, except for his eyes and lips, which seemed to float weirdly behind holes in the mask. I glanced at the house across the street again. Why was the house's occupant taking so long to call the police? Come on: two guys, one holding a gun and one wearing a Ronald Reagan mask. How much more of an impetus did he or she need?

"I don't care if it's hybrid or wheat bread," Ronald said. Gun Guy laughed appreciatively.

"Look, I don't know what it is you want," I said truthfully.

"I believe you do," said Ronald.

"I don't. Could you show me a picture or describe it? At least tell me what letter it starts with?"

Ronald adjusted his mask, which had shifted to where I could only see his nose and one cheek through the eyeholes. I thought a ski mask would have been a better choice. The little black elastic band holding the mask in place didn't look too secure.

"Quit dicking around," he said. "Tangerine gave it to you this morning. We followed her to your office. She didn't have it with her when she left."

My senses went on high alert. "How do you know she didn't have it?"

Gun Guy snickered. "Let's just say I conducted a *very* thorough search."

I heard sirens in the distance. They seemed to be getting louder. Gun Guy looked at Ronald nervously. Ronald said, "Shit."

A few seconds later, flashing lights appeared at the subdivision's entrance.

"Fuck," said Ronald. Gun Guy threw my car keys on the grass, and both men ran toward the back of the house. I heard a car start, and then a large, white Mercedes, tires squealing, appeared and took off down the road with an impressive big-engine roar.

The police car passed by the house in pursuit of the Mercedes. I was in no mood to wait around and talk to the next wave of law enforcement, so I scrambled around on all fours until I found my keys, and then threw myself into the Honda, pointed it in the direction the police had come from, and floored it. My little hybrid engine sped down the road with a discreet whine.

It was obvious to me that the two men were looking for the thumb drive hanging on the cord around my neck. The little sucker was feeling heavier and heavier by the minute. At this point, though, I was concerned less about the thumb drive than I was for Tangerine's safety, not to mention mine. What Gun Guy said about searching Tangerine sounded ominous.

I searched the passenger seat for my cell phone, and then remembered it was in my purse, which I had last seen lying in the parking lot of the old hardware store. Knowing that area of town, I'm sure it wasn't lying there for long. It and its contents were probably for sale on eBay by now. I did have Mr. Goldman's phone, though. I knew what I was about to do constituted tampering with evidence, but I convinced myself that the exigencies of the circumstances excused my behavior. I searched one-handed on the floor behind the driver's seat and found it. It felt wet, but its keyboard lit up when I powered it on. I called my office, and it rang through. Beth answered using her businesslike voice, clearly not recognizing the name on the caller ID.

"It's me," I said.

"Thank God! Michele from Stranded called and said you'd been abducted. She said some guy with a gun forced you into your car and made you drive. I called the police and gave them your license number. You have no idea what we've been going through."

What *you've* been going through?

"The jerk who kidnapped me wanted something he thinks Tangerine gave me. We need to track her down. I think she's in trouble, and she may be hurt. See if you can get her on the phone. I'm heading back to the office. If you get hold of her, make her stay on the line until I get there."

"But ..." I didn't hear the rest of what Beth said because Goldman's phone died. I didn't blame it. It had been through a lot too.

I caught sight of myself in the rearview mirror and startled. I knew the urgency of finding Tangerine overrode all other priorities, yet I must admit that I briefly considered blowing off my client's needs and returning to Stranded to get my hair rehabilitated.

I pulled into the driveway of my office and screeched to a halt. Beth met me at the front door.

"I tried Tangerine's home, business, and cell numbers. No answer."

I ran into my office, opened the top drawer of my desk, and hauled out the black notebook Tangerine had given me earlier. I turned to the "personnel" section, found Tuwanda's number, and dialed. Tuwanda picked up after the first ring.

"Tuwanda here. I'm beautiful, black, and have a slot open from seven to eight tonight," she purred.

"It's me, Kate."

Nothing.

"The attorney you met at Stranded. I gave you my card."

"Oh, yeah. Kate. I heard you're our new attorney. That reminds me; I gotta put you on my speed dial."

"Do you know where Tangerine is? I need to speak with her right away, and she's not answering her phone."

"This time of day, she'd be at her office. She's there from nine to five every day, no exceptions. Why you need her? She in trouble?"

"I don't know," I answered honestly. "I ran into a guy earlier today who wants something from her, and he didn't seem too concerned about how he got it."

"It's her little black book again, I bet. A coupla times a year, someone goes after it. It's like the Holy Grail or somethin'. They oughta make a movie about it, with Indiana Jones."

I was thrown off for a second by the Holy Grail comparison, but I recovered quickly.

"Do you have a key to her office?" I asked.

"Sure I do. I'm kinda like Tangerine's second in command. She trusts me with everythin'."

"Can you meet me there in fifteen minutes?"

There was a pause at the other end of the line. "I gotta five o' clock downtown. You think this'll take long?"

"You should have no problem making your appointment. See you in a bit." I hung up, not giving her a chance to back out. Tuwanda didn't seem to have my sense of urgency, but maybe she was used to this kind of stuff happening. She did say quests for the little black book were fairly common, and to date Tangerine seemed to have foiled the treasure seekers. I hoped she had come out of it okay this time as well.

I sighed and picked up the phone again to make one more call. "Kate Williams for Detective Webber, please," I said, hoping I would get his voice mail again. I didn't.

"Webber here."

I skipped the social niceties and launched into a brief description of my kidnapping and my concern about Tangerine, leaving out any mention of what I believed my kidnappers were after, and where that something was.

"So what do you want me to do about it?" asked Webber when I was through.

A part of me had hoped that I had overreacted to his personality during our first meeting. I hadn't. He really *was* a rude asshole.

"The police took off in pursuit of the two men who kidnapped me. Did they find them?"

"I don't know off the top of my head, sweetie. Believe it or not, we do have other stuff going on around here. Hang on while I check the computer."

I heard a series of taps, and then Webber came back on the line. "Nothing in the system about a kidnapping report, pursuit, or arrest. Are you sure you didn't imagine the whole thing?"

"Actually, I made it up just to have an excuse to call you," I sputtered. "I sensed there was something special between us when we met. I haven't been able to think of anything else all day."

I slammed the phone down without mentioning that earlier I'd used Goldman's phone, an important piece of evidence. I would tell him later.

"Beth, I'm meeting one of Tangerine's employees, a woman named Tuwanda, over at Tangerine's office. Do we have an extra cell phone around here I can use?"

Beth, who had been standing in the doorway, listening to my conversations with Tuwanda and then Webber, was already on top of the situation. She pulled a small phone out of her pocket and handed it to me. "It's M.J.'s. I got it from her office after you called on that other phone. I figured you'd need one."

Something in her expression told me that M.J. had no idea that her phone was now my phone. I would leave it to Beth to explain it to her. I had to get going.

I'd started to head for the door when Beth called out, "Wait, you don't have a purse. You're gonna need some cash. She unlocked the lower left drawer of her desk, dug around, and pulled out a fistful of ten- and twenty-dollar bills. "Take this," she said, thrusting it at me.

"Oh, Beth, I can't take your money," I said.

"It's from petty cash," she said, waving me away.

I'd had no idea we had a petty cash drawer. I would have to remember to ask her about it later.

"Could you call Stranded and reschedule my hair appointment?" I called over my shoulder as I shot out the door. "Anytime tomorrow is fine."

Today would be better, but life was not proceeding according to my plans. I would have to stay a redhead for at least another day.

I backed my car out of the driveway, spinning the wheels in the gravel in my haste, and then headed toward Tangerine's office, which is located in the south-central part of town. I called Bryan as I wove through traffic.

"M.J.?" he answered, sounding surprised. "Is everything okay?"

"It's me," I said. "I'm using M.J.'s phone because mine was stolen." I gave Bryan a summary of the day's events. I said nothing about the thumb drive, though.

"So you hair's still red?" he asked.

"I tell you about Tangerine hiring us, Larry and the dead guy, meeting with the police, being kidnapped, and basically getting snubbed by Webber, and you ask about my hair color?"

"Well, I was just curious …"

I cut him off before he could dig himself in any deeper. "Webber said the police records didn't show anything about a reported kidnapping and pursuit. I thought the car chasing the kidnappers was from the Phoenix Police Department, but could it possibly have been a sheriff's car? Could you check to see if your department received any reports on this?"

I heard rapid tapping at Bryan's end.

"Nope. Nothing. Maybe it hasn't been put into the department's system yet, although usually the dispatcher would make an entry as soon as the call came in."

"Do you have access to the police logs?"

"Not unless we're working together on a matter that's part of a multijurisdictional task force or it's a case where we've got dual jurisdiction, and even then our access is limited to information relating to that particular case. All other requests for information need to be made formally and signed off on by both departments. I take it you don't want me to go the formal route on this one."

"You got that right. I don't have time for formalities. I think Tangerine may be in real danger," I said worriedly, glancing at my watch. Too much time had already gone by.

"So your plan is to try as best as you can to put yourself in danger too. Isn't that a bit above and beyond the call of duty?"

I growled both in frustration and for effect.

"Okay, okay. I know some guys at the police department who will help me out. I'll give them a call and see what they can find. But I want you to call me as soon as you get inside Tangerine's office and let me know what's going on."

"Deal," I said, then ended the call. A few minutes later, I arrived at Tangerine's office. Pole Polishers' corporate headquarters were housed in a nondescript two-story beige stucco building with a red tile roof and no signage. No cars were parked in the area, and the building had a vacant after-hours feel about it. Apparently, the employees at Pole Polishers either enjoyed a short workday or started much earlier than most folks.

After a few minutes of waiting, an older model pink Cadillac convertible cruised down the street and backed into the space next to me. The sole occupant of the car waved at me. It was Tuwanda. I lowered my window, and she did likewise.

"Have you heard from her yet?" I asked.

"Nope. I even swung by her house and knocked on the door on my way over. She ain't there. But she never is durin' work hours." Tuwanda head jerked toward the office building. "Let's say you get out of that nasty piece of metal and we go in together."

I got out of the nasty piece of metal and eyed Tuwanda's car. "I get good mileage with this car," I said defensively. "These older model cars," I said, gesturing toward her Cadillac, "must be real gas hogs."

Tuwanda snorted derisively as she slid out of the capacious front seat. "This here is a nineteen eighty El Dorado with a chopped top, custom paint, custom leather interior, kicker subwoofers, amplifier, chrome spinners, an' dual exhausts. This here's not a car. It's a work of art. Callin' it a gas hog is like sayin' Michelangelo wasted too much paint doin' the Sistine Chapel, or he wasted marble on David that coulda been used for bathroom tiles."

I wasn't sure I understood her similes, but I decided to back off the car issue. We were wasting precious time. I needed to smooth Tuwanda's feathers so we could move off the topic.

I pretended to study the El Dorado again. "It *is* lovely," I said. "When we have time, I'll have to get the name of the shop that customized it for you."

This seemed to mollify Tuwanda. "My cousin did it. He got skills when it comes to trickin' up rides. He learned in prison. I'll give you his number later, but we got to get down to business. You wastin' time talkin' about car shit."

I followed Tuwanda to the front door of the office building. She looked elegant in a brown leather pantsuit, matching boots, and a cream-colored high-necked blouse. I stared enviously at her neatly coifed shiny black hair.

She pulled a plastic card out of a purse the size of a suitcase and swiped it through a metal slot next to the entrance. A buzzer sounded, and we walked in. The furnishings were sparse, the minimum necessary for a business operation: two faux green leather couches with a desk and chair in the reception area, behind which were two rows of cubicles. Each cubicle was equipped with a desk, chair, and a PC.

"Tangerine owns the whole building. Her office is on the second floor. The first floor's administrative staff. We'll take the elevator to her office."

An elevator in a two-story building? Tangerine apparently eschewed exercise. I admired that quality in a woman.

The elevator rose silently, gently stopped, and then the doors slid open. We stepped out into the dark room. I couldn't see where I was going, so I stayed put and waited until Tuwanda reached around and flipped on a light switch. The lights blazed on, and I let out an involuntary gasp.

The room in which we were standing had thick red carpeting and red-flocked wallpaper. Red silken ceiling-to-floor blackout drapes covered the windows. The red silk theme was carried throughout the room, with translucent banner-length swags hanging from the ceiling. The walls were covered with Baroque gilt framed oil paintings depicting women in explicit and creative sexual positions. An ornately carved gold gilt desk and a tufted red leather chair dominated the center of the room. Two enormous red and gold poufs sat in front of the desk. The overall effect was overwhelming. It looked like Hollywood's idea of a house of ill repute circa 1890.

Tuwanda had obviously been in Tangerine's office before because she showed no reaction to the décor. Plus, she seemed to know her way around. She moved quickly around the room, searching behind the desk and curtains. I was staring at a painting of a woman smiling down happily at her vagina when Tuwanda hissed to get my attention. She'd opened a side door and turned on the lights to an adjoining room. She jerked her head to the side to indicate that I should come over.

"Look here. This ain't good. There's blood everywhere," she said in a tight voice.

I joined her at the door and peered apprehensively over her shoulder, into a bathroom with the same color scheme as the office. I scanned the room but didn't see anything out of the ordinary (if you didn't count the gold gilt toilet), so I slipped in front of her to take a closer look. It was then that I saw the dark brown stains on the wall and mirror. I had to give Tuwanda credit. She was quick to spot the blood, despite the red wallpaper and paint camouflage.

"Do you think it's Tangerine's?" I asked shakily.

"How the hell am I supposed to know? I ain't never seen Tangerine's blood before, and even if I did, I can't tell the difference between one blob of blood and another. You need to be one of them CSI-ers to figure it out."

"I'm going to call the police," I said, pulling M.J.'s cell phone out of my pocket.

"Like hell you are," asserted Tuwanda agitatedly. To my surprise, she grabbed the phone and threw it hard against the wall. It shattered on impact, and its pieces ricocheted across the room. I was not having any luck with cell phones lately.

"No police has ever been in this building, and they ain't gonna get in now. There's confidential stuff all over this place. Tangerine'd go crazy if they was police in here. Uh-uh. No way. No police. We gotta find out where she is an' let her handle this her way."

I forbore from pointing out the obvious: that if this was Tangerine's blood, she might not be in any condition for decision making. The same thought should have occurred to Tuwanda, but I guessed she had entered the deep denial zone and wasn't coming back until she found Tangerine.

I made a quick and, upon later reflection, stupid decision. "So where do we look for her next?" I asked.

Tuwanda sat down heavily on the toilet seat and appeared to consider the issue.

"We could look at her appointments an' see if that helps," she said at last.

"Where do we find them?" I asked excitedly.

"She writes them all down in a little book she keeps on her desk or in a drawer. She don't use a computer for that kinda thing; says there's too many Net spies."

I trotted over to Tangerine's desk and searched the top. No book. I opened the upper left drawer and found an assortment of candy bars, but nothing else. I opened the upper right drawer next, and pulled out a small book covered in brown leather with *Appointments* stamped in gold letters on the front. Not subtle, but I figured Tangerine didn't think anyone besides her would be looking at it. I placed the book on top of the desk and turned to today's date. Tuwanda, who had emerged from her temporary think tank, nudged in next to me to take a look.

Tangerine's small, neat handwriting covered the page. Her appointment with me was recorded, as were several afternoon appointments with people Tuwanda identified as employees of the company. The name written in the one thirty slot threw her.

"It jus' says 'Asshole.' Who the hell is Asshole?" she said, half to herself.

"It's definitely not a name, and probably not a nickname. Maybe it's a description. Does Tangerine have an especially negative opinion of anyone in particular—that you know of?"

"Yeah. Your former boss, for one, but he's locked up, right?"

I nodded yes.

"Then there's her ex-boyfriend Freddy. He's a real turd. He threw her over for a twenty-year-old with no brains and a big butt. Freddy moved to Hawaii with Big Butt, but I heard he's back in town an' workin' for Tangerine again. I have a hard time believin' that, though.

"Then yesterday she was complainin' about some guy who was tryin' to shake her down, but hell, someone's always tryin' to shake her down. It gets to be kinda a joke. Someone comes along 'bout once a month an' threatens to tell the police about Tangerine's business. She just tells 'em to go ahead 'cause it's not like the police don't already know what she's doin'."

Tuwanda took a Snickers bar out of the left hand drawer. "I need thinkin' food," she said, as she opened the wrapper. While Tuwanda munched and went into thinking mode, I searched the remaining desk drawers. I found binders filled with meticulous time records for each employee, pens arranged in neat rows, and, oddly enough, a rubber hot dog. I'd purchased one like it for Ralph, and it was his favorite chew toy. I lifted the hot dog out of the drawer and looked questioningly at Tuwanda.

"Tangerine uses that for demonstrations," she said.

I put it back and wiped my hand on my skirt. I did not pursue the matter.

The bottom right drawer was locked.

"Do you know what's in here?" I asked.

"Nope. Can't be that important, though—just kinda important—'cause those locks don't hold worth shit."

Tuwanda daintily licked the vestiges of the candy bar from her fingers and then took a letter opener off the desk, inserted it in the space between the drawer top and the desk, and worked it around. There was a small click, and the drawer rolled open.

I looked at Tuwanda admiringly.

"I got a gift," she said, shrugging modestly.

A locked metal box lay inside the drawer.

"Go ahead," I said. "Have at it."

This time she took a small nail file out of her purse, worked the sharp end into the keyhole, and wiggled it around. The little box opened with even less resistance than the drawer. I would never again store anything important in something other than a bank safe. I doubted Tuwanda would have a problem with a bank safe either, but at least the guards and alarms would slow her down.

Inside the box was a gun—a .38 Smith & Wesson, to be exact. It was lying on top of a folded piece of paper, which I pulled out with a two-fingered grip, being careful not to touch the gun. I held the paper by its corners and opened it.

"Tag, you're it" was written in large letters.

Tuwanda and I looked at each other.

"That ain't at all helpful," she said.

I was about to agree when I remembered that Larry said Goldman had the word "tag" written on his cheek. I told Tuwanda about Larry finding Goldman's body and the statement he gave to Webber.

"Richard Goldman? Dead? Jesus, I just saw him last week. He done what you're gonna do: he represented us in court whenever we—well, whenever. Tangerine said he retired." Tuwanda sounded genuinely shocked and sad. "Anyway, he committed suicide? I mean, he was gettin' kind of morose in his old age, and no matter how much it pays, attorneyin' ain't the easiest job in world ."

According to the birth date of Goldman's license, he was forty-eight, which *is* old for a practicing criminal defense attorney. Burnout usually occurs around forty-five. Being morose is part of the job description, though.

"I don't think it could have been suicide. He was shot in the back of the head," I said.

"I see what you mean. Plus that thing about 'tag' bein' written on his cheek. Suicides usually leave notes with lots more detail. I know I would. I'd include a list of every piece of shit that did me wrong, so's they could live with the guilt. Then I'd have a section for SECRETS I HAVE KEPT, and I'd tell everythin' bad I know, and some stuff I'd make up about people I don't like. Ain't no one gonna question the word of a dead woman."

I made a mental note to keep on Tuwanda's good side, and to keep her away from pen and paper if she seemed depressed.

"So what's the deal with this tag thing, anyways?" she said. "Sounds like some kinda sick game. If you're tagged, you're out—real out. But who's still in the game? That's what we need to know."

A scary thought occurred to me. "What if the game is over, and the only one left is the murderer? What if Tangerine is dead and ..."

"Don' *say* that. Uh-uh. Do *not* go there. She's fine. She's gotta' be fine. We jus' need to find her. Did Goldman have anything else on him that could help? I don't mean more graffiti; I mean, like, other stuff."

I remembered Goldman's cell phone, keys, and the damp bit of paper under my car seat. I told Tuwanda about them.

"But the cell phone's battery died," I added.

"What kind is it?" asked Tuwanda.

"Samsung, I think."

"I got one of them. We can see if my car charger will work on it."

"I'm going to take Tangerine's appointment book with us. It may have more information we missed. Do you think she'll mind?"

"I think she'd mind dyin' more."

I shoved the book into my jacket pocket and followed Tuwanda into the elevator.

Once outside, we walked to my car, and I dug around under the seat for Goldman's things. I found his phone and handed it to Tuwanda. Then, with slightly more effort, I was able to locate the still soggy piece of paper and keys, as well as a tube of lipstick I thought I'd lost, two pens in addition to Goldman's, and a pack of gum. I shoved the keys and pen in my pocket.

In the meantime, Tuwanda had taken Goldman's phone to her car. She whooped triumphantly when the charger fit. I opened the folded note as I walked over to her, being careful not to rip the wet paper.

The message, written in blue ink, was streaked, barely legible in some places and illegible in others. The light was fading as the late afternoon sun sank into the horizon, making it even more difficult to make out what it said.

"Tuwanda," I called out. "Do you have a flashlight?"

"I don't got no flashlight. What d'ya think I am, a goddamn burglar? Wait a minute. Maybe I got somethin' else that can help."

Tuwanda plumbed the depths of her handbag and a few seconds later held up a small, oblong object.

"Use this," she said.

"What is it?" I asked, not able to identify it in the dim light.

"It's a Bic, an' it's special: it's a heirloom. So be careful with it."

"An heirloom?"

"Yeah. My momma gave it to me, and I used it to light her last cigarette just before she passed on."

"I'm sorry about your mother. What did she die from?"

"Lung cancer. She went to heaven halfway through a Marlboro."

I took the Bic and, as respectfully as I could, flicked the flame on. I held it behind the note, being careful not to singe the paper. It was bad enough that I was withholding evidence. I didn't need to dig myself in deeper by destroying it.

Tuwanda and I peered intently at the writing. It looked like an address. The numbers seven, four, and two were visible, but the next number could have been a three or a five, depending on how you interpreted the streaks. The name of the street looked like it could be Central or Columbia. The name of the town was clear, at least: Glendale. The city of Glendale is in the western part of greater Phoenix, and it's identical to the other towns and cities on the west side. Strip malls, two-story office buildings, and gas stations dominate the commercial areas, and houses representing styles popular in each of the last six decades ring the downtown area, with bungalows from the forties in the innermost ring and stucco Taco Bell houses built in this millennium in the outermost ring.

"Do any of those computers on the first floor have Internet access?" I asked, gesturing toward Tangerine's office building.

"Why? Internet's good for only one thing, and this ain't no time to go shoppin', which is sayin' something for me 'cause I love shoppin'."

"No, of course not shopping. I want to locate a mapping site and find out where and what our address options are," I said, holding up the faded note.

"Whooey. That's a *good* idea. That's why you get paid the big bucks. C'mon."

We started back across the street to the office when suddenly I felt light-headed and shaky. I grabbed Tuwanda's arm for support.

"You okay?" she asked. "Dear God, don't nothin' happen to *you* now."

I thought Tuwanda's concern was surprising but sweet; after all, we barely knew each other. I rushed to reassure her.

"I'm fine. I just haven't eaten all day, and I think my energy reserves just gave out. Let's keep going, though. I'll get my second wind after I sit down for a while."

"Good. 'Cause I got enough problems without needin' to take care of some white girl."

I reversed my previous impression of concern.

Tuwanda supported me into the building and led me to a chair in one of the myriad computer stations.

"I'm gonna go up and get you somethin' outta Tangerine's candy stash. You got a preference between Milky Ways and Snickers? I personally think you should go for the Snickers since they got peanuts in 'em, so they're more healthy an' all."

"A Snickers would be great." I didn't add that at this point anything short of a piece of leather sounded good to me, and I might even consider the leather if I had to wait any longer.

Tuwanda headed off to the elevator, and I powered on the computer in front of me. The screen flickered, and a picture of a man dressed as a woman flamenco dancer appeared. I figured Tangerine's employees had to be a bit offbeat to work here, so his or her choice in screen wallpaper came as no surprise to me.

I hit the Internet icon, and the search page appeared immediately. The incredibly efficient Tangerine had made high-speed Internet transmission available to her employees.

Tuwanda returned as I was punching one of the possible addresses into a mapping site. She dumped an assortment of candy bars next to the computer.

"I figured what you don' eat, we can take for later," she said, ripping the wrapper off a Snickers and handing it to me. I bit into the bar and swallowed the piece without chewing. Tuwanda had to pound my back to keep me from choking.

"Pace yourself, girl," she said.

We turned out attention back to the computer screen, and I finished inputting the address and hit "search." The information that popped up indicated that an elementary school was located at that address. An elementary school seemed inconsistent with the prostitution, murder, and kidnapping themes we were working with, so we tried the next address possibility. This one looked more promising. It was a residence in an area the Glendale civic leaders had officially designated the "Historic District," which, in a county where no structure was more than sixty years old, usually referred to a decrepit area of town dominated by bars, gas stations, and antique stores.

I wrote the address on a notepad.

We checked each of the remaining addresses, eight in all, and came up with two more possibilities: one was a lightbulb warehouse and the other was a horse stable.

"Where do we start first?" asked Tuwanda.

"The house in the historic district is the closest. Let's start there. We can take my car."

"Uh-uh. No way are you gettin' me in that li'l tin can. It's got no class. I need a ride with class. We're takin' my car."

I shrugged. "Fine. We'll take your car, then." I did not point out that a pink Cadillac with a burgundy interior didn't fall within *my* definition of class, because I didn't want to get back into the same argument with which we'd started.

Once we were outside, Tuwanda tried the door to make sure it was locked before walking to her car, where she politely held the passenger side door open for me. I slid in, having to bend only slightly to clear the car's roof. The spacious interior was remarkably comfortable. As soon as she was seated behind the wheel, Tuwanda buckled her safety belt, demanded that I do the same, and then grabbed her cell phone. "I gotta make a few calls. Do you mind if I talk while I'm drivin'? I know that kinda thing makes some people real nervous."

I assured her that I had no problem with multitasking, and we took off with Tuwanda steering with one hand and speed-dialing with the other. I tried not to listen, but I couldn't help picking up that she was rescheduling several of her evening appointments. Between calls, she said, "You think we can tie this thing up by midnight ... 'cause if not, I gotta cancel a whole slew more of appointments, and there's gonna be some real disappointed men at the bakery supply convention."

"I certainly hope things are figured out by then, but I honestly don't know. We have no idea what we're dealing with here."

"I think I'm gonna call Yolanda. Maybe she can cover for me. She ain't as good as me, but at least they'll get to the same place, though gettin' there won't be half as fun."

While Tuwanda continued to make calls, I picked up Goldman's phone, which was, thanks to the car charger, now completely recharged. I was startled to notice several new calls had come in over the last hour. All of them were from the same number. On impulse, I hit redial. The person at the other end picked up immediately.

"Kate? It's me, Larry."

I needed to learn how to control my impulses.

"Larry, how did you get this number?"

"I've been trying to get hold of you all afternoon. Beth told me you called in on this number before, so maybe I should try it."

I reminded myself again to talk to Beth about the screening process.

"What do you need to talk to me about?"

"That Goldman guy. I found something else in his pocket."

"What? You told me you'd given me everything you found."

"That was the truth at the time. I didn't find this until after I saw you. It was in the lining of my jacket."

"Your jacket or his jacket?"

"Like I said before," explained Larry patiently, "when someone's dead, they can't own nothin' no more. So ..."

"Never mind. Just tell me what you found," I said through gritted teeth.

"It's a photograph of two people havin' sex doggy style. I can't see the other person's face, but the one on top looks a lot like that guy Webber we talked to today."

"That can't be right. Are you sure?"

"I'm pretty good with faces, and I think it's the same guy, or maybe his brother."

"Maybe the other person is his wife," I said hopefully, although why Goldman would have a picture of Webber and his wife in his jacket was a complete mystery.

"I don't think so, unless his wife is a man."

I was quiet for a few seconds while this sunk in.

"You can't see his face. Maybe it's a woman with short hair."

"I can see his dangles," Larry replied promptly. "It's a real artistic shot. The angle is amazing. I'd say the guy who took the picture was lying on the floor in front of them and kinda shooting up. I woulda used a different background, but ..."

"Enough," I said. I had no interest in Larry's critique of the photographer's work. "Where are you now?"

"I'm at the Sacred Bleeding Heart Shelter over on Washington."

"What's the exact address?"

He told me. "You gonna come by for the picture?"

I turned to Tuwanda, who had finished her calls and was listening to my conversation with interest.

"Can we swing by 2020 West Washington on the way to Glendale?" I asked.

She nodded.

"Who's in the car with you?" asked Larry. "If it's family, I should probably be there too."

"It's not. We'll be by in ten minutes. Meet us in front of the shelter."

I ended the call before Larry could get into the custody issue again.

"I know what's at that address. I spent some time there myself. So why we goin' to some nasty-ass homeless shelter?"

I briefly explained the situation to her.

"Well, okay. But I gotta tell you, we are way overdressed for that place." She glanced over at me. "You might wanna take off your watch and put it in the glove compartment if you're gettin' out."

I did as she suggested.

We got to the shelter in five rather than ten minutes, but thankfully Larry was already waiting outside. Tuwanda pulled up in front of him, and I opened the window and stuck out my watchless arm. I wiggled my fingers in a give-it-to-me motion. Instead of handing me the photo, though, Larry opened the rear door and got into the backseat of the car.

"Larry, give me the photo and then get out of the car!" I demanded.

"Uh-uh. I'm going with you."

"You are not," I said firmly.

"Come on, Larry," I said in my let's-be-reasonable voice. "You don't even know where we're going. Believe me; we're not going to be having much fun."

"It's better than stayin' at the shelter," he said.

"He got you there," Tuwanda interjected. "Like I said, I been in that place before. One time somebody took a piss on my bed with me still in it. That's not right."

I did not consider her contribution at all helpful.

After briefly wondering if Tuwanda meant to imply that it would be okay if someone peed in her bed provided she wasn't in it, I let out an exaggerated sigh.

"Larry, you can come with us, but you have to promise to not do or say anything."

"You're stifling my creative young mind. You are such a lame parent."

"He's your son?" gasped Tuwanda.

"No! Larry is confused between short-term custody, for a specific purpose, and permanent child custody."

"Well, which kind of custody do you have of him, then?"

"I have custody solely for the purpose of getting him to court when he's supposed to be there, period."

"I don't know 'bout that. Either way you look at it, sounds like you're stuck with him."

"You are not helping at all," I snarled. "Just drive and don't offer any more opinions."

Tuwanda turned around to look at Larry. "You're right. She's a shitty parent."

"Drive!" I yelled.

CHAPTER FIVE

▼

We drove for five minutes in silence, with Larry hanging his head out of the back window again, like a cocker spaniel. I took advantage of the quiet and opened the envelope Larry had handed me. I slid the picture out. Because it was inside a plastic Ziploc bag, it had suffered no ill effects from being in the water. The face of the man who Larry described as looking like Webber, and whom I felt without question was Webber, wore an expression of ecstasy. You could only see the top of the other man's head, but Larry was right; you could definitely tell it was a man. There was something familiar about the guy's hair. I just couldn't put my finger on it. In any event, I now had a reason—better than mere personal dislike—to avoid Webber. It seemed as if Webber was not a disinterested public servant. In fact, the picture pretty much put him at the top of the list for best motive in the Goldman murder case.

I held the picture up for Tuwanda to see. She took a quick look, and said, "I know the cowboy on top. He's a cop. I seen him hangin' around Tangerine's office a few times. He tried to ask the girls questions about Tangerine's new man-ho division, until Tangerine told him that if he was there in an official capacity, he had to talk to her, and if he wasn't, he should go the hell away."

"I know there's not much to go on, but do you recognize the guy on the, er, bottom?"

Tuwanda glanced at the picture again. "I never seen them balls before, if that's what you mean. I do have a good memory for that kind of thing, especially if the client orders a number nine, 'cause your eyes get real close on a number nine. His 'do looks like Chris's, though."

"Chris?" I asked.

"Yeah, you know, the dude at Stranded. The one you made dye your hair red. You oughta get that fixed, by the way."

I started to deny that I had *made* Christopher color my hair red, but decided it was best to let it drop. The less I talked about it, the better. The subject made me too emotional.

"Does Christopher know Webber?" I asked instead.

"Damned if I know. I do know Chris's gay—it don't take no Dr. Phil to figure that one out—an' how many guys out there got a blond-tipped Mohawk? I wouldn't say it to Chris's face, but that punk shit went outta style a long time ago."

"I can't believe it's Christopher. That would be too much of a coincidence."

I made a decision and punched Bryan's number into my, or rather Goldman's, cell phone (I needed to watch myself; I was starting to adopt Larry's theory of entitlement). I cupped my hand protectively around it in case Tuwanda tried to grab it and destroy another phone. I guiltily remembered that I promised to call Bryan once I got to Tangerine's office. He would probably be ticked off, and for good reason. Bryan did not answer. My call went directly to his voice mail.

"Bryan, it's Kate. I found something that ties Webber to the murder of a man named Richard Goldman. At the very least, it will justify your office taking the Goldman case over from the police. I will drop it by your apartment later tonight."

"Who's Bryan?" asked Tuwanda after I ended the call.

"Bryan Turner."

"Bryan Turner? You mean Sheriff Bryan Turner? What the hell, girl? You said when we was at Stranded yesterday that you didn't have no more to do with that side of the law."

"I don't professionally. Bryan is a personal acquaintance."

"You mean your boyfriend's the sheriff? You must be one of them schizophrenics. Like a Dr. Jekyll and Mr. Hyde kinda thing. In the day, you defend the weak an' oppressed, and you makin' out with one of the oppressors at night."

"Bryan is not an oppressor. He's just a cop doing his job. And you are hardly weak and oppressed. Where do you come up with that rhetoric?"

"I'm weak and oppressed," Larry piped up from the backseat, although his voice was somewhat muffled by the sound of the air rushing through his open window.

Tuwanda turned to look at Larry. "You ain't so much weak as you reek." She then focused narrowed eyes on me. "And as for what you call rhetoric, I'm jus' a student of life, and I tell it like I see it."

"If you're a student of life, you must be in kindergarten!" Larry yelled from his wind tunnel.

"Larry, what did I say were the rules if you are to stay in this car?" I said.

"No doin' or talkin'," he said sulkily.

"Larry, I swear. I have a dog with better manners than ... oh my God! Ralph." I had forgotten about Ralph. It was long past his walk time. He must be frantic or, more likely, had already redecorated my condo in shades of brown and yellow.

I called Macy, who had a key to my condo in case of emergencies. "Hello?" she answered.

"Macy, thank goodness. It's Kate. I'm stuck at ... uh ... work, and I won't be able to get home until much later. Could you take Ralph out for me?"

"No problem, sweetie. Ain't it past his pooping time, though? I don't wanna have to clean up his mess if he couldn't hold it."

"That's fine. Leave the mess. Just make sure he's okay."

"Will do, sweetie, but you know I'll probably clean up. I can't leave that kinda stuff on the floor. It's against my religion. No Jew can walk away from a dirty floor."

"Thank you, Macy. I owe you."

I ended the call, and we continued driving in silence. Tuwanda finally slowed and took a right turn into an older residential area. She drove slowly, creeping along the curb and calling out street names as the signs appeared. She turned right again, stopping in front of a white two-story house with gingerbread trim, a front wraparound porch, and a picture-perfect yard surrounded by low shrubs. A small stone path wound through neat flower beds to the front steps. A painted wood welcome sign hung on the door.

"This doesn't look like a drug dealer's house," whispered Larry.

"That's 'cause it's not," Wanda hissed. "We're lookin' for a kidnapper."

"It doesn't look like a kidnapper's place either," Larry said stubbornly.

"What's it s'posed to look like? A big ol' rickety dark house with bars on the windows an' 'kidnapper' written on the mailbox?"

"Enough, you two," I interjected. "I'm going to go knock on the door."

"An' do what? Ask whoever answers if they got someone stashed in the bedroom?"

"No. I'll make something up. I just want to get a look inside."

"Okay, and if you see Tangerine tied up in the parlor, you be sure an' tell us."

I shot Tuwanda a dirty look and got out of the car, but by the time I reached the front door, I'd lost my nerve. What exactly *was* I going to say? I didn't have a chance to think of anything brilliant, or anything for that matter, because the door opened. A short, heavyset white-haired woman, who looked to be in her eighties, peered at me through thick lenses. She was wearing a pink flowered dress, an old white cardigan, and yellow flip-flops.

"May I do something for you, dear?" she asked pleasantly.

"Oh, um, I apologize for disturbing you, but I was trying to find a home offered for sale, that our real estate agent suggested we take a look at. I could only remember part of the address, though. I thought this might be the house." I looked behind the woman into the interior of the house as I spoke. The only area visible was an empty sitting room and the bottom of a staircase.

"Oh my, no. I've lived here for years, and I plan on staying here until the undertaker carries me away. Why, do you know something I don't?" she asked with a mischievous sparkle in her eyes.

We both chuckled at her little joke. "I must have the wrong house. I'm sorry. I'm Kate Williams, by the way," I said, sticking out my hand.

The woman shook my hand and introduced herself as Margaret Canton.

"Would you like to use my phone to call your agent for the right address, dear?" she asked.

"That would be nice. Thank you so much," I said. Things were going remarkably well. As I followed Margaret through the sitting room into a small, neat kitchen at the back of the house, I silently congratulated myself for quick thinking under pressure.

She pointed to an analog phone on the counter. The telephone, along with the other appliances in the kitchen, looked to be forty to fifty years old. Either Margaret had not introduced modern technology into her home due to a desire to maintain historical accuracy or because she could not afford to update.

I called Tuwanda's number with some difficulty, in that my finger was trained to punch, not dial.

"Hello?" Tuwanda answered uncertainly, probably because she didn't recognize the number I was calling from.

"Hello," I responded. "This is Kate Williams. We spoke earlier today. I was trying to find that house for sale, the one you told me about in the historic district, but I seem to have gotten the address wrong. Could you give me the address again?"

"What the hell you doin'? I'm sittin' out here with a stinky-ass homeless guy while you take your time inside. I saw that nice ol' lady who answered the door. She don't look like no kidnapper. Unless you found Tangerine in there sippin' tea, I say we move on."

"Yes, I think I have it now. Thanks so much for the address and directions." I hung up and called out to Margaret, who had been politely waiting in the hall to give me my privacy.

"I'm all set, Margaret. I was off by four blocks. Thank you again for letting me use your phone."

She came into the kitchen and beamed at me as if I'd done something incredibly clever. "I'm glad you got things figured out, dear. Could I offer you some coffee and cookies before you go?"

The word "cookies" vibrated happily through my mind, body, and soul. Cookies were my manna. I was convinced that the Holy Grail, if found, would turn out to be a cookie jar. It took every ounce of self-control I was capable of mustering to decline Margaret's offer.

"No, you've been kind enough. Might I use your bathroom before I go, though? It's been a long day."

"Of course, dear. It's up the steps and to the left. I'm afraid they weren't big on bathrooms in the forties, so it's the only one in the house."

I climbed the narrow stairs, taking another look around the sitting room as I ascended. The furniture was a bit shabby, but the overall effect was one of welcoming comfort. A copy of *Fortune* magazine lay open on the seat of an overstuffed chair upholstered in a floral pattern. Margaret must have been reading it when I knocked. I thought it was a strange choice for a sweet elderly lady, but to each his or her own.

I quickly scanned the rooms upstairs before going into the bathroom. There were two bedrooms, both of which looked like they were in use. The larger one was clearly Margaret's. It was sparsely furnished, with a neatly made canopied bed, a dresser, and a night table. A pink robe hung on the door, and matching fluffy scuffs sat next to the bed. A copy of *Better Homes and Gardens* lay on the nightstand. A suitcase sat on the floor of the smaller room, and men's pajamas were draped over a chair. Maybe a male relative, boarder, or friend was staying there. If so, possibly the *Fortune* magazine belonged to him.

The windows of both bedrooms were open, and a soft breeze blew through the rooms.

The part about my needing a bathroom had provided an excuse to search the second floor, but it also reflected a sincere need. I shut the door, sat on the toilet, and looked around while performing the necessary functions. The two toothbrushes in the holder and the separate tubes of toothpaste were consistent with the theory that another person was staying in the house with Margaret.

I didn't think the other person could be Tangerine, though. Based upon what the guy in the Reagan mask had said, and what we saw at her office, Tangerine's disappearance was not voluntary, and was probably accompanied by violence. People kidnapped under such circumstances were rarely allowed to bring suitcases, and there were no signs of anyone being kept here against his or her will. The doors and windows I'd seen were unlocked, and whoever the other occupant was, he seemed to have free run of the house. Finally, the pajamas I saw in the bedroom were, after all, men's.

I came back downstairs and thanked Margaret again for her hospitality. My reiterated thank-yous took on greater intensity when she handed me two cookies wrapped in a napkin.

"Here, dear, take these for later," she said.

I surreptitiously slipped the cookies into my jacket pocket on the way back to the car. I was not willing to share when it came to cookies.

During my absence Tuwanda had moved over into the passenger seat.

"You can drive for a while. I'm gonna sit up here with my head out the window like Fido back there," she said, jerking her head in Larry's direction. "I'm sick of breathin' in his smell."

Clearly, tensions had grown during my absence.

I got into the driver's seat and said, "You have to be the navigator, then. I don't know this town as well as you seem to."

"Tha's fine with me, but ..." Tuwanda stopped in midsentence and sniffed the air suspiciously. "You smell like cookies. You either got fed cookies, or that ol' lady gave you some to take with."

"We had some coffee and cookies. Which direction do I take from here?" I asked, trying to shift her attention away from the subject. I felt bad about not telling her about the cookies in my pocket, but the need to protect my stash trumped being honest.

"Turn around and drive 'til you come to Union, then take a left and head over to Grand. At Grand you take the right left."

"What's a right left?"

"You'll get it once you're there."

I followed instructions until we got to Grand Avenue, a five-way intersection where which direction was which was anybody's guess.

"So here's where you take the left that's right of the first left," Tuwanda clarified.

"You mean the left that's south of the other left?"

"Yeah. Goddamn, you lawyers are difficult, picky sons-of-bitches, ain'tcha. No matter what anybody says, you gotta tweak it."

"I like to think we're precise, not picky."

"Right. So when the Titanic's sinkin' and the captain yells 'Abandon ship,' all the attorneys onboard start arguin' an' tryin' to pin down the details, like who gets in which lifeboat, what you c'n take with, and the number of people you gotta let on the boat with you, and then they hunker down and draft an agreement *and* a letter demandin' a refund plus damages for all the shit that's happenin'. In the meantime, all the sane people are sailin' away in the lifeboats."

I didn't try to defend my profession in response to Tuwanda's critical commentary because she pretty much had it right.

We were finally on our way again after stopping for a red light at Grand, which lasted so long some of the drivers behind us, who were no doubt regular commuters along this route, got out, picked up coffee and soda at the 7-Eleven on the corner, and were back in their cars before the signal turned green.

We crossed the railroad tracks into an area dominated by huge, windowless warehouses surrounded by chain link fences topped with barbed wire. Interspersed among the warehouses was the occasional junkyard littered with car skeletons where parts were offered for sale. A wide array of hubcaps decorated the fences and the front wall of each of the wood shacks that served as sales offices. I wished we had come to the warehouse district first, before the sun disappeared completely. There were no street lamps here. The only light was the eerie green glow of the warehouses' security lights.

I pulled up in front of the building to which Tuwanda pointed, and turned the motor off. None of us made a move to get out.

"I think Larry should go check things out," said Tuwanda.

"Why me?" Larry shot back, which surprised me because he'd been so quiet during the ride from Margaret's house that I'd assumed he'd fallen asleep. It never would have occurred to me that he was actually following my orders to stay mute.

"Le's look at the facts here. You got two beautiful women here … an' you. Which one of us do you think would be less likely to be raped and murdered?"

Larry thought for a while. "If you take rape out of it, I think maybe we're all just as likely to get murdered, so it would end up the same way no matter which one of us it is. Dead is dead."

"Le's look at some more facts here. If you don't get outta this car an' take a look around I'm gonna kick your ass so hard you'll hafta poop through your mouth."

Larry looked at me, and I shrugged. I was staying out of this one.

"All right. I'm just gonna do a perimeter check, though," said Larry.

"A 'perimeter check'? You sound jus' like a cop. But then, I guess you been around enough police stations to pick up on the lingo," commented Tuwanda, as Larry got out of the car.

Larry walked around to her window and said, "You are not a nice person. I want you to think about that for a while." He turned on his heel and marched stiffly toward the warehouse, then disappeared into its shadows.

"Weird little dude," commented Tuwanda.

We silently watched the warehouse, straining to see through the darkness for any sight of Larry. The building looked like a slightly updated version of a Quonset hut. It had no signage indicating its ownership or function. The side facing us had two small windows, a long loading dock, and eight large metal garage doors. These doors appeared to be the only way to get into the building, at least from this side. No trucks or cars were parked in the adjacent lot, which from our point of view was a good thing.

An alarm went off, its sound ripping through the air like an air raid siren. Strobing red and white lights lit the building inside and out..

"We gotta leave," Tuwanda said urgently.

When I did not start the engine, she got out of the car, came around to my side, opened the door, and shoved me over.

"What about Larry?" I yelped.

"What about 'im?" she said. She started the engine and turned sharply. The car seemed to pivot on one wheel.. Maybe I would talk to Tuwanda's cousin about doing some work on my car after all.

As we roared off down the street, I turned to see Larry running out of the building. A police car siren sounded in the distance.

"Dang. I got beat up bad by a client 'bout a year ago, and it took the cops two hours to respond to my nine-one-one. A homeless guy looks into the window of a warehouse, and they're here just like that," she said, snapping her fingers. "We got fucked-up priorities in this country."

Tuwanda did not slow down until we got to a gas station adjoining one of the ubiquitous 7-Elevens, where she pulled in next to a gas pump. She filled up the car while I got us some sodas and an assortment of junk food.

"We'll just wait for a while and then go back to check on Larry," she said when I got back in the car with our groceries. She moved the car to a parking space, and we dug into the little pile of Fritos, potato chips, peanut butter crackers, and Ding

Dongs I'd purchased. I thoughtfully set aside a few sodas, a couple packages of crackers, and a package of Ding Dongs for Larry.

Tuwanda polished off the last of the Fritos and daintily wiped her hands on a Kleenex. If she and M.J. were in an eating contest, I wouldn't know who to bet on. How Tuwanda managed to stay so thin was beyond me.

"Let's drive by that last address where the horse stables is before we go back to the warehouse. We got time. It'll take the cops a while to figure out there's nothin' goin' on at that warehouse."

I nodded yes, a mouthful of crackers preventing me from giving a verbal response.

We drove north into a largely agricultural area. Irrigated fields of cotton and soybeans lay on either side of the road, interrupted from time to time by bladed tracts of brown soil with signs announcing the construction of new subdivisions with names like "Bellagio" and "Portobello."

"Damn, you'd think we're in Europe or maybe Las Vegas. Why don' they use the names of local shit, like Skunk Creek or Bloody Basin?"

"I think you just answered your own question," I remarked.

Tuwanda pulled off to the side of the road in front of a freshly graded area, where a sign announced the future site of the Grand Venetian Townhomes.

"There's the stables," she said, pointing to the sign.

I was actually relieved. I didn't feel like conducting any more clandestine property searches. The close call at the warehouse was too much for me.

Tuwanda turned the car around, and we headed back toward the warehouse.

"Is there anything more you can tell me about Tangerine that could help us find her?" I asked. "Does she have family in town? Who are her friends? What does she like to do?"

"You got anymore Ding Dongs left? I need more thinkin' food."

"I have one package left, and I'm saving it for Larry. Here, have a Coke. It's got enough caffeine in it to stimulate your brain cells for a week."

Tuwanda took the Coke and sipped for a while.

"I don't know about no family. It's hard to picture Tangerine havin' a mother, father, brothers, sisters, an' shit. There might be someone in town, though—someone who, if not a relative, is a good friend—'cause every so often Tangerine disappears for a little R & R, and goes to what she calls 'Mary's Cottage.'"

"That could be a hotel, maybe."

"I dunno. It ain't a local motel or hotel or one of them bed-and-breakfasts, that much I know. We needed to get hold of her while she was away once, and there ain't no listin' for Mary's Cottage, at least in Arizona."

Tuwanda sniffed and rubbed her eyes. "I hope she's okay. Tangerine's all business, but she's done right by us Care Bares. I can't stand the thought of her not bein' up in her office every day talkin' on the phone or readin' one of her boring-ass *Fortunes*."

I patted Tuwanda's arm sympathetically. "There's something very human and vulnerable about people who read their fortunes every day; it's as if they trust fate more than themselves."

Tuwanda glared at me through watery eyes. "What the hell you talkin' about? Tangerine doesn't read no fortunes. She thinks all that stuff is bullshit. I mean, she reads *Fortune* magazine."

I thought of the magazine I'd seen at Margaret's. But many people read *Fortune*, so it probably didn't mean anything.

"Say, Tuwanda, this may sound like a strange question, but have you ever seen Tangerine in her pajamas?"

Tuwanda's grip tightened on the steering wheel. "What you tryin' to imply? 'Cause I like my employer, it don't mean I'm sleepin' with her. Tha's the trouble with you civilians. You think everythin' we do or say in my industry is about sex."

"Geez, you're defensive. I only asked because I saw men's pajamas in Margaret Cantor's guest room."

Tuwanda seemed to settle down a bit. At least it didn't look like she was trying to strangle the steering wheel any more.

"As a matter of fact, Tangerine does wear men's pj's. She sleeps at the office once in a while when things get real busy, an' I seen her goin' into the coffee room early in the morning wearin' 'em. But that don't mean nothin'. Lots of people, men especially, wear men's pj's."

I told Tuwanda about seeing the *Fortune* magazine in the parlor, and thinking at the time that it did not seem like the kind of reading material Margaret would choose.

"It ain't much to go on, but it's somethin'. Unless Larry found somethin' at the warehouse, I say we go back an' talk to Mrs. Cantor."

I checked my watch. It was just before eight, still early enough for a social visit. I didn't want to scare Mrs. Cantor by pounding on her door late at night at a time when visitors only brought bad news or were themselves bad news.

Tuwanda slowed down as we neared the warehouse, and we both looked around nervously for any sign that the police were still in the vicinity. About a block away from the warehouse, a man dashed out from the shadows, plastered his face against my window, and pounded on the door. Aside from his extremely agitated demeanor, Larry didn't look as if he'd suffered any ill effects from his adventure.

I reached behind me and unlocked the rear door. Larry opened it and threw himself into the backseat.

"You left me!" he screamed. "You left me there to die!"

"Well, if we did, we fucked up, 'cause here you are, alive an' screamin' an' stinkin'," said Tuwanda, unfazed by his dramatic performance.

"Here, have something to eat and then tell us what happened," I said, tossing him the packages of crackers and Ding Dongs I'd saved for him.

"Nothing to drink?" he asked sulkily.

I handed him a Coke.

"You're paying my dental bills," he said.

Tuwanda headed back toward Mrs. Cantor's house. Tuwanda and I waited with varying levels of patience for Larry to finish eating before we peppered him with questions. As soon as he'd devoured the last bite of his junk food feast, I asked, "So what happened back there?"

"Nothin," Larry answered promptly.

"Did you see anything inside the warehouse?"

"Nope. Cops came before I could look."

"Did you go back after they left?"

"Didn't think it was necessary."

I sighed in exasperation. "Larry, it's important that we know what's inside that warehouse. Someone's life could be at stake here."

"Yeah, well *my* life was at stake, and no one seems to care."

Tuwanda and I glanced at each other. I knew I was wearing a guilty expression, but Tuwanda's appeared unrepentant.

"Larry, we felt sure you would be okay. We never would have taken off like that if we thought you couldn't handle the situation."

"Damn. I am *not* goin' back to that place again tonight. It'll jus' hafta wait 'til mornin'. What was you thinkin', you dumb li'l man?" raged Tuwanda.

We were silent for a while, and then a thought occurred to me. "Larry, did the police search the warehouse?"

"Yup. Every damn square inch."

I now understood what he had been trying to tell us. Larry felt it was unnecessary to search the warehouse because the police had done it for him. If the police had found Tangerine inside, more law enforcement and emergency vehicles would have shown up and the area would be blocked off as a crime scene. The police's response to the building's alarm was the best thing that could have happened under the circumstances, because it was doubtful whether Larry could have gained access to the locked warehouse anyway.

I told Tuwanda what I was thinking.

"I love that. For once, the cops actually did somethin' helpful. Course, they don' know that, and it's jus' as well 'cause it would piss 'em off."

I turned toward the backseat and said, "You did good, Larry," although I'm not sure he heard me because his head was hanging out the window again.

Tuwanda got us to Glendale's historical district in record time, a feat made possible by the near-miraculous cooperation of the traffic lights at Grand Avenue. At Larry's request, we dropped him off at a 7-Eleven about three blocks away from Margaret's house so he could use the bathroom. I gave him some cash for more junk food, promising we'd be back for him in a half hour.

Both Tuwanda and I went up to the front door of Margaret's house this time. We had decided after a brief discussion in the car that the direct approach was best, and direct approaches were Tuwanda's specialty.

The house was dark, even though it was only about eight thirty. I rang the doorbell and, after waiting a minute or so, knocked on the door. Still no response. Tuwanda took over and pounded on the door while ringing the doorbell.

"Geez, Tuwanda," I hissed. "Lighten up. I don't want to scare Margaret. We don't even know if Tangerine's here. All we have to go on is a magazine and a pair of pajamas."

"I feel for the ol' lady. I really do. But we been drivin' around all night, an' so far we got nothin'."

I could hear Tuwanda sniffling.

"Tuwanda, we've done the best we can, and you've been wonderful. Tangerine would be proud of you if she knew everything you've done to try to find her," I said. I put my arm around Tuwanda and gave her a squeeze.

At that moment, the door flew open, and a very irritated, and then surprised, Tangerine stared out at us.

CHAPTER SIX

▼

Tangerine looked as though she had been just about to go to bed. She was wearing the blue men's pajamas I'd spotted earlier, covered by a blue and black striped man's robe, which she now wrapped tightly around her in a protective manner. She motioned for us to come inside. Once we'd entered, she quickly closed the door behind us. Tuwanda, unable to hold back anymore, threw her arms around Tangerine.

"You okay? We been so worried. We saw blood in your office, and …"

Tangerine winced and extricated herself from Tuwanda's bear hug. "I'm fine. I just needed a break. I'm sorry to have worried you," she said in an oddly strained voice.

"You're not fine," I said, pushing the sleeve of her robe up gently. Her wrist was badly bruised, and by the stiff way she held her arm and the rest of her body, I guessed the damage wasn't limited to her wrist. "Who did this to you?"

Tangerine stared at me for a while and then smiled slightly. "Attorney-client privilege?"

"Attorney-client privilege doesn't extend to third parties who are not otherwise covered by the privilege." Both Tangerine and I turned to look at Tuwanda.

"Hell no, Tangerine. I been drivin' around with a smelly old homeless guy in the backseat looking for you all night, and I been worried ev'ry second. Ain't no way you gonna tell her what's been goin' on and not me. After she invited the stinky dude into my car, she mostly just sat in the passenger seat and talked to her boyfriend. I'm gonna have to get my 'polstery cleaned 'cause of that bum. He smells like a week-old dead rat marinated in sweat and piss."

"Who are you talking about?" Tangerine asked. "Is this person out in the car now?"

"No. We dropped him off at the 7-Eleven so he could use the toilet and get somethin' to eat. I don' know about the toilet part, though. With his problem bein' inside places and all, he pro'bly likes to pee al fresco. He don' need no toilet."

Tangerine looked at me and raised an eyebrow.

"His name is Larry Larkin. He's … er … a client of mine. He came to my office this morning after he found a body in the canal. He didn't want to go to the police alone to report the incident, so I agreed to represent him for the limited purpose of his discussions with the police." I had to be careful of what I said about Larry. The attorney-client privilege belonged to him as well.

I softened my voice before delivering the next bit of news. "The police identified the body Larry found as that of Richard Goldman."

Tangerine swayed slightly and grabbed the staircase newel to steady herself, moaning softly through slightly parted lips. Her eyes reflected anguish as well as another emotion: fear.

I placed my hand under her elbow to give her extra support. She shook her head slightly and gently pulled away.

"Let's all sit down," she said weakly. She led the way into the small front parlor. Her gait was slow and stiff.

Tuwanda and I sat next to each other on the couch, and Tangerine sat in the chair where the *Fortune* magazine was lying before. I noticed dark circles under her eyes, which hadn't been visible in the dimly lit foyer. Her body radiated a combination of tension and exhaustion.

"Richard was supposed to meet me here tonight. He was late, and when I heard you ring the bell, I thought it was him.

What happened to him?" Her voice was soft and her hands shook. The woman sitting across from me was a far cry from the confident, businesslike woman I'd seen in my office earlier that day.

I told her the circumstances under which Goldman was found, without mentioning why Larry happened to be wading in the canal at the time, and I described the "tag" note written on Goldman's cheek. I didn't want to get Tuwanda in trouble, so I didn't mention that we'd found a similarly worded note while snooping through the locked drawer of Tangerine's desk.

"Did your client report his discovery of Richard's body to the police?" she asked.

"Yes. I took Larry to the police department on Washington, and he gave his statement to the detective assigned to the case."

Tangerine nodded wearily. "Which detective would that be?"

"Detective Webber."

Tangerine placed a hand over her eyes.

"Was anything else found on Richard's body?"

"Yes. The police had already recovered the body by the time Larry gave his statement, and I don't know what all the police found, but Larry, um, borrowed Mr. Goldman's jacket and found his billfold, cell phone, some keys, and a note with an address written on it in the pocket. He also found a photograph hidden in the lining of the jacket."

Tangerine plucked nervously at the end of the tie on her robe. "Webber has these items?"

"We delivered the billfold to the police. I still have the remaining items. In light of the content of the photo Larry found, I decided to turn them over to the sheriff's department instead of the police."

Tangerine's hands dropped from her eyes, and she sat back in her chair. It may have been my imagination, but she seemed to relax a bit.

"Why did you come to find me?" she asked next.

I told her about being kidnapped by Gun Guy and Reagan; how what Gun Guy said about searching her made me worry that she may have been harmed; how I got hold of Tuwanda and met her the office at Pole Polishers; and how we discovered the blood in the bathroom and feared that she might have been injured and kidnapped ... or worse.

"Why did you think the address in Richard's pocket had anything to do with where I was?"

I looked at Tuwanda, who gave me a slight nod.

"We searched your desk and found a message that said, 'Tag, you're it.' The word 'tag' was written on Mr. Goldman's cheek when his body was found. We were afraid whoever shot him was going after you next and may had already kidnapped you. The address on the note was the only lead we had.

Tangerine smiled briefly. "Are there any candy bars left?" she asked, looking at Tuwanda.

"No, ma'am. I will buy you some more, though," Tuwanda said earnestly.

Tangerine turned her attention back to me. "Do you have any idea who those men who kidnapped you were, or what they were after?"

"Both of them were white and on the short side. The guy with the gun was maybe five feet nine, tops, and the other guy was only about five-six or five-seven. Obviously, I couldn't see the masked man's face, but he had light brown hair with graying temples, light blue eyes, and an impressive beer belly. The other guy had curly dark hair, brown eyes, kind of a longish nose, and a mustache. He was wearing a flashy suit, white shirt, red tie, and a gold pinky ring."

Tuwanda and Tangerine looked at each other knowingly and simultaneously said, "Freddy."

I was briefly at a loss, but then I remembered that Tuwanda had told me earlier that Freddy was Tangerine's ex-boyfriend.

"Ain't Freddy in Hawaii?" asked Tuwanda.

Tangerine sighed. "He came back last week. I gave him a job. He said he needed the money."

Tuwanda shook her head and tsk-tsked. "Way that man treat you, you shoulda tol' him where to go, and what to do when he got there."

I cut Tuwanda off before she gave more relationship advice. After all, Tangerine was her boss. "Do either of you know who the masked guy might be?" I asked.

"That coulda been that lazy-ass friend of Freddy's that used to work for Pole Polishers as a bouncer at some of our 'Gettin' to Know You' functions. Tangerine, didn't you bounce his *own* ass out 'cause he was dippin' his pen in the company ink? Anyways, he and Freddy hung out all the time before Freddy left town."

Tangerine nodded in agreement. "It could have been him. Tom Fields is his name."

"If it is this Tom Fields, he was careful not to let me see his face. Freddy, on the other hand, didn't care if I saw his."

Tuwanda snorted. "Freddy's jus' stupid. Plus, he thinks he's so good-lookin' he pro'bly didn't want to hide his face behind a mask." Tuwanda paused, and her eyes narrowed. "Why's Freddy goin' after you?"

Tangerine answered before I had a chance to plead ignorance. "I believe he thinks I gave Kate some important information, and I believe he wants to get that information and use it against me, unless, of course, I pay him."

"Dang. Ol' Freddy's big-butt girlfriend must've spent all his hard-earned cash, and now he need to raise some more—a lot more—to keep her happy." Tuwanda put her hand over her mouth and glanced nervously at Tangerine, clearly realizing a little late in the game that Tangerine might be sensitive about the subject of Freddy's new girlfriend.

Tangerine responded with a soft chuckle. "Mercedes does have a rather large derriere," she said.

Tuwanda's shoulders relaxed, and she grinned. "I think Mercedes mus' be her nickname 'cause she's got a big trunk. I don' know how that bitch finds bathin' suits. There must be a special shop that sells size four tops and size sixteen bottoms."

A muffled voice called from upstairs. "Katherine? What are you doing down there? Is everything all right?"

"Everything's fine, Mother. You can go back to bed," Tangerine answered.

"You got a mother?" Tuwanda asked in disbelief.

A smile tugged at the corners of Tangerine's mouth. "I do indeed. I'm flattered that you believed I might be the product of immaculate conception, though." Addressing me, she said, "I think you met my mother earlier this evening. I thought her description of the lost house hunter fit you, but I couldn't see how you possibly could have gotten this address."

"Yes, we were here earlier looking for you. The address on the paper in Mr. Goldman's pocket was partially illegible. We narrowed down the possibilities to three addresses. This was the first place we looked. I was thrown off by the fact that no one in the house was tied up or locked in a room; and the only evidence that there was another occupant in the house was a *Fortune* magazine in the sitting room, which didn't look like the kind of reading material your mother would choose, and a pair of men's pajamas in the spare bedroom. So we left to check out the other addresses. We came back here after Tuwanda mentioned you are a loyal reader of *Fortune* magazine, and that you wear men's pj's. We figured it was a long shot, but here you are. Your mom is really sweet, by the way."

"She is, and she's a wonderful cook. She said she gave you a couple of her special Toll House cookies to take with you. Did you like them?"

Tuwanda harrumphed. "I knew I smelled cookies on you when you got back in the car. You said you didn't have no cookies on you. Here I been foraging for food for you an' sharin' packages of snack food, an' you hidin' fresh cookies. Tha's mean."

I had the common decency to look ashamed, but I still did not let on that the cookies were still in my pocket. I had plans for them. Personal plans.

"Let me get you some from the kitchen, then," said Tangerine, laughing, "although between cookies and chocolate bars, you two haven't had much real food tonight."

"Don' worry 'bout us. We got some healthy stuff at the 7-Eleven earlier—you know, like Fritos and Ding Dongs an' shit. O' course, I didn't know Red here was holdin' out on the cookies."

"Do you need any help in the kitchen?" I asked politely, bringing the focus back to Tangerine's offer and making it clear that at least I was still interested in more junk food.

"Uh-uh," interjected Tuwanda, jumping to her feet. "If anyone helps, it's gonna be me. You'd probably eat 'em all before you made it back. You got a problem, girl."

A few minutes later, Tangerine returned carrying a plate of cookies, followed by Tuwanda, who was carrying three cups and a full coffeepot on a little silver tray.

After everyone was seated again, I poured cups of coffee for the other two women and myself, and took a cookie after passing the plate to Tuwanda and Tangerine, all to prove, more to myself than to them, that I could control my cookie impulses, at least in a social setting.

We quietly sipped and nibbled for a while. The cookies were superb. Despite my best efforts, my nibbling transitioned into alligator bites.

I was the first to break the silence because I was the first to finish.

"Katherine, now that we've answered all your questions, could you please answer a couple of mine?"

Tangerine glanced at Tuwanda. "I would be happy to, but, as you mentioned before, Tuwanda is not covered by the attorney-client privilege." Addressing Tuwanda, she said, "It's not that I don't trust you. I just don't want to get you involved in this mess. I hope you understand."

"You don' gotta hit me over the head. I get it. You want ol' Tuwanda to leave the room."

"Yes, if you could, please," said Katherine.

"Fine. I'll be in the kitchen with the rest of the cookies and, if it's okay, with some of that cake I saw in the fridge."

Katherine nodded graciously. "Help yourself to cake, cookies, and anything else in the refrigerator that appeals to you."

Tuwanda practically ran to the kitchen. She obviously had no hard feelings about being excluded from our discussion when free access to food was offered as an alternative.

I waited until I heard the kitchen door close, and then I asked, "Who beat you up ... and why?"

Katherine sat back wearily and brushed her hand over her face.

"I don't know," she said. Whoever it was came at me from behind and shoved me into the bathroom. The blood you saw in there was where my head hit the wall." Tangerine raised the hair covering her forehead to show me a two-inch cut. "Then he grabbed my wrist and forced my arm behind my back. He demanded that I give him a copy of the electronic file I gave your earlier today. He also asked about a photograph. I didn't recognize his voice. That doesn't mean he wasn't someone I knew. It sounded as if he was disguising his voice by speaking in a falsetto.

I don't know anything about the photo he wanted, though. Could it possibly be the one your Mr. Larkin found on Richard? Did you by chance look at it?"

"Yes," I answered. "The photo is of two men appearing to be in the middle of a sexual act. I think one of the men was Webber. Do you think the man in your office could have been him? He certainly has a strong motive to recover the photo."

Katherine seemed to consider this possibility. "It could have been. I just don't know." Something in her expression made me think she knew more than she was telling me, though.

"Katherine, do you know where that photo came from?"

She sighed and stared at her hands. "If it's the one I'm thinking of, it was taken by an old client of Richard's. The client gave it to Richard, thinking Richard could use it as leverage to get the police to drop a string of minor drug charges against him. Richard immediately recognized the photo as having been taken at a launch party my company threw last night for a new subsidiary specializing in man-on-man services. He didn't want to do anything with the photo until he talked to me first. He called me, but I wasn't in, so he left a voice mail outlining the situation and told me he would meet me here tonight with the photo. I didn't listen to his voice mail until I came back from your office.

"Maybe Webber found out about it from Richard's client, and then came looking for me , thinking that since the photo was taken at my establishment, one of my people took it and I had the original. If that's what he was doing, though, why would he ask for copies of the files, too? Was he looking to blackmail me as well as recover the photo?

"In any event, when I said didn't have anything to do with the picture and did not have any files, he twisted my arm behind my back and grabbed me around the neck. I think he would have killed me, except he got distracted when the downstairs receptionist buzzed my office. I broke away and ran down the rear steps without looking back. Then I got in my car and drove to my mother's house. I don't think he followed me."

"Freddy seemed to know you'd been searched. Do you think he could be in contact with Webber somehow?"

Tangerine shook her head no. "I have no idea. As far as I know, Freddy's circle of friends does not include any police detectives, not even a corrupt one. I met Freddy when he applied for a job in our marketing department, and subsequently got to know him and his friends fairly well."

"Marketing department?"

"Yes. We hire people to hang out in bars and attend conventions and introduce our product to prospective customers."

"Freddy was a procurer."

"I believe vocabulary is an individual choice. I prefer to call him a marketing executive, and whatever my other feelings toward Freddy are, he was excellent at his job."

I looked at Tangerine speculatively. "What *are* your other feelings about Freddy?"

It was if a mask slid into place, covering her face, making it difficult for me to read her emotions. "Freddy and I became lovers about a week after he started working for me at Pole Polishers. After about a month, our relationship cooled off, and Freddy moved on."

"Did you move on?"

"If you are asking whether I have a new man friend, no. If you are asking if I have made a mental as well as physical break from Freddy, the answer is yes. I cannot afford to let emotions run my life. I am far too busy."

I understood what Tangerine was saying, but I'm not sure if I believed it. I am plenty busy too, yet from time to time, my emotions get the better of me. Unless you are a complete stone, it's hard to avoid. I didn't share these thoughts with her, though. It wouldn't have helped. She was clearly in emotional lockdown mode.

"Getting back to Webber, have you met him before?"

This must have been safer territory for Tangerine because the mask slipped slightly, and her face acquired a look of disdain. "Yes. About three months ago, he started hanging around my office building and questioning my people about what they were doing. I contacted Detective Joe Binder, Mr. Webber's supervisor, and asked if an official investigation of my operation had begun, and asked that, if this was the case, I be notified of the focus of the investigation. I also asked that all requests for information be directed to me rather than my employees. Joe assured me that he knew of no investigation of my operation, and he was kind enough to note that since I had assisted in other investigations unrelated to my business, it made no sense for Webber to be nosing around without contacting me directly to engage my cooperation.

"After my conversation with Joe, I confronted Webber. He had no explanation for his snooping, other than a vague reference to a an illegal immigrant smuggling operation, which is ridiculous because I check all my employees' papers and run their names and social security numbers through the government's E-Verify system. In any event, Webber stopped hanging around, and I didn't see him until the opening party for As You Like It, Inc."

"As You Like It?"

"That's the name of our new man-on-man services company."

"How come I didn't see any reference to your new company in the corporate information you brought to my office?"

"Because I retained separate counsel to handle matters relating to As You Like It. I wasn't wholly truthful with you. While it's true that Richard had given up a large part of his practice in order to retire, he agreed to represent our new subsidiary until it got off the ground. Neither of us anticipated that it would take much of Richard's time because we were starting small. When I couldn't get hold of him earlier this week to discuss the transfer of the Pole Polishers' files to new counsel, I just assumed he'd gone on the vacation he's been threatening to take for the last six years. Pole Polishers is an established operation and has a great deal of ongoing business, so I moved quickly to find you to take over. I didn't know he was still in town until I got his voice mail."

"Did you save Richard's voice mail?"

Tangerine put her hand to her head. "No, unfortunately, I did not. I deleted it out of habit. Most of my callers would not appreciate it if I saved their messages. They trust me to keep records of their contacts with me to a minimum."

"How many of your clients know about the electronic file you gave me?"

"None. The file is rumored to exist, but no one knows for sure it does. Richard knew about it, and you and some of my more trusted employees know about it. That's all."

"Was Freddy among those trusted employees?"

"Yes. However, except for you, no one knows where the file is—only that it exists."

"So it's possible Webber found out about the file from Freddy."

"Yes, but once again, I have no reason to believe Freddy knows Webber."

A darker possibility occurred to me. "Maybe Webber got the information from Richard."

"Richard would never have said anything about it to Webber or anyone else."

"Even if he had a gun pointed at his head?"

Tangerine's eyes reflected sudden understanding. "You mean Webber ..."

"I mean it *could* have happened that way. We just don't know."

"When are you two gonna be done talkin' behind my back?" called Tuwanda from the kitchen.

"We'll be done in just a few minutes. Eat some more food," I yelled back, then addressed Tangerine in my normal voice. "How does she do it? She can't be more than a size four, yet she eats nonstop."

Tangerine's sorrowful, worried expression transformed into a grin. "She just burns off a lot of calories, I guess. Tuwanda's been with me since the start of the company. I've always envied her amazing metabolism. I eat one square of chocolate, and I immediately gain weight. I don't even think my body tries to digest it. It just assigns it to a spot on my hips. Tuwanda, on the other hand, treats candy bars like hors d'oeuvres and doesn't gain an ounce."

Tangerine and I smiled at each other, and I nodded to indicate I understood and empathized with the near-universal feelings of all women concerning weight gain and weight distribution inequalities. Then I got back to business.

"Katherine, I think we need to contact the sheriff's department, tell them what we know, and let them take it from there. Your options after that are to either seek protective custody or continue to hide out and hope that Webber, Freddy, or whoever it is, is arrested before he or they are after you again. Even though they didn't find the file in your office or on you, they know you know where it is."

Tangerine reached over and covered my hand with hers. "They're looking for you as well," Tangerine said softly. "Maybe you should think about going underground for a while too."

Tangerine's comment caught me by surprise. Of course, she was right; I had been so focused on assessing the risks to my clients that I forgot to assess the risk to me, which was substantial.

Tuwanda chose my moment of self-realization to walk into the room. "Your few minutes of private time are up," she announced, "an' you need to buy more groceries, Tangerine. Just so's you know, in case I need to come here again, I'm partial to stuff with chocolate in it. Hell, I'd put chocolate sauce on roast beef. As a matter of fact, I think I jus' did.

"I'll keep that in mind," said Tangerine sardonically.

Tuwanda, apparently oblivious to the tone of Tangerine's response, said, "That's real nice. Thanks." She then turned to me.

"You think it's time we picked up Stinky? Not that he'd mind if we left him at the 7-Eleven all night; it's an improvement over the homeless shelter. I jus' think we owe it to the store employees an' patrons to get him outta there. They been nice toleratin' him this long."

I had completely forgotten about Larry. "Oh God, you're right. Could you pick him up and then come back here and get me? I just need a few more minutes with Katherine."

Tuwanda delicately wiped a crumb from the corner of her mouth. "He's your responsibility. You gonna pay me for babysittin' your kid?"

"What? He's your child?" asked Tangerine, looking startled.

I explained the custody situation to Tangerine. "Tuwanda, I wouldn't ask you to pick up Larry if it weren't important that I have a bit more time with Katherine."

"Yes, Tuwanda. As a favor to me too, do as Kate asks," Tangerine said in a businesslike tone that made it clear that she was still Tuwanda's employer.

"Yes, ma'am," Tuwanda responded, all but saluting. "I'll be back in a jiff."

After Tuwanda left, I commented, "I wish my employees responded to direction like that. I've got a paralegal that treats my requests like they're suggestions or abstract descriptions of possibilities rather than orders."

"In my business, I need to be careful who I hire. I screen them good. I'm not saying you don't, but I even go so far as to hire a detective to follow prospective employees around for a month before I decide whether or not to bring them on."

"You didn't have *me* followed, did you?" I asked, half kidding ... but only half.

"No, I only do that for company employees. I did a good background check on you, though."

Tangerine started at the distant sound of a car horn, and then glanced around nervously. I could see the fear return to her eyes.

"Will you excuse me for a second, Kate?" she asked, standing quickly. "I need to make a work-related call. I'll be right back, and then we'll discuss how to go forward in light of our ... situation."

I attributed Tangerine's abrupt announcement and departure not to a sudden overwhelming need to attend to business, but rather to her need to compose herself and take time alone to think about where she went from here.

I am one of those people who cannot sit quietly and wait. I have to write, read, watch television—anything to avoid an unproductive void. I'm a Zen master's worst nightmare. I looked around the room and found the magazine Tangerine had been reading earlier. She'd placed it in a magazine holder filled with several other periodicals, most of which related to home decorating and cooking. I passed over articles on "Best Investments for Your First Million Dollars" and "Luxury Autos for the Super Rich," settling on an article titled "Bankruptcy: Should You Choose Chapter 7 or Chapter 11?" I figured the last was more relevant to my lifestyle.

I finished the article on bankruptcy and skimmed most of the rest of the magazine as well before I looked at my watch. Tangerine had been gone for twenty minutes. I got up to go look for her to see if she was all right. She was not in the kitchen. I couldn't see how she could have gone upstairs without me noticing; the bankruptcy article wasn't all that absorbing. I tiptoed up the stairs, not wanting to wake Margaret. The door to Tangerine's room stood open. The bed covers had been thrown back, and the pajamas no longer hung over the chair, but otherwise the room looked the same as it had earlier in the evening. I knocked softly on the closed bathroom door and waited. Hearing nothing, I opened it and looked around. The area was tidy and clean and, most importantly for my purposes, empty. I eyed the door to Margaret's bedroom. I hated to bother her, but I was getting more concerned about Tangerine by the minute.

I tapped on the door softly, then louder when I heard no response. Finally, I heard Margaret's sleep-muddled voice. "Yes? Is that you Katherine?"

"No. It's me, Kate. Kate Williams. We met earlier today, and I came back to talk to Tan ... er ... Katherine. She seems to have disappeared, though."

I heard the rustling of bedclothes and then the sound of soft footsteps crossing the floor. The door opened, and Margaret peered out at me nearsightedly. "Katherine's not downstairs or in her room?"

"No, and as far as I know, she was still in her pajamas when she left. Did you hear her go into her room within the last half hour?"

"No, dear. I usually wake up whenever someone comes up the stairs. But I didn't awaken when you came up, so maybe I am a sounder sleeper than I realized. I don't mean to be inhospitable, but do you mind if I go back to bed now? And don't worry about Katherine. I'm sure she'll show up safe and sound."

"Please go back to sleep. I'm so sorry to have awakened you." As Margaret's door closed in my face, I reasoned that if her own mother wasn't worried about Tangerine, maybe I shouldn't be either.

I heard someone in the front entryway and assumed it was Tuwanda returning from the 7-Eleven. I headed down the stairs to meet her. The figure standing at the bottom of the steps wasn't Tuwanda, though. It was my kidnapper, whom I now knew to be Freddy. He still had the gun.

"We meet again," he said, running his free hand through his heavily moussed hair. He was wearing the same suit he'd worn earlier, except it looked a bit more rumpled now, and his white shirt was smudged with dirt. It didn't look like Freddy was having a very good day.

I retreated a couple of steps up the stairs and sat down. "I'm beginning to see what Tangerine saw in you. I know *I've* always been a sucker for witty repartee."

Freddy looked pleased and eyed me suggestively. He was obviously unaware that I was being thoroughly sarcastic. Freddy was either vain or stupid or both. I'd put my money on the last.

"Are you looking for Tangerine?" I asked innocently.

"Not anymore. I think you got what we need." He started to climb the steps toward me. I stood and tried to back up, but he reached out, grabbed my arm, and pulled me toward him. I stumbled in my effort to stay out of his grasp, and he caught me neatly around the waist, still holding the gun in his other hand. I could smell booze, tobacco, and garlic on his breath. The combination of odors was powerful. Even in my panicked state, it occurred to me that the military should look into its weapon potential.

I tried to pull away, but Freddy had a good grip on me. He shoved his gun into his waistband and moved his hand over the front of my sweater, stopping at the slight bulge made by the thumb drive. He smiled and whispered, "Bingo" in my ear. Thank God ears don't have olfactory cells.

He pushed his hand down the front of my sweater. Freddy was so excited about the hand down the sweater thing that he'd left his gun exposed, unguarded, and within reach. I went for it.

Just as I was going for the gun, I heard a door open on the second floor. Margaret peeked around the door and screamed.

"Freddy, Kate, what's going on here?"

Freddy and I both froze, he with his hand down the front of my sweater, while I was going for his waistband. It probably looked more like an amorous encounter than assault and robbery.

"Freddy's trying to rob me," I squeaked.

"She's lying, Maggie. She wants to hurt Katherine," he snarled.

I had to hand it to Freddy. He was rather quick with a cover-up.

"I am not!" I wasn't so quick. But you had to give me a gold star for truthfulness.

Finally realizing my hand was dangerously close to his gun, he let go of my waist and snatched it out of the way. His remaining hand was still down my sweater front.

Margaret moved to the top of the steps and stared down at us. "Why do you have your hand down Kate's shirt?"

"I, er, I … I think she has a weapon hidden in there," stuttered Freddy.

I guess he wasn't that quick after all.

I pushed Freddy away from me, leapt up the steps to the landing, and stood next to Margaret.

"Please put that gun away, Freddy." Margaret's voice was steely.

"Freddy immediately complied. I saw where some of Tangerine's toughness came from.

"I think you should leave now, Freddy," Margaret continued. "Katherine isn't here right now. I'll let her sort all this out when she gets back."

Freddy smoothed his moustache nervously and then backed down the steps. When he reached ground level, he swung around and barged out the door. I waited for the door to close behind him before turning to Margaret.

"Good job. How do you know that guy?"

"He's one of my daughter's past indiscretions. He's a well-meaning boy, but he has no future."

Yeah. And he carries a gun, kidnaps people, and assaults women on stairs.

Just then, Tuwanda strolled through the front door. Spotting Margaret and me, she said "You know, you should lock that door. No tellin' who's gonna walk in off the street."

No kidding.

"Where's Larry?" I asked.

"Out in the car with his head hangin' out the window. That boy don't like inside places. Says he has to be able to breathe fresh air. It took me a while to find him at the 7-Eleven. I finally found him sittin' next to the Dumpster in the back, so I don' know what kinda fresh air he's talkin' about. I guess if you smell like him, you gotta different definition."

"Margaret, we should probably leave," I said. We've caused you enough excitement for tonight. Will you be okay here alone? I don't think Freddy will be back. He's after me, not you."

"I'll be fine, dear," said Margaret, and after the way she'd handled Freddy, I knew she would be.

"I'll write my number down for you, and if you hear from Katherine, please let me know."

I trotted downstairs to the kitchen and found a pad and pencil next to the phone. I ripped off a sheet of paper, wrote down both my office number and the number of Goldman's cell phone, then returned to the stairs and handed it to Margaret.

"Please call me anytime, night or day, if you hear from Katherine," I reiterated.

"I'll give your numbers to Katherine … should she contact me, dear. She can decide whether to call you. I try to stay out of Katherine's business affairs."

I wondered if Margaret knew what Tangerine did for a living. I know it's not the kind of thing I'd want my mother to know. But then, I hadn't seen my mother since I was eighteen, and I didn't even want her to know where I lived, so my nondisclosure rules were quite restrictive.

"I understand. Thank you for your hospitality, Margaret. Your cookies are wonderful," I said, trying to be as gracious as possible under the circumstances.

"Yeah, an' your potato salad, coffee cake, fried chicken, an' pot roast are pretty good too," added Tuwanda.

I followed Tuwanda out, giving Margaret a little wave just before I closed the door behind me, being sure to push in the button lock first. I noticed there were no other locks on the door and wondered at Margaret's lackadaisical attitude toward security. Perhaps it was evidence of her attachment to a past when unlocked doors were the rule rather than the exception.

I got into the passenger seat of Tuwanda's car and glanced back at Larry. Just as she'd said, he had his head hanging out the window. There was a little pile of Ding Dong wrappers next to him on the seat, and a bigger pile on the floor.

"I thought you hated junk food," I said.

Without changing his position, Larry shot back, "You don't take me anywhere I can get healthy food. The 7-Eleven doesn't have much of a vegan section, in case you didn't notice."

I sighed. There's just no pleasing some people.

As Tuwanda started the car and pulled away from the curb, I told her about Tangerine's disappearance and Freddy's appearance.

"Hell, no," she moaned. "We lost her again? I figgered she was just upstairs in bed. An' that asshole Freddy's hangin' around too?"

"Margaret doesn't seem to be worried. Maybe Tangerine decided to take my advice but found a better place to hide out, which is probably a good idea in light of Freddy's visit. She probably thought we could contact law enforcement and fill them in, and she could stay out of it until the dust settles."

"But you said you an' her mom didn't see or hear her go upstairs. Does that mean she's wanderin' around in her jammies? That don' make no sense."

"Good point." I gave it some thought. "There's a laundry room off the kitchen. Maybe she had some clothes in there and changed into them. I didn't think to check to see if she'd left her pajamas in there."

"It coulda happened that way, but I'm not thinkin' any happy Pollyanna thoughts 'til we hear from her."

"Well, since there's nothing we can do until we *do* hear from her, I say we all go home and get some sleep."

Tuwanda glanced at her watch. "It's ten o'clock, girl. The evenin' has jus' started accordin' to Tuwanda time. I'm gonna go back to work. You gotta call me, though, if you hear from Tangerine. It's gonna be hard concentratin' while I'm worryin' about her. I may have to give some discounts to make up for that. I gotta reputation to think about."

"Are you taking me back to the shelter?" Larry asked.

"Yes," I answered in a tone intended to convey that this was an absolutely unequivocal and nonnegotiable fact.

"Good, 'cause I'm getting car sick, and bad as it is, I would prefer to be at the shelter."

"Uh-uh. Don't you *dare* puke in my car. You think you're gonna hurl, you tell me so's I can throw your stinky ass out before you upchuck vomitty Ding-Dongs."

"Larry," I interjected, trying to get the image of vomitty Ding Dongs out of my mind. "How is it that you stay at the shelter? I thought you didn't like being in closed spaces."

"I have a space on the roof, right next to the heating vent, with a cot and a solar cooker, and a tarp in case it rains. I even hooked up a television, although I don't watch it much. I enjoy some of the programs on Discovery, but most of the channels just have one reality show after another, and reality shows are crap."

"That jus' shows you how ignorant you are. Some of them reality show's got drama you just don't see in regular fake shows. Like that show about the kids out in California havin' breakdowns 'cause they can't find a pair of two-hundred-dollar jeans that fit just right. I feel for them kids. It's not like they can pack their butts in a pair of Levi's an' go out. They got high standards. I seen one show where a sweet girl's boyfriend dumped her for a girl with pants jammed so tight up her ass, it didn't take no imagination to picture her naked. Takes a long time to find a pair of pants like that. Takes focus, determination, and no fear of yeast infection to wear 'em, too."

I ignored the digression into reality TV and got back to Larry's living arrangements. "So they let you live on the roof?" I asked.

"Dunno. I never asked anyone about it."

"And no one has noticed you up there?"

"Sure. Lotsa people. But you gotta remember most of the guests at the shelter have drug issues and lots of paranoia, so they'd think it was weird if *no* one was on the roof. They just assume I'm from the CIA, Homeland Security, the FBI, ICE, or their HOA board."

The fact that this actually made sense to me was further evidence that I needed to get some real food and go to bed.

We dropped Larry off in front of Sacred Bleeding Heart. Even though the night air was cool, Tuwanda insisted that we keep the windows open to get rid of Larry's residual odor.

"So, you wanna come with me and see what a real woman can do for a man? You could even help out by hangin' up clothes and tidying up while I apply my expertise. You could be like an apprentice or somethin'."

"No." *Hell no.* "Just drop me off at my car. I'll call you if I hear anything about Tangerine. In the meantime, I'm going contact the sheriff's office and tell them everything I know."

"Do you mean you're gonna call the sheriff's office or do you mean you're gonna call *your* sheriff?"

I felt my face go hot, and I knew I was blushing. Fortunately, it was too dark for Tuwanda to notice.

"I can feel you blushin'," she said.

We arrived at the corporate offices of Pole Polishers, and Tuwanda dropped me off next to my car. As I was searching my pockets for the keys, she said, "I'm gonna check on you a few times to make sure you ain't in no trouble, so keep that phone you got from the dead guy with you." She handed me the phone charger from her car. "An' take this. I got another one at home."

"Thank you, Tuwanda, and thank you too for all you've done tonight."

"No problem. Tangerine's my boss, but she's also my friend, an' I like to consider you a friend too, an' once you're Tuwanda's friend, you're Tuwanda's business. According to all the facts I got at my disposal, you're in a deeper pile of shit than Tangerine. You gotta be careful."

I nodded weakly and gave her a slight wave. I'd found my keys, so I opened my car door and got in. Tuwanda waited until I started my car before driving off. As I watched her drive away, I noticed a bumper sticker for the Phoenix Symphony next to a bumper sticker that read UNLESS YOU'RE PAYING, GET OFF MY ASS. Tuwanda was a bundle of contradictions, to say the least.

I glanced up at Tangerine's office as I was pulling away from the curb, and then slammed on the brakes. I thought I'd seen a light moving around inside. I'd just lowered my window to make sure it wasn't a reflection from the streetlights when a hand snaked through the window and grabbed me by the shoulder. I stifled a scream.

CHAPTER SEVEN

▼

"Where the hell have you been?" demanded Bryan.

"I called and left you a voice mail!" I countered defensively.

"Yeah. You just left out some minor details: like where you were, who you were with, and what you were doing."

"Phones work both ways, you know. You could have called me."

"I did, dammit."

I pulled Goldman's cell out of my pocket and looked at it. Sure enough, it showed five missed calls from Bryan's number. "I must have had it on vibrate."

"Then your whole body must have been shaking. Pay attention to the cues, Kate."

"Sorry."

My apology seemed to placate him somewhat because his shoulders dropped out of angry into neutral mode. "What is this number, anyway? Did you get another cell? If so, that makes three today."

"Actually, it's Goldman's phone."

Bryan was silent for a while, and his shoulders went back into the angry position. "That's evidence," he said tersely.

"I know, I know. It was an emergency, though. M.J.'s phone got smashed."

"How many calls did you make on this phone?"

"Four: one to Beth, one to Macy, and two to you."

Bryan grabbed Goldman's phone from me and hit a few buttons. "The last call by Goldman was made two days ago. Do you recognize the number?" he asked, shoving the lighted screen under my nose.

"That's Tangerine's office number. She said he called her and left a voice message early today, but he must have used another phone."

"Maybe. You stay here. I'm going to check on something." Bryan walked to his car, which was parked behind a hedge of oleanders. That explained why I hadn't noticed it before. I could hear him talking on his cell. I was slightly miffed that he didn't want me to overhear what he was saying after I told him everything I knew. Well, almost everything. Or maybe half of everything. Anyway, I was sharing more than he was, which gave me extra points in our personal relationship, though I was still behind in the tally when it came to the cop and witness situation.

I looked up at Tangerine's office to see if the light was still there. I didn't see anything at first, but then I noticed a pinpoint beam moving over the curtain. I glanced over at Bryan and saw that he was still immersed in whatever conversation he was having that he wouldn't let me listen to. I slipped out of the car and tiptoed over to the front door. I tried the knob, but it was locked. Then I remembered Tangerine saying something about leaving through the back door after Webber or whoever else it was roughed her up.

I slipped around to the back of the building, being careful to stay in the shadows, which wasn't too hard because there was only one working streetlight on the block. I ran my hand over the building's rough stucco until I felt a hard metal door frame. I didn't need to try the door to see if it was locked because it was standing open, a fact I established when my head smacked against it. I climbed the stairs quietly, then stopped outside the metal fire door on the second floor and listened intently. I could hear sounds of movement coming from inside Tangerine's office. Then I heard a different sound.

"Shit!"

I recognized the voice and the vocabulary. "M.J.?" I said tentatively, opening the door.

"Kate! Thank God."

I found the power switch Tuwanda had used earlier and turned on the lights. M.J. stood in the middle of the room, blinking in the sudden glare. She was holding a penlight and was dressed in tight shiny blue pants and an equally tight sweater with a picture of the Eiffel Tower, the latter of which was distorted by M.J.'s bosom and was a squashed version of the landmark.

"We didn't know what happened to you. We haven't heard from you since you left the office to come here. Crap, when I saw this," she said, holding up the remnants of her cell phone, "not to mention the blood in the bathroom, I didn't know what to think."

I looked around Tangerine's office. All the drawers of her desk had been pulled out, their contents dumped on the floor; the drapes had been ripped down; the poufs were torn and gutted; and the paintings had been removed from the wall and piled haphazardly in a corner.

"Geez, M.J. Did you do this?"

"No! It was like this when I got here. I thought maybe there'd been a fight or something."

"I don't think it was a fight. It looks more like someone searched the place. People usually don't take the trouble to rip apart sofas in a fight," I said, tilting my head toward the destroyed poufs.

"Hell, those things are so ugly, I'd rip 'em apart just on general principal."

"Can't you just once do what I ask?" Bryan had come up the stairs and was standing behind me, arms akimbo and looking disgusted.

"Hi, Bryan," said M.J.

"Hi, M.J. I don't know why, but for some reason I'm not at all surprised to see you. Is Sam here too? Beth maybe?"

"Beth had to babysit her granddaughter," Sam called from the bathroom.

"I'm officially declaring this a crime scene area. I want you all out of here," said Bryan in his sheriff voice. "Although I don't know why I'm bothering. You've left your prints everywhere."

"I had to use the toilet," said Sam, walking out of the bathroom. "So, technically, I left more than fingerprints."

"Bryan ...," I started to say.

"Out! All of you. Now. Out!" he shouted.

We walked single file down the stairs, with Bryan in the rear, talking on his cell to the dispatcher at his office. Once we were outside and he'd slammed the door shut and jiggled its knob to make sure it was locked, I tried again.

"For security reasons, Tangerine doesn't want the police to search her office," I said.

"Security reasons?" asked Bryan.

"Yes. You know ... the security of her clients."

Bryan let out a long sigh. "Look, Kate," he said. "I'm going to take a wild guess and say that whoever searched her office and left that mess was likely looking for information on Tangerine's clients. Judging by the thoroughness of their search, either they already found it or it isn't there." He paused and looked meaningfully at me. "That *is* what they were looking for, isn't it, Kate?"

I nodded. "Seems so."

"Do you think the guys who kidnapped you were looking for the same kind of information?"

"I don't know. Could be."

"Did Tangerine give you something to keep for her?" Bryan persisted.

"That's privileged information," I answered evenly.

"Are you going to give a direct answer to anything I ask?"

"Only if in doing so, I would not be violating the tenets of attorney-client privilege."

"I'll remember to put that on your tombstone," Bryan remarked dryly.

"I refuse to be intimidated, Sheriff."

"Goldman's dead, Tangerine's missing, and you were kidnapped. Yet you say *I'm* the one trying to intimidate you. I'm the good guy, remember? I'm trying to help you.

"Look," he continued, "is there any way I can try to get hold of Tangerine? Do you have any idea where she is?"

"No. I haven't heard from her since I spoke to her earlier this evening."

"You spoke with her?" he asked, surprised.

"Yes. Tuwanda and I found her at her mother's house, and I spoke with her for maybe thirty minutes. But then she left, and I don't know where she went. Her mother, Margaret, said she'd call me if she heard from her."

"You were at her mother's house? What the ...? Okay. Start at the beginning and tell me everything; I mean, everything you feel you can without violating the almighty attorney-client privilege."

"Can we at least go somewhere where there are chairs and more light so we can all sit down ... and maybe even get a cup of coffee?" interjected Sam, who, with M.J., had been observing my exchange with Bryan like spectators at a tennis match.

M.J. said she thought that was a great idea, and while I did not verbalize my opinion, I thought it was a great idea too. Bryan was clearly impatient to find out what I had to say, and he probably would have preferred to stay where we were and finish the interview, but he must have taken pity on us or realized he was outnumbered because he gave us the address of an all-night restaurant in the area, ordering us to be at the restaurant in fifteen minutes or he would have warrants issued for our arrest.

At that moment, several cars from the sheriff department pulled up in front of Tangerine's office building, and Bryan went over to talk to the deputy driving the lead car. As I left for the restaurant, they were putting up crime tape and placing traffic barriers around the building entrance.

Sam and M.J. were already inside when I got to the restaurant, which was a shabby truck stop painted an unsettling shade of green, located just off Interstate 17. The large number of semis parked in the lot outside indicated that, despite its appearance, the food must be good.

Spotting Sam sitting in a booth in the back, I wove my way through tables full of truck drivers of both sexes. Those who had not yet been served bantered back and forth with each other, while those with plates in front of them were silently absorbed in their meals, which was another sign that the food was good.

I slid in next to Sam. "Where's M.J.?" I asked.

"She's in the little girl's room. She really had to go bad, but unlike me, she waited to get to a place where her butt wouldn't destroy evidence. By the way, your boyfriend is getting testy. If I were you, I'd make a better show of cooperating."

"I *am* cooperating," I snapped. "Can I help it if he doesn't ask the right questions?"

M.J. appeared and sat down facing us. Without preamble, she said, "Kate, tell us quick what's going on, before Bryan gets here, and don't pull that attorney-client privilege crap, because you can't violate it talking to us."

I reminded myself that this was true because, with a few limited exceptions, the privilege extended to members of an attorney's staff. Speaking at the pace of an auctioneer, I described what had happened, starting with my kidnapping, and was just finishing when Bryan arrived. He waited until we had all ordered before starting his questioning, which was a good thing because I was famished, the Ding Dongs being no more than a distant memory by now. I ordered the blue-plate special, which included fried chicken, mashed potatoes, green beans, and blueberry pie for dessert. Sam, M.J., and Bryan all ordered the same. The down-home food described on the menu made me feel like I was in Mayberry. But the sheriff was Bryan Turner, not Andy Griffith, which was unfortunate because Andy would have been a lot less irritated.

His eyes bored into mine. "Start at the beginning," he commanded. I did, and since I omitted the privileged stuff, even though I was speaking slower than I had to Sam and M.J., it took me less time to get it all out.

His eyes still locked on mine, Bryan said, "Give me everything you have that belonged to Goldman: the picture, the keys, the paper, the pens … any pocket lint, gum wrappers, everything. I don't care where you found it, who gave it to you, whatever. Just give it to me. Now." He pronounced each of his words slowly and with emphasis, as if I were a small child, and not a bright one at that.

I searched around in my pockets and produced the folded paper with Margaret's address on it, Goldman's keys, and his pen. I hadn't noticed until then that the keys were attached to a keychain that read I LOVE MY PENIS. I was about to pull the picture of Webber out of my waistband when the food came. Like the other diners, after our first bites of food, we all fell silent. None of us wanted anything to distract us from what was probably the best cuisine in the state for plain food aficionados like me. The chicken was crispy on the outside and tender on the inside. The potatoes were real mashed potatoes, not the powdered stuff my mom used to call "masked potatoes." The beans were fresh and cooked al dente. Warm biscuits rounded out the presentation.

M.J., as usual, was the first to finish. "Does this place deliver?" she asked, wiping her mouth carefully and inspecting the napkin, no doubt hoping to find a few more crumbs to enjoy.

"You can ask," mumbled Bryan through a mouthful of mashed potatoes, "but I doubt it."

M.J. rubbed an imaginary stain on the tabletop, and in so doing, brought her hand within inches of Sam's plate. Sam's reaction was quick and decisive.

"Ow!" yelped M.J. "Did you see that? He stabbed me with his fork."

"Stay away from my food," growled Sam, placing an arm protectively around his plate.

"I wasn't going to take your damned food, you paranoid freak," responded M.J., as she popped the biscuit she'd managed to snag from his plate into her mouth.

"Since you're finished eating, why don't you tell me how you and Sam came to be at Tangerine's office tonight?" asked Bryan, moving his plate a few more inches away from M.J.

"Fine. But when the pie comes, I'm gonna stop whatever I'm in the middle of saying and eat, and don't go all cop on me when I do." M.J. glared at Bryan and waited to make sure he understood the conditional nature of her cooperation. Bryan just nodded and continued to eat.

M.J. straightened her back, folded her hands in her lap, and went into professional mode. "There's not much to tell about Sam's and my involvement in this whole mess. We heard from Beth about Kate being kidnapped and then going out to look for Ms. Paar. We were worried, of course"—here, M.J. paused and looked at me sweetly for effect, no doubt intending to underline the sincerity of her concern—"and we waited anxiously for Kate to call. Beth even stayed late in case she called in after hours."

M.J. paused again to let us ponder the magnificence of Beth's gesture. "Beth called me at about seven. She needed to get home and watch her grandkid, and she still hadn't heard from you. She asked if Sam and I could try to track Kate down.

She said Kate had my cell phone, but she'd been calling that number for over an hour, and Kate hadn't picked up. She gave me Ms. Paar's office address and asked me and Sam to do a drive-by, and if Kate wasn't there, to call you. It took Sam a while to get ready, after which he picked me up and we drove to Tan … I mean, Ms. Paar's office. We found Kate's car parked outside, but there were no other cars around, and no lights were on in the building. We got out and tried the front door, but it was locked. Then we walked around to the back of the building to see if maybe there was another entrance. There was, and it was open. We looked around the first floor and didn't find anyone, so we went up to the second floor. We were still searching up there when Kate showed up."

Sam had been watching M.J. with a look akin to horror on his face. When she concluded her presentation, the vein in his forehead was bulging, and he was holding his fork like a dagger.

"May I offer my statement now?" he asked. His voice shook with barely contained rage. M.J. shot him a warning look and slowly shook her head no.

"Certainly," Bryan said wisely. I was sure Sam's head would have exploded had he answered otherwise.

"I wish to point out a few discrepancies in Ms. Polowsky's rather fanciful recitation of events. First, Beth called me, not M.J., when she couldn't get hold of Kate. I immediately called M.J. She did not answer, so I left a voice mail telling her I was coming by to pick her up in ten minutes, and she'd better be ready. When I got to her apartment building, she wasn't waiting outside, so I went up to her unit. No one answered when I knocked, so I tried the door and it was open, and, well, the rest is just awful. She was in the living room dressed in a black thong. Loud music was playing—I think it was Barry White—and she was sliding up and down this pole thing. She looked like King Kong trying, unsuccessfully, to climb the Empire State Building."

"Oh, for God's sake," interjected M.J., "I was exercising." Addressing me, she said, "You know, it's that workout program where you pole dance and prance around like a stripper."

I drew a blank on that one and stared at her dumbly, struggling to quash the image of M.J. in nothing but a black thong that had popped into my brain.

"Oh yeah," said Bryan. "I saw a show about that on *Oprah*."

I turned to look at Bryan. Who *was* this man?

He must have seen the look on my face because he hastily added, "Someone had it on in the break room."

"What*ever*," said Sam. "The point is, I'm going to have nightmares for weeks."

"So what happened next, Sam?" I asked, wanting desperately to move away from the subject of M.J. and her pole dancing.

"He fainted," supplied M.J. with a shrug. "I heard a thump and turned around. Sam was lying on the floor, out cold."

"Do you blame me?" blurted Sam.

I didn't. I probably would have done the same thing, but I didn't say so.

"It took me a while to bring him around," said M.J. "Every time he opened his eyes, he'd scream and pass out again."

"You were hitting me on the chest," said Sam indignantly.

"I was trying to resuscitate you. That's how you're supposed to do it now. No more mouth-to-mouth—just chest pumping."

"You were not pumping, you were *hitting*, and you could have at least put on a robe."

Thankfully, our waitress came by at this juncture and removed our dirty plates, replacing them with slices of blueberry pie. M.J. and Sam fell silent and dove into their desserts, but continued to glare at each other over their rapidly moving forks. Although the pie looked wonderful, I'd lost my appetite, and I offered my slice to Bryan. When he declined, M.J., her hand shooting out quicker than a lizard's tongue, grabbed my plate.

Once the pie was gone, the waitress cleared the table and refilled our coffee cups. Bryan, who no doubt felt he'd lost control of the interrogation during the Sam/M.J. controversy, refocused his attention on me.

"I believe you have an additional item belonging to Goldberg," he said brusquely.

I dutifully pulled Webber's picture out of my waistband and placed it face up in the middle of the table. Bryan, M.J., and Sam all leaned forward to look at it.

"This is why I asked that the sheriff's department get involved," I said.

"I see your point," said Bryan. "I recognize Webber, but do any of you know who the other guy might be?"

We all turned expectantly toward Sam. "What, because I'm gay, I'm supposed to know every gay man in Phoenix?" he asked defensively. "I recognize Webber only because he was the detective on a couple of cases I worked on at the county attorney's office. I have no idea who the other guy is."

"Actually, he kind of looks like the stylist who did this to me," I said, gesturing to my hair. "But I can't see enough of his face to be sure."

"What's his name?" asked Bryan, who seemed unable to tear his eyes away from the photo.

"Christopher. I don't know his last name, but it would be easy to find out. He works at Stranded. Why are you staring at that picture so intently?"

"There's something weird about it," he said thoughtfully.

"You're an insensitive homophobe," huffed Sam.

"No, no, I mean there's something weird about Webber's position."

"I repeat, you are a homophobic asshole," said Sam.

"I mean the position of Webber's head. It doesn't quite match up with the positioning of his neck."

We all looked at the photo again.

"I see what you mean," I said. "It's barely noticeable, but if you look at the way his neck muscles are, he should be facing more to the side."

"It could just be the camera angle. Or maybe his head and neck were kind of contorted because of his, um, emotion," offered M.J.

"Or it could be that the photo's been altered. I'll give it to the guys in our lab. If it's been Photoshopped, they'll be able to tell. In the meantime, I need to get hold of Darius Johnson, the Phoenix chief of police. I think the sheriff's department should step in on the Goldman case until this thing with Webber is cleared up."

"Hasn't your department already stepped in? Weren't those sheriff's cars I saw pulling up in front of Tangerine's place before we came over here?" I asked.

"The burglary at Tangerine's office is different. Her building is located on a county island, which means the sheriff has primary jurisdiction, and there's no reason yet to believe it's related to the Goldman case, so we don't need to coordinate with the police. It's only when crimes occur within the city limits that jurisdiction gets fuzzy."

"What about Tangerine? She's missing, and she's in danger. What is your department going to do about that?" I pressed.

"No one has filed a missing person report on her, and even if someone had, she hasn't been missing twenty-four hours. You said yourself that you saw her earlier tonight. As for your little confrontations with Freddy, it's clear he was looking for you or something you had, not Tangerine."

"*Little* confrontations? The man kidnapped me at gunpoint and then showed up at Margaret's house and groped me in the stairwell. 'Little,' my ass." I considered throwing the rest of my coffee in his face, but I decided to wait for a hot refill. A couple of tablespoons of lukewarm liquid weren't going to make the dramatic impact I was looking for.

"And just what was Freddy groping for?" Bryan asked quickly.

I set my jaw and glared at him. We'd been over this before, and I still wasn't about to tell him about the thumb drive Tangerine gave me.

Bryan sighed. "Fine. That's that, then." He slid out of the booth. "I'll let you know if I hear anything about Tangerine's whereabouts. In the meantime, if I were you, I'd stay low. Why don't you leave town for a while? Go visit some friends in Chicago, maybe."

"And who would cover my practice in the meantime?" I shot back.

Bryan dramatically threw his arms in the air in mock frustration, then turned on his heel and stomped out of the restaurant.

"He didn't pay," noted M.J. She and Sam looked at me expectantly. I dug in my pocket and pulled out five dollars and a quarter, which was all that was left of the cash Beth had given me.

"This does it for me," I said, tossing my paltry contribution on the table. "You guys will have to cover the balance."

Clearly, this was a novel concept for M.J. Her face reflected surprise, confusion, and then panic. "I never carry cash or credit cards," she said.

"Bullshit! You do too," exclaimed Sam, making a grab for M.J.'s purse. M.J. blocked him and deftly delivered a hard blow to his upper arm. Sam reflexively recoiled, then balled his hand into a fist and aimed for M.J.'s jaw.

I figured I'd better say something before things got out of hand—or, rather, *more* out of hand. "I'm tired, and I want to go home. It's been a tough day. Either one of you is going to have to pay the rest of the bill, or we'll be washing dishes all night."

Sam stopped his fist in mid-flight and let it drop on the table. M.J. hit his arm again.

"Shit, stop it. That hurts," he said, rubbing the point of contact.

I picked up the bill our waitress had dropped off at the table and looked at it. M.J. and Sam watched me nervously. "How bad is it?" asked M.J.

"Thirty dollars plus twenty percent for the tip," I said, unable to keep the surprise out of my voice. "That's a heckuva deal. I may have to move in here. I wonder if they allow dogs."

Sam pulled a couple of twenties out of his wallet. "I've got his one. M.J., you can get the next one. I'm thinking lobster at Morton's."

"In your dreams, buddy," sniffed M.J.

I volunteered to drop off M.J. My motives were purely selfish. I was too tired to deal with the homicide investigation that would inevitably result if she and Sam rode in the same car.

"Listen, M.J.," I said, once we were on our way, "I'm sorry about your cell phone. I'll get you another one tomorrow. I'm going to need to buy one for me too. Maybe the store gives volume discounts."

"I'll go with you. I want one of those new phones that does everything except wipe your butt. And, of course, I need to see the color choices. The color is important. It tells a lot about you. You don't want to give people the wrong impression 'cause of the color of your phone. I have a friend who got a red one with sparkles. It looked okay in the store, but it took on a hot pink glow outside in the sunlight. He almost had to quit his construction job."

We fell silent for a while, and I let my mind wander over topics unrelated to cell phone color. I hoped Ralph and Macy were doing okay, and that Tangerine, wherever she was, was all right. Thinking of Tangerine reminded me that I had to remember to call Tuwanda and Margaret as soon as I got home to let them know I no longer had Goldman's phone, and they needed to contact me through my home or office line until further notice. Life was so much simpler when all we had were carrier pigeons and snail mail.

M.J. cleared her throat to get my attention. "Kate, I just wanted you to know that all of us—Sam, Beth, and me—were worried about you. I'm glad you're okay," she said softly.

I smiled and patted her knee. "We joke around a lot, but I know you guys always have my back. Thanks, M.J."

CHAPTER EIGHT

▼

I dropped M.J. off in front of her apartment building and then headed for home. I made good time due to the lack of traffic at that hour, as well as the surprising cooperation of the traffic lights, which, before now, I'd assumed were each equipped with a sensor that triggered a red light every time it recognized my car.

I didn't want to bother Macy at this late hour. I would wait and pick up Ralph in time for his morning walk. Macy's condo is right across the hall from mine, though, and Ralph started to bark as soon as I put my key in the lock.

I heard Macy's door open. "Who the hell are you?" she said in a sleepy voice.

I turned around just as Ralph bolted through the door and hurled himself at my legs. Macy had a kitchen knife raised above her head. It occurred to me then that Macy had not seen my hair yet, and she had likely taken me for a burglar, although burglars don't typically wear heels and St. John suits on the job.

"Katie?" she asked incredulously. "Is that you? I guess it's gotta be you, 'cause the doggy ain't snarlin'."

The doggy was now leaning against my leg and drooling on my shoe.

Macy squinted and stared at the top of my head. "Why's your hair red?"

"It's auburn," I answered defensively.

"Auburn? I suppose Bozo was auburn too, then."

"The point is that it was a mistake, and I'm going to go back to being a blonde just as soon as I can get another appointment with my hairdresser. I don't know why everybody keeps making such a big deal about it."

"Maybe because unless you walk around lookin' in a mirror all day, you can't see it, so it don't bother you so much. As an onlooker, though, I can tell you it's pretty out there."

I was too tired to have this conversation again. "Thank you for taking care of Ralph, Macy. I'll take over from here. I need to get to bed now. It's been an exhausting day and an even more exhausting night." I opened my door and shoved Ralph inside.

"So the red hair's getting you some action? Maybe I should try it. I could—"

"Good night, Macy," I interrupted. I went into my apartment, restraining the impulse to slam the door. I switched the light on and then froze. The furniture was upended, and the couch cushions were ripped open. My only table lamp lay shattered on the floor. Admittedly, the couch wasn't much of a loss. It had red plush upholstery rubbed to pale pink on the armrests, and suspicious stains on the seat cushion. The previous occupant had left it, and I never seemed to find the time to look for a replacement. I'd brought the lamp with me from Chicago, though, and I really liked it. Maybe I could glue it back together.

I checked the kitchen and the bedroom, both of which had received the same treatment as the living room. Nothing seemed to have been taken, which made sense because there was nothing worthwhile to take. I'd left my laptop at the office, so the only electrical gadgets in the apartment were a coffeemaker and a television, and the latter was one of the huge box varieties popular about twenty years ago. Any self-respecting burglar would be embarrassed to try to fence the thing.

Ralph, who had followed me from room to room, lay down and curled up on a stack of my underwear lying on the floor. He seemed to like the new feng shui. I guess from a dog's point of view, mess is a good thing.

"You barked your head off when you heard me put my key in the lock, but I bet you didn't make a peep when someone broke in and trashed our home!" I muttered, pointing an accusing finger at him.

Ralph's big brown eyes calmly assessed me, and then he rolled over and proffered his stomach for a tummy rub. I groaned out of a combination of exasperation and exhaustion, and collapsed on the floor next to him. Ralph nudged my hand with his nose, and taking the hint, I gently scratched his belly. This activity had a calming effect on me, and my thoughts and heartbeat slowed down, enabling me to think more clearly about my next move. "Move" was definitely the operative word here. I needed to find another place to stay. I had already figured out that the burglary was not a run-of-the-mill smash and grab. The thief had been after something specific, and based on the day's events, I guessed it was the thumb drive. The search of Tangerine's office and my condo either occurred before Freddy accosted me at Margaret's house, or was done by someone working independently of Freddy, because Freddy seemed to be convinced that the thing hanging around my neck was what he was looking for, and I hadn't had time to try to convince him otherwise. Regardless of the details, though, two things were clear: the bad guys knew where I lived, and at least one of them knew what I had.

I stood and walked over to the phone, or at least to where the phone used to be. In its place was a hole in the wall and a mess of tangled and torn wires. This was the unkindest cut of all. It would be months before the telephone company sent someone out for repairs, during which time I would spend huge amounts of time calling, only to listen to a menu the length of a novel, but which would not include the department

I need. After that, they would pass me around from extension to extension and put me on hold each time, forcing me to listen to ads for additional services. If I slammed the phone down, which is the normal and appropriate reaction under such circumstances, I would lose my place in line because "all calls are answered in the order in which they are received." As a further indignity, a recorded voice would tell me prior to each transfer that "this call may be recorded to ensure quality customer service," which always has the effect of chilling my vocabulary. Of course, I would need to give my account information and explain why I was calling to each new person I was transferred to because, for some reason, the technology necessary for the current employee to pass the information along does not exist. Placing me at the mercy of the telephone company was beyond cruel; it was sadistic.

I had few options as to where I could go. I didn't know of any hotels in the area that would accept Ralph as a guest, and Bryan's building didn't allow pets. I hated to wake her again, but Macy was my best bet.

Finding my suitcase lying open near the hall closet, I hauled it into my bedroom. I threw in underwear, shoes, skirts, jackets, and blouses, basing my choices not on fashion, but on whether the items were useable. The bathroom was the biggest disaster area: all my makeup had been smashed, smeared, or otherwise rendered useless, but I managed to find my toothbrush and a comb on the floor of the shower. I grabbed Ralph's leash and a bag of his dog food on the way out, and then I lined up the suitcase, dog food, leash, and Ralph in front of Macy's door and knocked.

We went through the same routine as before, except this time Macy was holding a wooden spoon instead of a kitchen knife. She must have grabbed the least-effective utensil because of her sleep-addled condition.

"Good God; you look like refugees from a circus," she said upon seeing us.

I sighed. Enough with the hair jokes, already. "Macy, someone tossed my apartment, and I need a place to stay. Could you take us in for the night? I promise I'll find a hotel for Ralph and me tomorrow."

"Sweetie, come in! I had no idea. I didn't hear nothin' goin' on in your place. Course, we had the TV on kinda loud. We were watchin' that show where folks try to outdo each other losing weight, and there's lots of screamin' and cryin' and stuff. I think Ralph understands emotions about food."

Macy took my suitcase and ushered us in. "You want something to eat, doll?"

"Thanks so much, Macy, but it's enough that you're giving us a place to stay tonight. You don't have to feed us too. Besides, I just ate, and Ralph looks pretty well fed to me."

"You'll stay in the guest room, then. You know where it is, right?"

I nodded. I'd been in Macy's apartment enough to know the layout, plus where she kept just about everything.

"The doggy has to sleep on the floor, though. I'll find some nice soft towels for him to lie on."

I took my suitcase to the guest room and set it on the floor. Macy had decorated the room consistent with the taste of her one and only grandchild: a six-year-old girl with a passion for pink and Barbie dolls. There were pink ruffles on the curtains, the bed skirt and bedspread, and the pillow shams. Even the sheets had pink ruffles, a fact I discovered after I turned back a quilt covered with a huge portrait of Barbie that matched the Barbie images on the curtains and rug. A Barbie doll on the top of the dresser stared at me with a supercilious half smile.

I hated Barbie. I wanted to rip her perfectly coiffed blond hair off her head and use it for dental floss. I'd always thought her impossible proportions and clothes obsession had a negative effect on young minds. I'd explained this theory to Macy, but she'd just shrugged and said, "Marisa likes Barbie, and whatever Marisa likes, I got no problem with. Let her mother worry about raising her right. I'm the grandma. The only job I got is to spoil her rotten." I'd complimented Macy on her job success and left it alone after that.

Macy came in with a stack of towels and made a nice nest of them (blue, in deference to Ralph's manhood) on the floor. Ralph circled and sniffed, and then curled up on top of them, although we both knew he would jump up on the bed as soon as Macy left. I meant no disrespect to Macy's house rules, but I understood from experience that any attempt on my part to un-bed Ralph would fail, and it was likely I, not Ralph, who would be sleeping on the towels.

After Macy said good night and left the room, I went into the small pink bathroom off the bedroom, washed my face with a Barbie washcloth, and then changed into a pair of old shorts and a T-shirt. A shower would have to wait. I was too tired to make the effort. Ralph was already asleep on the bed, snoring loudly, when I came back from the bathroom. I shoved him over an inch or two and lay down, and I was asleep seconds after my head hit the pillow. Despite the fact that my day had provided a wealth of material, my slumber was dreamless.

I was awakened by a soft knock on the door, to which Ralph responded by bolting off the bed and onto the towels. I felt as though I had only been asleep for a few minutes, but it must have been more like several hours because the early morning light was coming through the window.

Not waiting for a response, Macy tiptoed in with Ralph's leash. "No need to get up, doll. I'm just gonna take the doggy out for his morning pish."

I gratefully fell back to sleep. According to the grinning Barbie clock on the nightstand, it was nine thirty when I woke up again. "Damn," I said, throwing back the covers. I had a lot to do, and oversleeping wasn't part of my plan.

I must have spoken louder than I thought, because Macy called out, "What, this is how you greet the day God made? You scream 'damn'?"

"Sorry," I called back. I scrambled out of bed. Ralph was not in the room. I figured he was with Macy, probably stuffing his face with people food. Macy is an excellent cook, and she treats Ralph like a human when it comes to meals.

I managed to shower and get dressed in under five minutes. I had to be creative with my wardrobe. Although I'd grabbed as many clean clothes as I could find the night before, the selection not affected by the burglar's makeup, shampoo, and shower gel graffiti was limited. As an afterthought, I grabbed a necklace, à la Marisa, out of the dresser and added it to my ensemble. Accessories are important.

Macy was waiting for me when I emerged from Barbieland. She was holding a plate filled with scrambled eggs, bacon, and pancakes. Ralph was sitting on the floor next to her, staring at the plate. A string of drool hung from the corner of his mouth.

"Macy! Thank you so much, but I don't have time to eat. I have to get to the office. I have a lot of calls to make."

"The world won't come to an end if you take a few minutes to eat. Come in the kitchen. I'll pour you some coffee."

The offer of coffee did it. I needed caffeine. Badly. My brain was still suffering from the misapprehension that its job was to sleep, not think.

I followed Ralph and Macy into the kitchen. I wasn't surprised to see our neighbor Cal sitting at the kitchen table, reading the paper and eating a stack of pancakes the height of a three-tiered wedding cake. Cal always tried to act aloof around Macy, but I knew that deep down he was fond of her; and not so deep down, he loved her cooking. I sat in a chair next to him and Macy slid the piled-high plate and a mug of coffee in front of me.

Cal looked up from his paper. "Interesting outfit," he pronounced, after giving me the once-over. "Aren't you a little young for a midlife crisis, though?"

"What do you mean?" I asked, nonplussed.

"You're wearing Mary Janes, white tights with a black kitty cat pattern, a short yellow dirndl skirt, a sweater with a big red heart in the middle, a black watch plaid jacket. You look like you're going to a junior high dance."

Cal has impeccable taste in women's fashion. Sam considers Cal a style icon and frequently calls him for advice.

"Thank you for your input, Mr. Blackwell," I muttered through a mouthful of eggs. I paused to swallow, and added, "My apartment was trashed last night, and I could only salvage a few pieces of useable clothing out of the mess lying on my bedroom floor."

I looked down at my tights. They'd been part of a cat costume I'd worn to a Halloween party last fall. I'd hoped the kitty cat motif was too subtle to make out. Apparently, it was not.

Cal nodded sympathetically. "Macy told me what happened. She said you didn't think anything was taken, though."

"I haven't fine-tooth combed it yet, but none of the obvious stuff was missing; the television, VCR, my watches, and my earrings are all still there. But whoever broke in went Jackson Pollock with my bath and beauty products. I'm going to be the dry cleaner's favorite customer."

"Have you called the police yet?" asked Cal.

"Not yet. I was too tired to deal with it last night. I'll call from my office."

"Do you want me to call the police? I can wait in front of your condo and let them in so they can do whatever on-site investigation needs to be done. They'll want to talk to you at some point, but unless you know who did it, I doubt there's any hurry."

"Thank you, Cal. It would help me out if you could handle things." Cal's offer was more than kind; I knew how long it could take the police to get around to investigating a low-priority complaint like burglary. I almost forgave him for his unfair fashion critique.

"Sure, and Cal can stay here until the police arrive," said Macy, clearly seeing an opportunity to spend more time with him.

"Why, thank you. I believe I will take you up on that offer," said Cal in a formal voice. He exchanged grins with Macy.

I hoped Macy and Cal didn't enjoy their visit so much that they didn't hear the police knock.

"Kate, before you go to your office, why don't you come down with me to my condo and attire yourself in something more suitable for your professional image?" Cal suggested.

Cal's wardrobe is strictly haute couture. I coveted one pink Chanel suit in particular. The problem is, Cal is over six feet tall and wears a size eleven shoe. If I wore Cal's stuff, I would look like a five-year-old playing dress up in her mom's clothes.

"I'd love to, Cal. Your taste is superb." Cal preened in response to the compliment. "But you and I are not even close to the same size. Besides, everything you have is expensive. With the way my life is going lately, anything I wear is at risk. I wouldn't want to ruin any of your things."

A flash of concern crossed Cal's face. I was sure it had less to do with my possible fate than that of his clothes.

"I understand," he said. He looked me up and down again, and then smiled teasingly. "I guess it's not too bad. Besides, people will be so distracted by your hair that they won't notice what you're wearing."

I threw a piece of toast at him.

"You two remind me of the way me and my brother used to be when we were kids," said Macy. She paused, looking thoughtful, and then her benign gaze sharpened and focused on Cal. "My brother is and always has been a schmuck. Be nice to Katie. She's been through a lot."

Cal looked at me apologetically. "I'm sorry, Kate. Ignore me. I'm just a critical old bastard." He paused, and then added "But those socks ..."

He ducked as another piece of toast sailed by his head.

For the remainder of breakfast, we stuck to safe topics, like sports. Macy was a die-hard Jets fan, and Cal rooted for the Miami Dolphins. I wasn't sure what game these teams played, so I was neutral.

After we finished, I called M.J. and told her to meet me at the mobile phone store in fifteen minutes. Macy gave me a thermos full of coffee to tide me over until I got to my office, and Cal walked me to my car as a safety precaution, and probably also to make up for his earlier fashion critique. Cal held the car door open for me and slammed it shut once I was inside. He motioned for me to lower the window.

"Something tells me you haven't told Macy and me everything," he said, bending over so his eyes were level with mine. "I think you have a good idea who broke into your apartment last night. I'm going to get a couple of buddies of mine to take turns with me watching your apartment twenty-four seven until this thing is resolved. In the meantime, I suggest you tell the police *everything*."

Cal's cop radar was pretty damned good. I thought I'd successfully left Macy and him with the impression that the assault on my apartment was a random break-in.

I met his gaze and slowly nodded my head. "Thank you, Cal," I said softly.

CHAPTER NINE

▼

I met M.J. at Phones Plus, one of the ubiquitous tech stores dotting the city. She was already inside, looking at an iPhone. "Look!" she said, showing it to me. "You can listen to iTunes and play games on it and all sorts of stuff."

"All I want is something with a calling function," I said flatly.

"You are so twentieth century when it comes to technology. I don't even know if they make any single function cell phones anymore. Even the most basic ones have cameras, e-mail, and texting."

E-mailing capability would be nifty, I thought. *I don't know about the camera, though. With my luck, I'd lose the phone, and my pictures would end up on the Internet.*

I waved down a clerk, which wasn't too hard to do since there were about twenty of them milling around. The young man who came over to help us looked no older than fifteen and smelled like Clearasil. The Clearasil was not working.

"Do you have any phones that just have telephone, text, and e-mail capabilities?"

"Do you drive a car with just three wheels and half a motor?" he smirked.

I did not find the analogy amusing. "What is the least expensive cell phone you have?" I asked.

"The best deal for the money is that iPhone she's holding," he said, jerking his head in M.J.'s direction.

"I did not ask what the best deal for the money was. I asked which is the least expensive."

His expression evidenced confusion over the distinction.

I sighed. "Is there someone else here who can help us, like your manager?"

He shrugged and said, "Sure." He then waved at someone in the back of the store. "Hey, Randy," he yelled. "Can you come over? This lady wants a cheap phone."

Randy, who looked thirteen, trotted over, stopping to grab a phone off the Nokia display along the way. "Here," he said, handing it to me. "It comes in red, pink, black, or white. They're real popular with the high school kids."

We'll take two. One in black and one in ..." I turned questioningly to M.J.

"Pink," she said promptly.

It took us another half hour or so to get the phones set up, after which we left for the office in our respective cars. The sky had clouded over, and it looked like it was going to rain. This was unusual enough for Phoenicians to slow traffic. Actual rain would bring the city to a halt.

I arrived at the office before M.J. I had a suspicion she'd stopped off for a snack. Beth met me at the door. "Look!" she wailed, standing back and waving her arm in an arc to indicate the reception area.

It looked a lot like my apartment.

"I got here this morning and found it like this. All the offices look the same. I thought I'd better wait to talk to you before I called the police, but I didn't know how to get hold of you."

"Can you tell if anything's missing?" I asked, staring at Beth's upended desk.

"I don't know for sure what all was in your office"—I was sure she did—"but nothing seems to be missing."

"Is Sam here?" I asked.

"Can't you hear him?"

I stopped to listen. I could hear loud sobbing coming from the back.

"Sam?" I called out.

Sam emerged from his office looking as if he'd just discovered that his favorite Armani suit had been eaten by moths.

"It's awful," he sobbed. "They destroyed everything. Even my Brad file."

We all knew that over time, Sam had assembled an extensive collection of Brad Pitt photos about which he was very proud. He stored it in one of his desk drawers, but took it out to show anyone who expressed an interest in Brad, as well as anyone who, while not expressing a direct interest, indicated he or she knew who Brad Pitt was.

Sam was clutching the remnants of Brad's publicity photo for *Thelma and Louise*. Dropping to his knees and holding the torn photo aloft, he cried out plaintively, "Why, why, oh God, why?"

I felt sorry that his collection was destroyed, but I thought his performance was a bit over the top. But then, much of what Sam did was over the top.

I patted his head and said "There, there, Sam. It will be all right. We'll all help you replace the photos in your file. We can search for them on eBay."

"It's not the same. The memories attached to these photos make them irreplaceable," he groaned. But he seemed to have brightened up a bit. I thought it was the prospect of spending hours and hours looking at pictures of Brad on the Net. At least he cut the Scarlett O'Hara pose and got off his knees.

"What the hell happened here?" demanded M.J., who had finally decided to show up.

"It looks like someone was searching for something and got emotionally involved. Maybe he or she was upset about not being able to find whatever they were looking for. My apartment got the same treatment last night," I said dolefully.

M.J., Beth, and even Sam were immediately sympathetic and said how sorry they were. Sam, who apparently had recovered enough from the Brad Pitt catastrophe to notice what I was wearing, asked solicitously if the burglar had hit me on the head, "because sometimes concussions result in bizarre behavior." When I answered that no, I hadn't been there when the apartment was tossed, he looked confused and pointed to my clothes. "Then why are you dressed like that? You look like Little Orphan Annie on crack or, worse, like M.J. on a bad day, or on a good day if you're coming from M.J.'s point of view."

This brought a harrumph and a slap to Sam's head from M.J.

"Whoever trashed my apartment dumped all my clothes on the floor and then added my makeup, shampoo, and whatever else he could find to the pile, and hit puree. The clothes I'm wearing are some of the few that survived," I explained somewhat defensively.

"It could all be part of this demon's heinous plan: reduce your apartment to rubble and, by forcing you to wear absurd clothing, subject you to public ridicule that will result in you taking your own life. Oh my God, are those cats on your tights?"

First Cal, and now Sam. I was feeling especially abused.

"Should I go ahead and call the police?" asked Beth.

Bless her for changing the subject. "I don't know. This is a criminal law defense firm, and I don't want law enforcement personnel poking around in our files." Plus, I'd had enough input on my appearance for one day. I didn't want to invite the troops over for more. I knew cops; they'd never let me forget it. I figured I should be democratic about the decision, though. This time it wasn't just my stuff and peace of mind were destroyed. "How do you guys feel about it? If it makes you feel safer, I say we call the police."

Beth, M.J., and Sam looked at each other. M.J. spoke first.

"I vote no on calling the cops," she said. "I mean, every idiot and his grandmother knows enough to wear gloves when they break into a place, so it's not like the police are going to find any fingerprint evidence. And this is the Phoenix PD we're talking about here, for God's sake, not an episode of *CSI*. Five detectives aren't gonna rush over and crawl around looking for DNA samples."

Sam and Beth nodded their agreement.

"Good. Now let's see what we can do about cleaning up this mess. Maybe you guys could start with the reception area. I need to go into my office to make a few calls, but when I'm through, I'll come back and pitch in on the cleanup."

Since I had already seen the havoc wreaked on my condo, I wasn't too shocked at the condition of my office. It actually wasn't that bad. At least the phone hadn't been ripped out of the wall.

The first call I made was to Tuwanda. She picked up on the seventh ring.

"Tuwanda ain't here. Leave your name and phone number after the beep, or the buzz, or the ring, or whatever the hell noise you hear," she said in a sleepy voice. "After a short pause, she said, "Beeeep."

"Nice try, Tuwanda," I said sardonically.

There was a pause. "Kate?"

"The one and only. Have your heard anything from Tangerine or Margaret?"

"Not a thing. I tried callin' you to see if you knew somethin', but I got no answer. I called both numbers: the cell and your home."

I sighed. "It's a long story. Let's just say I have a love-hate relationship with telecommunications."

"You need a date if you're lookin' to phones for a relationship. Anyways, did you hear somethin'?"

"No. Nothing. I'll call Margaret to see if she heard from Tangerine or found out something new. I call you back if she has anything to say."

"Well, unless it's real vital, wait 'til after noon. My workday don' start 'til then."

We hung up, and I dialed Margaret's number. She picked up just before I was about to give up. "Hello," she said sweetly.

"Hi, Margaret. It's Kate Williams." Prompted by the subsequent silence, I ruefully added, "One of the people who invaded your privacy last night."

"Oh, yes. You're Katherine's attorney, as I recall."

Margaret apparently had some problems in the memory department. I certainly would have remembered anyone who got into my home by misrepresenting herself as a homebuyer—someone I later caught on the stairway with my daughter's ex-boyfriend. But maybe with Katherine as a daughter, last night's events were relatively tame.

"Have you heard from Katherine?"

"No, but I am sure she's fine. My darling Kat is always going off somewhere or another. She's a very important businesswoman, you know. She takes care of her old mother, though. She pays all my bills. She has since she was eighteen. I would know if she was in trouble."

Because your bills wouldn't be paid, I thought. Margaret probably won't raise the alarm until Tangerine misses a payment.

But then I chastised myself for thinking such a cynical a thing about a sweet old woman who obviously loved her daughter.

"Did you talk to Katherine yesterday about why she came to stay at your house?"

"Oh my, no. Katherine pops in and out all the time. She was quieter than usual, but I assumed it was because she was tired. She works so hard ... and such long hours."

"Did you notice she was bruised and cut?"

"I asked her about that. She said she fell at her office, but she insisted she was fine. I made her tea and cookies. She loves chamomile tea and my Toll House cookies. It's a family recipe … the variation of the cookies, I mean. You take one cup of flour, a stick of margarine …"

I started writing the recipe down and then caught myself. I wondered if there was something like methadone for cookie addicts.

Through massive exercise of willpower, I cut Margaret off at the vanilla (one teaspoon), thanked her for talking to me, and asked again that she call if she heard from Tangerine orFreddy. After I gave her my cell number, I signed off.

The next call I made was to Larry's homeless shelter. Again, as seemed to be the procedure for the day, the phone rang numerous times before someone picked up. "You the CIA?" a man with a low whiskey voice asked without preamble.

"No. I need to speak with Larry Larkin. Is he around?"

"He's on the roof. I ain't gonna go git him, though. It's too far. Plus, there's Martians in the stairwell, and there's a ton more on the roof. I dunno how Larkin takes it. They eat your brains, ya know. Mebbe that's why Larkin's on the dumb side of stupid."

"Could you post a message by the phone asking that he call me?"

"Sure," he said, and hung up.

I sighed and dialed the number again. A different person answered. "Hello?" a voice, obviously a woman's, asked suspiciously.

I thought I'd try a more direct approach. "Please tell Larry Larkin that Kate Williams is on the line."

"Are you with the CIA?"

"Yes."

"I'll let him know right now."

I heard the receiver hit the wall and bounce several times until it settled into inertia, and waited. After a minute or so, I heard scurrying feet.

"Hello? Hello?" Larry said breathlessly. "Is this really the CIA? Are you finally gonna do something about the extraterrestrials?"

"It's Kate, Larry."

"You're with the CIA? Wow. My mom is a member of the CIA. Wait 'til I tell the folks in my therapy group."

Maybe I could get my old job back in Chicago. I'd have to do some groveling, but it would be worth it.

"Look, Larry, I just called to see if you're doing okay."

"I know how the CIA operates. That's code for whether I talked to the aliens last night."

"No, it's not code." I didn't want to take the time to explain my little lie to his housemate about being in the CIA, and I plowed ahead with my original line of questioning. "I'm calling to check up on you. I want to verify that none of the people inside the Glendale house we went to got a good look at you in the car."

"Just that guy I seen earlier."

"Which guy?"

"The guy runnin' out of the house. Tuwanda and me were comin' down the street, and he jumped right in front of the car. Tuwanda had to turn real sharp to avoid hittin' him. Instead of thankin' her for havin' such good reflexes, he swore and shot me the middle finger. I guess because he couldn't see Tuwanda very good, and I had my head out the window, he took all his negative emotions out on me. That's what my therapist calls 'em—negative emotions. I personally think some people are just mean."

"You said you saw him earlier?"

"I'm pretty sure, yeah. He was takin' a piss on the Dumpsterdumpster behind the 7-Eleven. I happened to be sittin' there at the time, so I took exception. He ruined a perfectly good Twinkie. He looked like he was gonna hit me, but then he saw the lady in her pj's get into a car and drive away, and he took off after her."

"Lady in her pj's?" I asked weakly.

"Yeah. She was in the store when the pisser drove up and relieved himself on my dessert cake. I saw her go in earlier. She was wearin' pajamas and a robe. I didn't think too much of it. She coulda been in bed, got a hankerin' for some snack food, and didn't want to go to the bother of changin' clothes. Heck, with the robe and all, she had more coverage than most of the women on the street today."

"Do you remember what the lady looked like?"

"Nope. She had a scarf on, and she was facing the other way. The robe was real bulky, so I couldn't tell if she was fat or if it was just the robe. I can't remember what color it was either. I just remember it wasn't pink. I hate pink. I woulda remembered pink."

"Did she seem upset?"

"No, not at all. She was chattin' up the store clerk and lookin' through magazines when I left to go outside to enjoy some repast."

Tangerine wasn't wearing a scarf when I saw her, and I didn't recall the robe she was wearing as being particularly bulky, but she could have had a scarf in her car, and Larry could have mistaken a plump figure for bulk. *One thing's for sure: if the woman in the store was Tangerine, had she known how dangerously close she'd come to running into Freddy, I doubt she would have been so calm.*

"When the pajama lady left, did you see which direction she went?"

"She took a left out of the parking lot. That's all I know."

"Do you know what kind of car she was driving?"

"White."

"That narrows it down," I said wryly.

"Coulda been one of those Japanese cars. They all look the same to me."

All cars looked the same to me too—Japanese, American, European, whatever. I doubt I could have given a better description.

"Larry, if you remember anything more about the guy near the Dumpster or the pajama lady, will you give me a call?"

"Sure."

I gave him my new cell number and signed off.

It wasn't good that Freddy had seen Larry in Tuwanda's car, but it probably all happened too quickly for him to remember much detail. I would have to check with Tuwanda, but it's possible Freddy didn't know what Tuwanda's car looked like, he couldn't connect Larry to Tuwanda.

I went out into the reception area to see how the cleanup effort was going. Stu Napolitano, the World's Slowest Contractor, had come in while I was on the phone, and he was uprighting an end table. Beth was sitting on the floor, checking files to see if anything was missing. M.J. and Sam weren't in the room. I guessed they had gone to straighten up their offices.

"Hi, Stu," I said unenthusiastically. I noticed Stu didn't have any tools with him, and that usually meant he was here not to work but to ask for another check.

"Hey, Mrs. Esquire." No matter how many times I told him to call me Kate, or at least Ms. Esquire, he still referred to me as Mrs. Esquire. I didn't bother to correct him today because our conversation had already gone on too long as far as I was concerned.

I turned to ask Beth a question, but Stu wasn't finished.

"I dropped by to see if you could give me another check so I can get started on the rest of the demo. Looks like you already started, though. Ha-ha." No one except Stu seemed to find this funny.

I looked at him stonily. "Maybe you could finish the kitchen first. Half of it is missing." The most important half: the half with the oven. Stu had come in yesterday and taken everything out. No oven, no cookies.

"I'm waitin' on a part," Stu said.

"What do you mean you're waiting for a part? It's a kitchen, not a car engine." I snapped.

"The light for over the sink ain't in yet," Stu said, sounding hurt.

"Then finish everything except for the light above the sink."

"Okay, but it ain't gonna look right." Stu sighed and finished uprighting one of the file cabinets. "I'll go get my tools."

I knew he wasn't going to come back anytime soon.

"Dang," said Beth, who was still sitting on the floor next to a pile of papers and folders. "You *know* he ain't comin' back today, right? It's some kind of contractor's code that you have to stop a job until you get all the supplies in. I bet Stonehenge was supposed to be a big ol' house, but it never got finished because the idiot contractor was waiting on a roof tile. And all these years, we've been thinking it's some religious site."

I nodded in agreement. "Have you found anything missing yet?" I said, gesturing to the files.

"Nope. But then, I'm only about a tenth of the way through this mess. It's gonna take awhile."

"Do I have anything on my schedule for this morning?"

"You had two new client appointments, and I cancelled them both. I don't think this is at all reassuring to a client," she said, sweeping her arm around the room.

"You're a wise woman, Beth."

"I know. Why don't you see about getting your hair situation taken care of? There's not much you can do around here."

It didn't seem right to desert the fort in the middle of a crisis. "I should stay here and help you with the files."

"Uh-uh," said Beth, shaking her head. "No one touches these files except me. I can't keep it all straight otherwise. That's why I sent M.J. and Sam to their offices."

"Okay, then," I said reluctantly. "I'll give Michele a call. It's probably too late for her to fit me in, but I'll give it a try."

I punched in the number of Stranded and, wonder of all wonders, managed to get a twelve forty-five appointment—about a half hour from now. I assuaged my guilt over leaving Beth, M.J., and Sam to deal with the office situation by telling myself that while at Stranded, I could question Christopher about the photo Larry found on Goldman, which was technically work. I wasn't sure how I was going to find a way to bring up the photo in my conversation with Christopher, though. Figuring out a smooth segue from hair style to doggy style was going to be tricky.

I made a halfhearted attempt to straighten my office and then stuck my head into M.J.'s and Sam's offices to see how they were doing. M.J. seemed comfortable with the chaos, which made sense, because her office was always a disaster; Sam was trying to tape his photos together and was muttering a continuous stream of obscenities, but at least he'd stopped crying. I then headed out to my car. A sheet of paper was stuck under my windshield wiper. I pulled it out, expecting it to be an advertising flyer. Instead, it was a handwritten note.

Leave the information in locker number 112 at the Greyhound Bus Station on Third and Washington by 1:00 today. Thank you. Have a nice day.

A smiley face was scribbled in at the bottom.

Pretty polite for a demand note; no "or else." And the smiley face was kind of nice. Polite or not, though, I had no intention of going to the bus station. I had more important things to do. I pocketed the note and automatically felt to make sure the thumb drive was still securely in place. I had removed it from around my neck, and tucked and taped it under my waistband. The lump was barely noticeable.

Immediately after I entered Stranded, Christopher delivered a quick assessment of my wardrobe. "Omigod! It's Pippi Longstocking."

I ignored him and walked over to Michele, who had been sitting at her station reading a magazine, but raised her head upon hearing Chris's comment. She hopped lightly out of the chair and motioned for me to sit down.

I was the only person in the shop other than Christopher and Michele.

"We don't have a lot of time. I fit you in over my lunch hour. My next appointment is at one fifteen," said Michele. She shook out a plastic cape, arranged it over my clothes, and then tied it around my neck. She took a step back and eyed my hair critically.

"I don't think you should try to go back to blond right away. Red hair won't take blond. We'll have to try something like chestnut, and move gradually back to blond over time."

"I don't want to be chestnut. Chestnut is a horse color. I want it back to what it was before the evil warlock turned it red," I said, glaring at Christopher.

Christopher tossed his head. "I'm not a warlock. I'm a witch, bitch. Take a look."

He held his fingernails out for my inspection. They were painted black and were long for a woman's, much less a man's. I silently chided myself again for letting this person near my hair.

"They're acrylic," he said proudly. "Some of us know how to try out new things without making it permanent."

Michele pressed down on my shoulders to keep me from jumping up and taking a swing at him.

"I guess I could try to strip the color out completely, and then take it blond," she said doubtfully. "But that's awfully hard on your hair, and it still may not work."

"Start stripping!" I ordered.

She gave me a mock salute and said, "Yes, ma'am. I'll go mix the secret potion."

She disappeared into a room in the back, leaving me alone with Christopher.

Screw segues. He didn't deserve a segue.

"Did you have sex with a man named John Webber?" I asked.

"Jesus. As if it's any of your business!" said Chris, indignation oozing from every pore.

"Actually, it is. Webber's part of a murder investigation I'm involved in." Not exactly the truth, but close enough. "I'm surprised the police haven't contacted you about it yet."

"Some guy from the sheriff's office dropped by this morning—really gorgeous, by the way—and showed me a picture. Is that what this is all about?"

I made a mental note to tell Bryan he was very attractive to a certain type. "What did you tell him?" I asked.

"I told him I was one of the guys in the picture, but I didn't know—or at least didn't remember—who the other guy was. You see, there was this party, and I met lots of people. I mean *lots*. It's not like I can remember all of them."

"Where was the party?"

"It was Tangerine's grand opening for the men's division. You were here when Tuwanda was talking about it."

"*Where* was it," I repeated, although I did appreciate the additional information.

"On the southwest corner of Third and Central," he said.

I pulled up a snapshot of the area in my mind. Coincidentally, this was the same intersection where Larry was arrested a few months before for exhibiting his privates to passersby. As I recalled, the only building on the southwest corner was an abandoned Lutheran church.

"The new men's division is in the old Lutheran church? Isn't the milieu sort of a mood killer?"

"No!" exclaimed Chris excitedly. "It's a real turn-on. It makes us all feel so *naughty*."

I imagined millions of Lutherans turning over in their graves.

"Just so I have this clear: you didn't recognize the other man in the picture the sheriff's guy showed you, and you don't know anyone named John Webber."

"Correct. But that's not to say everyone uses their real names at these events," said Chris. "I, for one, prefer to be called 'Fantasia.'"

Walt Disney rolled over in his grave.

Michele emerged from the back room wearing plastic gloves and carrying a small bowl filled with something that smelled like rotten eggs.

"What is that?" I asked doubtfully.

Christopher mumbled something about lunch and escaped out the front door. This was a wise move on his part. My desire to kill and/or maim him, temporarily forgotten while I was questioning him, revived at the sight and smell of the gunk in the bowl.

"The stripping solution," Michele said, as if she were introducing a relative she disliked.

"You mean like bleach, right?"

"Yeah, only lots stronger. The idea is to strip all the color out of your follicles. Bleach isn't enough to do the job. Like I said, red ..."

"I know, I know. Red is hard to get out. It's even harder to live with, though."

I eyed the goo nervously. "Will it make my hair fall out?"

"Only if you leave it in too long, and I don't plan on doing that. Also, I'm going to condition the hell out of your hair after we're through with the stripping and redyeing. Even when done by a professional, this process is hard on hair."

Michele divided my hair into sections and started to apply the stripping solution with what looked like a paintbrush. I silently apologized to my follicles for getting them into this situation.

Probably in an effort to get my mind off the mess on my head, Michele asked what she probably thought was a benign question. "How are things going at work?"

The memory of the break-ins at the office and my apartment, temporarily displaced by my hair issues, flooded back. Then, of course, there were the problems of the missing Tangerine and Freddy the stalker as well. The good news, I guess, is that the nostril-burning smell of the stripping solution didn't seem so bad by comparison.

I gave Michele a quick rundown of yesterday's events. "By the way, I forgot to thank you for calling the police after I left here yesterday."

"Yeah. I didn't buy that part about you coming by to cancel your appointment when a simple phone call would do the trick. Besides, the guy with you didn't look like your type. Too flashy."

"Christopher thought he looked like *his* type."

"Christopher thinks every man is his type."

We both got a chuckle out of that.

"In Christopher's defense, though, he was just trying to have a bit of fun with the guy. Christopher recognized him immediately. His name is Freddy, and he works for Tangerine. As soon as Christopher told me that, I knew there was trouble. When Christopher mentioned this morning that you now represent Tangerine, I thought maybe I'd made a mistake in calling the police."

"How does Christopher know Freddy?" I asked, and thought, but did not ask, *and how does he know I represent Tangerine?*

"Christopher's job is hair styling, but his passion is in knowing everything about everyone. I think he mentioned that Freddy was managing Tangerine's new men's division, or at least he was at the opening party in *some* official capacity."

This was news to me. I wonder why Tangerine hadn't mentioned that Freddy was involved in her new venture. She probably didn't think it was important, but it could tie Freddy to Webber and the photograph taken at the opening of As You Like It.

Michele finished applying the stripper. "You need to let it sit for twenty minutes," she said, as she set the little chicken-shaped egg timer she kept at her station. "If it's okay with you, I'm going to dash across the street and grab a sandwich. Do you want something?"

"Sure. Ham and cheese, if they have it. I'll pay you back. Just add both our lunches to my bill."

"Thanks," she said. "I'll be back in a jiff."

"Please don't get hit by a car," I called out nervously, as she dashed out the door.

I picked up a fashion magazine and paged through pictures of heavily made-up, pouting fourteen-year-old models dressed in clothes no woman would leave the house wearing unless she had a highly developed sense of irony and was impervious to criticism and laughter. Gradually, the magazine photos faded into background imagery and were overtaken by mental images of my hair follicles writhing in pain and screaming helplessly as the chemicals did their work. My scalp had become the Abu Ghraib of hairdom.

I glanced nervously at my watch. I was only ten minutes into the stripping process. I told the paranoid half of my brain that Michele still had lots of time ... and not to worry. Five minutes later, my paranoid half had grown into three quarters. I heard the door open and gave a silent prayer of thanks.

"Hey," I said, without looking up from my magazine, making a pretense of nonchalance I did not feel. "I was about to start rinsing without you."

"That would be a shame," said Freddy. "I'd hate to miss out on an opportunity like that."

"No, not now!" I yelled, hurling the magazine at him.

Freddy dodged the flying spring fashion issue. "What?" He looked nonplussed.

"Not now!" I repeated. "I do not have whatever it is you are looking for, and I can't deal with you now. In five minutes, my hair will fall out."

Freddy did not appear to be at all enlightened by my explanation. He continued to stare at me, confusion now tinged with concern, whether for him or me I couldn't tell.

"You're insane," he said sincerely. Having come to this conclusion, he nervously took a step back, as though insanity were contagious, and then tried to bring our conversation back in line with his original subject.

"You had it on you last night. I felt it. It was hanging around your neck."

"You mean this?" I wrestled with the tie to the plastic cape, only managing to pull it into an unyielding knot, and so I bunched the cape up under my chin. I pulled a locket out from under my sweater. A flash of wisdom I'd attributed at the time to undue paranoia, and now recognized as a realistic assessment of my life, had prompted me to put the locket on this morning in the event just this sort of thing happened. The pink plastic locket, which hung from a long silk cord, belonged to Macy's granddaughter. It bore the ubiquitous image of Barbie on its large oval face. If you hit a button on the bottom, it lit up and a cheery mechanical voice said, "Barbie loves you."

Freddy walked rapidly across the room and grabbed the locket. Since the cord was still around my neck it hurt like heck.

"Ow," I yelped.

"Shut up," growled Freddy.

"Barbie loves you," chirped the locket.

"What? What did you say?" asked Freddy in a startled voice.

"I didn't say anything. You hit the button on—"

"Barbie loves you."

Freddy stared in awe at the blinking locket as if it were magic. Watching Freddy struggle to figure it out was like watching a chimp trying to solve a Rubik's Cube. He turned it over and over, and even lifted it to his nose to sniff it.

"This isn't what you had around your neck last night," he finally said.

Brilliant deduction.

"The one last night didn't talk or blink."

"You didn't hit the button on it last night," I said helpfully.

The egg timer went off, and Freddy jumped. "What the hell was that?"

"Dammit!" I screamed. "Where's Michele?"

Freddy dropped the locket and grabbed my arm. "You're coming with me," he commanded.

"No," I said firmly. "We are going to wait for Michele."

"If Michele is the lady who was in here earlier, I locked her in a port-a-potty on an empty lot across the street. She's not getting out anytime soon."

Before I could stop myself, I slapped Freddy across the face. "Get her out! Get her out now! Getherout, getherout, getherout, getherout …"

"What the fuck is the matter with you?" Freddy said, massaging his reddened cheek.

"My hair! I have to get this stuff out of my hair or it will fall out."

"No shit. Really?" Freddy asked. He sounded genuinely interested.

"Yes, really. Michele put stripper on it to remove the red color, and if I don't get it out when the egg timer goes off, my hair will fall out."

"The timer already went off," Freddy pointed out.

"Thank you, Mr. Obvious. Go get Michele now!" I screamed.

"Oh, no. I'm not leaving you in here by yourself. You'll take off." He grabbed my upper arm again and tried to haul me out of the chair.

"Then let me wash it out." I thrashed around wildly, trying to loosen Freddy's grip.

"You're crazy," gasped Freddy, as he warded off a kick to the groin.

"Think about it, Freddy. What if it were your hair?"

What was I doing? I'd just asked Freddy to think. I didn't have time for that. I stopped struggling and looked up at him. He appeared to be taking his assignment seriously. His brow was furrowed, and he was frowning slightly. His synapses were no doubt engaged in a heroic effort to overcome inertia.

After what seemed like an eternity to a person in my particular circumstances, he said, "I see what you mean." He stroked his oily black hair protectively. "Where's the sink?"

"There," I said, pointing to the back of the shop.

Freddy hauled me to my feet and marched me to the sink. "You do it. I don't want to touch that stinky crap on your head."

Freddy apparently had flashes of wisdom after all.

I turned both faucets on full blast, kneeled on the chair facing the sink, and then stuck my head under the gushing water. I covered my face with my hands to keep the stripping solution from running into my eyes and dissolving my pupils.

Freddy dropped my arm and shuffled back a few steps to get out of splash range.

"Shampoo!" I yelled, after about five minutes of rinsing and scrubbing.

"What kind?" Freddy asked

"Anything that says it's for color-treated hair."

"Coconut, vanilla, or banana?"

"What?" It was hard to hear over the rushing water.

"The shampoo. They got three kinds for color-treated hair: coconut, vanilla, or banana?"

"Dammit, I don't care. Hand me the … vanilla."

"I think you should go for the banana. I smelled 'em all, and the banana's the best."

"*Whatever.* Give it to me. *Now.*"

Freddy placed a plastic bottle into my outstretched hand, and I squeezed most of its contents on my head.

"Jesus! And people think *I'm* kinky," said Christopher. Freddy must have forgotten to lock the front door, or maybe Christopher let himself in with a key.

Freddy whirled around to face him. "What are you doing here?" he demanded.

"Umm, I *work* here. *Helllooo.*"

"Look, Chris. This is none of your business. Shut the door behind you when you leave."

"It's *Christopher*, not Chris. Where's Michele?"

"In the ladies' room." Freddy's growing impatience was evident in his voice.

I stopped lathering my hair long enough to lift my head and say, "Christopher, call the police."

"Oh, for gawd's sake. Your hair got dyed a color you didn't like. Get *over* it."

"Leave, *Christopher*," interjected Freddy, who undoubtedly felt he was losing control of the situation.

"Yes. Leave and call the police." I was in the rinsing stage, so it came out somewhat garbled.

"Stay," ordered Freddy. I wasn't clear on whom he was addressing, but I assumed he meant both of us.

"Make up your mind, boy toy. Do you want me to go or stay?" asked Christopher.

"Who the fuck are you calling boy toy?" snapped Freddy.

"You. Aren't you Tangerine's poodle?"

I grabbed a towel and wrapped it around my head, but I left the water running so the two geniuses would think I was still rinsing. I didn't want to distract them from their duel of wits.

"A poodle's a pet, not a toy! shouted Freddy. Then, as an afterthought, he added, "And Freddy Scilli is not anybody's toy *or* pet." He took a few steps toward Christopher, fisting his hand threateningly.

Christopher started to laugh hysterically. "Silly? Seriously, your last name is Silly?" he managed to choke out between guffaws.

"It's S-C-I-L-L-I, not S-I-L-L-Y," Freddy shot back defensively.

"Not hearing the difference," replied Christopher, who was then seized by another paroxysm of mirth.

I edged toward the back door as Freddy launched into a defensive riff about his heritage. I'd gotten to the door and reached out to turn the door handle when the towel slipped from my head.

"Jesus, Mary, and Joseph!" screamed Christopher.

Freddy whirled around, and his features froze into a look of shock. "Gawd," he said. "What the fuck did you do to yourself?"

I stared at them in bewilderment. Christopher, ever helpful, grabbed a hand mirror, dashed over to me, and held it up in front of my face.

"Urk," I said, looking into the mirror. My hair was no longer fire engine red. It was bubble gum pink.

A stunned silence followed as all three of us stared at my hair. Reacting to an irrational surge of hope, I thought maybe the pink color would disappear as my hair dried, but the first wisps of dry hair looked even pinker than the wet stuff.

I whacked Christopher over the head with the hand mirror.

"Owww. Why'd you do that?" he whined.

"You started this!" I screamed. "Look at me. I look like Frenchie in the malt shop scene in *Grease*."

Freddy snapped his fingers. "Right! *That's* what I was trying to think of."

"What?!" I said, waving the mirror threateningly in his direction.

"I was trying to think what you reminded me of, and that was it: the scene in *Grease* where ..."

"*Shut up!*" I yelled.

Christopher, who was still rubbing his head and staying out of range of the mirror, said, "The stripper must not have got all the red out. That's why it's pink."

"Red! You said red! You admit it! It was red, not fucking auburn." I was vaguely aware that I was completely out of control, but the insane part of me took the position that I was merely being assertive.

A knock sounded at the front door, and someone tried the knob. Freddy motioned for us to be quiet and hoarsely whispered, "Everyone, out the back door. We're going for a ride."

"Who made you the group leader?" Christopher snapped in a normal voice.

"Smith and Wesson," said Freddy, taking a .38 out of his pocket. I was wondering when he'd get around to that.

"That is so Clint Eastwood," quipped Christopher. Although he probably intended to sound flip, I could hear the unsteadiness in his voice.

Following Freddy's orders, we trooped out the back door with me in the lead. "Get in the car," he said, pointing to a white Mercedes; it was either the car I'd seen leave the Happy Hollow house the day before or its twin.

I started to get into the backseat but Freddy grabbed my arm and pulled me out. "You're driving," he said, pushing me toward the driver's side.

"At this rate, I'm going to need to get a chauffeur's license," I grumbled.

"What did you say?" demanded Freddy

"May I at least take off this plastic sheet? It's hard to move my arms around with it on."

"Sure," he said, then added with a leer, "and anything else you want to take off too."

Yeah. Like that was going to happen. I pulled the plastic cape over my head and discarded it on the ground next to the car.

"Jesus," said Freddy.

"I know, right?" said Christopher.

"You're a lawyer, aren't you? I mean, lawyers are supposed to dress in matching shit, like suits or something." Freddy sounded genuinely concerned. Apparently, haberdashery was something very close to his heart.

"You of all people should know why my clothes selection was extremely limited this morning," I snapped.

"What? What are you talking about?" I couldn't tell if the surprise in Freddy's voice was faked or real.

"Someone tossed my apartment and my office last night. I'm guessing it was you." I retorted.

"I was at home watching TV last night. They had an episode of *Law and Order* on," said Freddy.

"Oh for God's sake, Freddy. First, we both know you were at Margaret's house last night. Second, there's *always* an episode of *Law and Order* on, so that's a stupid alibi."

"Start the car," Freddy said nonresponsively.

I did as I was told. "Who's Margaret?" Chris asked from the backseat.

"Shut up, Christopher," said Freddy.

"Tangerine's mother," I answered.

"Tangerine has a *mother*? God, that's got to make for some interesting conversations around the mahjong table: 'So, Maggie, how's your daughter's ho business doing these days?'"

"Yeah, kind of like with your mother: "So, Mable, how's the *fagala*? Still taking it up the ass?'"

Both Christopher and Freddy used falsetto voices when imitating Margaret and Mable, respectively. I felt like I was in the middle of a Milton Berle routine.

"My mother's name is *not* Mable," Christopher huffed. "It's Sophia, and the woman is a saint."

I cracked open the driver's side window. "What are you doing?" Freddy barked.

"I am trying to defog the windshield. You two have been yapping so much the windows steamed up," I said, and indeed the windows had turned opaque in spots.

Freddy flipped the car's defroster on. "Close the window and get going," he ordered.

"I don't want to pry, but where the heck am I supposed to go? I'll settle for general guidance if you don't want to divulge detail. You know, like, take a right, go left ..."

"God, you're a sarcastic bitch. Take a fucking right." Freddy waved his gun around agitatedly. Christopher dove down and flattened himself on the car's backseat. I took a right.

A few other drivers gave us—or, to be exact, me—strange looks, but for the most part, our entourage garnered little attention. Phoenix is a big city, and the locals have adopted a New York City attitude toward the unusual.

We followed the same route we took yesterday and, sure enough, ended up at the Happy Hollow house again. I wondered if the guy in the Reagan mask would come out and meet us again. What did Tangerine say his name was? Tom Fields?

This time Freddy had me pull around to the back of the house. He'd probably learned his lesson about nosy neighbors. He marched us into the house, through a large, well-appointed kitchen, and into an ostentatiously appointed living room. Burgundy and gold brocade floor-to-ceiling drapes covered the window. A huge couch and two overstuffed chairs upholstered in complementary colored fabric, along with an elaborately carved gold gilt-covered coffee table, occupied the center of the room. Several small tables were scattered about the room, and every available surface was covered with what Macy would call *tchotchkes*—except these trinkets looked expensive.

Christopher and I sat on the couch, sinking about a foot into the fluffy cushions. Freddy took one of the chairs opposite us and kept the gun trained on us.

"Crank!" Freddy yelled out. Both Christopher and I jumped at the sudden, unexpected sound.

A man, presumably Crank, came down the stairs. He had sharp features and thinning gray hair. I tried to imagine him with a Regan mask on. He had the same body type as mask-man.

"Are you Tom Fields?" I asked.

The man stopped short, one foot on the last step and the other poised in the air above the landing. He glanced nervously at Freddy. "How does she know my name?"

If I wasn't sure before, I know now, I thought. Tom and Freddie were obviously intellectual soul mates.

"Don't look at me," said Freddy, whereupon both Freddy and Tom looked at me.

"Lucky guess," I said, shrugging. I didn't want to bring Tangerine or Tuwanda into this.

"You're a smart-ass, aren't you?" said Tom, a.k.a. Crank. I figured it was a rhetorical question, so I didn't bother to answer.

"Just wait 'til she gets started," grumbled Freddy. "She's really sarcastic."

"I second that," piped in Christopher. "Plus, the way she carries a grudge makes John Gotti seem like a Buddhist."

"Why's her hair pink?" asked Tom, as if noticing it for the first time. I felt an odd sense of gratitude that it had taken him so long to bring it up.

"Because she tried to change the color herself and screwed it up. She should have let a professional handle it," said Christopher.

"Okay, that's it!" This nonsense had to stop. "This is the second time I've been kidnapped and held at gunpoint, and I still don't know why. Now, to top things off, a bunch of retards are conducting a critical analysis of my hair and personality as though I weren't in the room."

"See what I mean?" Freddy said, looking meaningfully at Tom.

"Freddy, just shut up!" I yelled. It occurred to me that I'd just screamed at a man pointing a gun at me. I took a few deep breaths to calm down, and then, addressing Tom/Crank in my normal voice, or in as normal a voice as I could manage under the circumstances, asked, "Mr. Fields, could *you* please tell me why I am here?"

Tom plopped down on a chair next to Freddy. The leather upholstered seat cushion made a noise like a whoopee cushion, and we were suddenly back in junior high. Freddy and Christopher took turns accusing Tom of flatulence, air pollution, chemical warfare, and other indiscretions involving intentional release of gas onto innocent bystanders. I endured the riotous exchange stone-faced. When things quieted down, I repeated the substance of my previous question.

"Mr. Fields, what is this all about?"

Tom and Freddy exchanged looks, and Freddy rolled his eyes.

"I think you know damned well what this is all about," said Tom. He shifted his weight and leaned toward me. The chair burped. I shot Christopher a dark look and cut him off in mid-giggle. "We want the list of names Tangerine gave you. We gave you the option of dropping it off at the bus station, but it don't look like you're gonna make the deadline." After a dramatic pause, he held up his wristwatch and pointed emphatically at the dial.

I looked at his watch. "It's six o'clock?" I asked.

"Dammit. I must've forgot to wind it this morning."

"Look, I don't know about any list of names," I said, which was technically true. I hadn't opened the thumb drive, so, although I had a good idea what was stored on it, I didn't have any direct knowledge.

The front door flew open, crashed against the wall, bounced back, and slammed shut. I heard Tuwanda swear, and then the door opened again, more gently this time. Tuwanda walked into the room holding a .38 in a TV-style two-handed grip. Larry trailed behind her but stopped in the doorway. Seeing me, he waved. I responded with a two-fingered wave.

Freddy had turned around in his chair at the sound of Tuwanda's entrance and was now pointing his gun at her. The two tried to stare each other down. Since Freddy and his gun were, at least temporarily, not my problem, I heaved myself up, grabbed a large *tchotchke*—a gilt cherub holding a cut-glass fruit bowl over its head—and coldcocked Freddy. Tom yelped and, as Freddy slid to the floor, took off toward the back of the house. A minute later, we heard the roar of the much-abused Mercedes engine, and the squeal of its equally abused tires.

"Tie him up with somethin'!" screamed Tuwanda.

Christopher, who until now had been like Switzerland in his allegiances, fought his way out of the couch's thick cushions. He flopped down on his knees next to Freddy and removed his tie with the ease of practice. He then rolled him over, straddled him, and bound Freddy's hands together behind his back. When he was done, he threw his hands up like a cowboy in a calf-roping contest.

"I take it you have done somethin' like this before," remarked Tuwanda.

Christopher smiled mischievously and jiggled his eyebrows Groucho Marx-style.

Freddy stirred and opened his eyes. "Get off me, you little fag!" he shrieked. Christopher, who was still straddling Freddy's back, shifted into a more comfortable position.

"Come on, Christopher," I said. "Some other time."

He sighed, patted Freddy on the fanny, and then moved to the chair Tom had recently vacated. I plopped down in the chair next to him, whooshing a sigh of relief.

"Tuwanda, I've never been so happy to see anyone in my life. How the heck did you find us?" I asked.

"It wasn't that hard," she said, starting to sit on the couch. Clearly thinking better of it, she sat on one of its arms instead. "I was at Michele's for my one fifteen appointment. I was parked across the street when I saw you get into Freddy's car. So I followed you."

"Where did you get him?" I said, pointing at Larry, who was still standing in the doorway.

"I tried callin' you on your new cell, but you didn't answer," she explained, looking at me accusingly.

That's because my phone had been on vibrate—not because I didn't want to be disturbed, but because I'm a technology-impaired idiot and don't know how to change the setting to ring. I didn't bother to explain my shortcomings, but just nodded in acknowledgement and looked at Tuwanda expectantly.

"Anyways, I wanted to find out if anything new came up on Tangerine situation, so I swung by your office. There was a sign on your buildin' that said it was closed 'cause of construction work. Larry was standin' outside on the curb, lookin' all sad. He came over to get lunch, you bein' his mom and all, and you wasn't there. I felt sorry for him so I told him he could come with me to Stranded and I'd get him some food at the Quiznos across the street before my appointment. That's what I was doin' when I saw Freddy, Christopher, and you leave the shop; I was gettin' Larry a sandwich."

"I ordered humus with sprouts on whole wheat," said Larry. "It wasn't ready yet when Tuwanda spotted you guys. She made me leave and get in her car, so I still haven't had lunch."

Larry's priorities were unyielding, even in the face of an emergency. I refused to be sucked into feeling guilty about Larry's lack of nourishment, so I ignored his last comment.

"I'd better report everything that's happened to the sheriff's office and ask them to pick up Freddy," I said, pulling my phone out of my pocket.

Tuwanda leaped to her feet and grabbed my arm before I could dial. "You ain't callin' no cops, not even your boyfriend. We're leavin' here now! Together."

Tuwanda's antipathy toward law enforcement was understandable in light of her numerous arrests. Still, I thought Tuwanda's position was a tad extreme. I tried to be sympathetic, though.

"I know you are ... um ... uncomfortable around law enforcement personnel, so it's fine if you and Larry want to take off before they get here. I'll keep you both out of this to the extent I can."

"Uh-uh. Ain't no cops comin' to this house," Tuwanda said stubbornly.

"Why?" I asked, annoyance creeping into my tone.

"'Cause this here's Tangerine's house. Ain't no cops gonna go through Tangerine's house."

I was dumbfounded. Taking another look at the room in light of this new information, I recognized similarities between the styles of Tangerine's office and the house. The explicit art was missing, but the house's interior had the same color scheme and gilt furniture. It also made sense that Freddy would know where Tangerine's house was, and he would know that she wasn't there. It was the perfect hideout: he and Tom would be around if Tangerine tried to return, plus they got the benefit of luxurious accommodations without the downside of rental payments or hotel bills.

"How about you drive me, Christopher, and Freddy over to the sheriff's department and drop us off?" I said in a placating voice. "I'll call Bryan and let him know we're coming, but I won't mention your involvement, other than to say you're giving us a ride. I'll tell him about the kidnapping at Stranded but leave the details fuzzy for now, until we can find Tangerine. The important thing is that I have to deliver Freddy into the sheriff's custody so he won't be a threat to anyone anymore. Once he's locked up, we need to find some way to let Tangerine know what's happened."

"Sounds good to me," said Tuwanda.

"What about me?" demanded Christopher. "It's not as if I want to talk to the big bad police either. I think I should go with Tuwanda and her hummus-eating friend. After all, you wouldn't want me to spill the details of our little adventure to the police. I crack easily under pressure. Actually, I crack easily without pressure. I'm a very giving person, and God knows I hate to lie. Why, I—"

I cut him off before we had to hear any more about Christopher's self-proclaimed sterling qualities. "Fine, then. Just drop Freddy and me off at the sheriff's office. Does that work for you, Tuwanda?"

"I'll take Larry and the little freak with me," said Tuwanda, and then she addressed Christopher with a narrowed-eyed look. "But you're gonna reimburse me for gas, and I ain't goin' out of my way to take you home. I'll drop you off at Stranded."

"Oh my God … Michele!" I said, remembering that Freddy had locked her in a port-a-potty. I punched Bryan's number into my cell and was relieved when he picked up right away.

"Where have you been?" he demanded before I could say anything.

"It's complicated. I'm coming to your office and bringing Freddy with me. I can explain everything once we get there. In the meantime, could one of your guys check on Michele? She's locked in a port-a-potty at a construction site near Stranded."

"Michele?" asked Bryan, sounding bewildered.

"Yes, Michele. She's my hairdresser, remember?"

"You locked her in a portable toilet? Did *she* mess up your hair too?"

"No! *I* didn't lock her in there; Freddy did. Just get her out!" I ended the call and pocketed my phone.

Freddy was sitting up by this time, but he still looked dazed. "Come on, Christopher," said Tuwanda. "Help me get this piece of shit into the car."

"Why do I have to do it? *He* looks stronger than me," he said, pointing at Larry.

"'Cause Larry ain't gonna come into the house.. He don't like bein' inside places. He's … watchacallit … closetphobic."

"Claustrophobic," I corrected.

Larry nodded solemnly in agreement.

"Well, I'm assholephobic," groused Christopher. "I don't like touching assholes." After Tuwanda shot him the evil eye again, he grudgingly bent down and grabbed Freddy under one arm, while Tuwanda grabbed him under the other. With a chorus of grunts, they hauled him to his feet.

"What the fuck?" said Freddy, trying ineffectually to push Christopher away.

"You got too fresh with me, so we had to tie you up," said Christopher. "Don't worry, though. I'm still interested. We just need to take it slower. *Cats* is in town. Should I pick up a couple of tickets? We can do dinner after."

Freddy struggled weakly. "You little fruit. You're lucky you've got this big black bitch here to protect you. If she wasn't around, I'd rip you apart."

Christopher, Larry, and I sucked in air and looked nervously at Tuwanda with the joint realization that Freddy had just said something very, very stupid.

"Did he just say what I think he say?" Tuwanda said dangerously. She fisted the hand that wasn't hooked under Freddy's shoulder, and slugged him with an uppercut worthy of Ali in his prime. Freddy's head jerked back and then fell forward. His body slumped.

Christopher and Tuwanda towed Freddy to the car, with Christopher whining nonstop about how hard it is to drag dead weight, and that it was Tuwanda's fault if he strained some vital muscle and couldn't perform his duties as a hairstylist. I personally thought that outcome would be a godsend to humanity.

Christopher and Tuwanda, but mostly Tuwanda, got Freddy into the backseat of the car and shoved his inert body into the center.

"Larry, you sit on one side of him, and Christopher, you get on the other side. If he comes to, make sure he don't work that tie loose," Tuwanda directed, as she slid into the driver's seat. I got into the passenger seat.

"I ain't startin' this car 'til everyone's got their seatbelts on," she said, looking pointedly at the trio in the backseat. Tuwanda and my mother had a lot in common in this regard. No amount of urgency could override the seat belt requirement.

We all dutifully clicked our belts in place and waited while Christopher placed a belt around Freddy. Grunting her approval, Tuwanda started the engine and pulled out onto the road.

"So Freddy ain't a threat to Tangerine no more, an' if I know Tom, he's run as far away as he can to save his own sorry ass. But what happens if we can't get hold of Tangerine to let her know? Or she ain't in a position to be got hold of or get hold of anyone else? Even if you don't say nothin', the police are gonna figure out the connection between Freddy an' Tangerine, an' they gonna start lookin' around for her. They gonna search her house an' office an' suchlike—an' that ain't good. We need to talk to her before that happens and convince her she needs to explain everythin' to the police and clear things up before they come up with their own crazy-assed ideas 'bout Freddy an' Tangerine, and maybe even 'bout Goldman. That gives me concerns."

I saw Tuwanda's point. It wouldn't take the police or sheriff's department long to find out, at the very least, that Tangerine was Freddy's employer. They already knew about her connection to Goldman, and to me for that matter. For these reasons alone, the police would want to talk to her. I didn't want to tell the police everything I knew, and I sure as heck didn't want to have to give up the thumb drive as evidence in the kidnapping case against Freddy without talking to Tangerine first. Simply put, until Tangerine came in from the cold, I was in the position of having to choose between withholding evidence or violating my professional obligations to a client. I figured my best strategy was to put off the necessity of making that choice as long as possible.

"I guess all we can do is take it step-by-step and hope for the best," I said, even though "stumble-by-stumble" would have been a better description. "After you drop me and Freddy off, could you call and leave messages on Tangerine's voice mail and with Margaret, giving Tangerine the all clear?"

"Will do," said Tuwanda. "You want I should let you know when I'm done callin'?"

"No. I'll get hold of you for an update as soon as I'm through at the sheriff's office."

Tuwanda glanced in her rearview mirror, and then bellowed, "What the hell you doin'?"

I turned around to see who and what she was talking about—just in time to see Christopher hastily withdraw his hand from Freddy's side pocket.

"I was just searching for ID," he said innocently.

"You don' need to search for no ID. We *know* who this fucker is. You jus' keep your hands to yourself. Hey, you ain't jus' tryin' for a cheap thrill back there, are you?"

"No," said Christopher, sounding thoroughly offended. "I like my men alert and on top of things."

Tuwanda rolled her eyes and groaned.

"Actually, Christopher may have a point," I said thoughtfully.

"I do not! I just told you—"

"For crying out loud. Not *that* kind of point. Can we try to make it through a conversation without the double entendres for once? What I mean is, maybe Freddy has ID with an address. After all, it's possible he's holding Tangerine there. Larry said Freddy was at the 7-Eleven last night and that he left following a woman in pajamas. I can't believe there are that many women running around in public in their pajamas, so she could very well have been Tangerine. Maybe Freddy wasn't sure I had Tangerine's list, so he grabbed her and stashed her where he could find her in case he needed more information."

"How you figure Freddy had time to chase down Tangerine, take her someplace an' stash her, and then drive to Margaret's house so he could grope you?"

I gave that some consideration. "Maybe he handed her off to Tom before going to Margaret's house."

"You got an agile imagination, I'll give you that," said Tuwanda. "But I guess it wouldn't do no harm to find out where he lives so we can check it out if Tangerine don't try to contact us. I jus' think it would be unwise to let Christopher here search Freddy. That boy's got boundary issues."

"Larry," I said, raising my voice to get his attention because, as usual, his head was hanging out the window.

"Larry!" I said, jacking up the volume even more when he did not respond.

He pulled his head into the car and turned to me slowly. "Whut?"

"I need you to reach into Freddy's pockets and find his billfold. I know you have experience in this kind of thing, so it shouldn't be hard for you."

Tuwanda raised an eyebrow at my mention of Larry's special expertise, but I didn't elucidate. I didn't want to get into Larry's liberation of Goldman's pocket contents and his loose interpretation of the laws of inheritance.

Larry did a quick pat down of Freddy, who was awake again but had a shaky grip on reality.

"I didn't do nothin', Officer," he mumbled. No doubt Freddy had plenty of prior experience with pat down searches.

Reaching quickly into Freddy's back pocket, Larry produced a wallet and immediately flipped it open, checking the cash compartment.

"Larry!" I said. "Hand it over!"

Larry sheepishly closed the wallet and put it into my outstretched hand. "Sorry," he said. "Habit."

I searched through the wallet, looking for a driver's license. I found three MasterCards, two Visa cards, and an American Express Platinum card. One of the MasterCards was mine. The other MasterCards and the Visa cards were issued to people whose names I didn't recognize. Only the American Express card had the name Frederick D. Scilli on it. I found his driver's license in a side compartment. I scanned it quickly and found out Freddy's middle name was Dolphius, he did indeed have a local address, and he didn't photograph well, even by MVD standards.

"He lives on Desert View Lane in Scottsdale," I said.

Scottsdale, referred to by some of the locals as "Snottsdale," is an upscale suburb northeast of Phoenix. Although it used to be called the "West's Most Western Town," it was now more like the Arizona town most likely to be mistaken for LA. The men in cowboy clothes roaming the sidewalks of Old Town Scottsdale, whose numbers rose and fell according to current fashion trends, were more likely to be looking for other men than they were little dogies.

The population of North Scottsdale, where Freddy lived, ranges from the merely wealthy to the super rich. Obsessed with status, exercise, diet, and things with labels (brand names are appended as adjectives to clothes and accessories, cars, appliances, sports equipment, furniture, and even bath towels; and people are labeled parenthetically according to occupation or level of wealth), the folks of North Scottsdale rarely strayed beyond the "Welcome to Scottsdale" monuments marking the boundaries of the city.

"That's a nice part of town," commented Tuwanda. "How's someone like Freddy afford to live there?"

Freddy mumbled something that sounded like "chocolate covered graham crackers."

"Damn, Tuwanda. How hard did you hit this guy?" asked Christopher.

Tuwanda shrugged. "Tangerine had us Care Bares take a class on self-defense. The instructor said I had a real gift."

"It's possible Freddy used a false address," I said. "It certainly would be consistent with his MO to do so. He's got a load of credit cards belonging to other people, including me."

"No shit! How'd he get that?"

"He must have taken it out of my purse when he was looking for my keys the first time he kidnapped me. I canceled the card, though, so it didn't do him much good."

"Man. This kidnappin' thing must be getting' real old for you," Tuwanda said, reaching over and patting my shoulder sympathetically. "You oughta think 'bout takin' a self-defense class like I did. That an' get yourself a big ol' gun. Guns got a real chillin' effect on kidnappers."

"Don't you have to get a permit if you want to carry a gun?" I asked.

"Hell, girl. This is Phoenix. My dog groomer carries a Glock."

"You have a dog? You don't strike me as a pet person," I commented.

"Walter ain't jus' a pet. He's a watchdog. Nothin' goes down in my buildin' that Walter don't make a comment on."

"He barks a lot?" I guessed.

"Damn right. No one's gonna sneak up on ol' Tuwanda as long as Walter's around," she said.

I thought of Ralph, whose primary defensive weapons were drool and crotch sniffing. I think I preferred Ralph's more subtle approach over loud barking.

Tuwanda glanced into the rearview mirror, looked back at the road briefly, then looked into the rearview mirror again and kept her eyes there a few seconds.

"Is something wrong?" I asked, turning my head to see if perhaps Christopher, despite Tuwanda's warning, was pursuing his examination of Freddy. I wouldn't put it past him to do a body cavity search if he thought he could get away with it. But Christopher had his hands folded neatly in his lap and was staring quietly out the window.

"I thought I saw a car followin' us," said Tuwanda. "It looked like that white Mercedes Freddy made you and Christopher get into at Stranded."

I searched the traffic behind us. "I don't see it," I said.

"It jus' turned right at that last stoplight. Probably was a different car. Them Mercedes are everywhere in this town. It's worse in Scottsdale. Damn grocery store parking lots look like Mercedes dealerships in Scottsdale."

We were within a block of the sheriff's department by now, and I could see a couple of deputies standing on the front steps, surveying traffic. They must be the guys Bryan sent out to meet us. Tuwanda did not slow down but drove around to the back of the building and pulled up to the curb. Larry and Christopher hauled Freddy out of the back backseat and unceremoniously dumped him on the sidewalk next to a NO LOITERING sign. The letters were partly obscured by a spray-painted gang tag, though, so it read NO -----RING.

I reiterated my promise to Tuwanda to call her when I was through at the sheriff's office. She gave me a short wave and a heartfelt "Good luck," and then gunned the engine and drove away, barely giving Larry and Christopher time to jump back into the car before liftoff. Tuwanda had serious avoidance issues when it came to law enforcement facilities.

I called Bryan. When he picked up, I skipped the preliminaries and announced, "We're standing—or rather, I'm standing and Freddy's sitting kind of slumped over—on the sidewalk behind your building."

"I'll be right down. I have two deputies stationed at the front steps waiting for you. I'll tell them to come around to meet us."

As I pocketed my phone, I noticed an incredibly tripped out lowrider coming around the corner toward us. The car was bright red with a lunging lion, its fangs sunk into a bloodied zebra, painted on the side facing the curb. I couldn't see the artwork on the other side, but I'm sure it was equally dramatic.

Spinners on the hubcaps, through some optical illusion I didn't understand, made it look like the wheels were turning in the direction opposite to that in which the car was moving.

The driver was hidden behind narrow, heavily tinted windows. As the vehicle drew nearer, it slowed and then stopped next to me, bouncing up and down on heavy-duty hydraulics like a rocking horse. I figured the driver was putting on a show for my benefit. With my pink hair and street chic outfit, I must have looked like a woman ready for action.

The passenger side window opened a crack, and the barrel of a gun appeared. I didn't hear the shot, but the bullet hit Freddy squarely in the chest. His body buckled, and then he sprawled out on the sidewalk.

I went facedown on the concrete, trying to use Freddy's body and the insubstantial "No ...ring" sign as shields. I stared at a flattened piece of gray chewing gum near my nose, praying it would not be the last thing I saw.

Shots rang out from the direction of the parking lot, the sound echoing in the canyon created by the surrounding high-rise office buildings. The lowrider accelerated and fishtailed around the corner. Amid shouted orders and crackling radios, two sheriff's cars roared out of the parking lot in pursuit.

The chewing gum was now an island surrounded by Freddy's blood.

Someone grabbed me under my arms and hauled me to my feet. "Tell me where Kate is," demanded Bryan in his cop voice.

"Right here," I said shakily.

Bryan turned me around and peered into my face. "Kate? What the hell did they do to you?"

An emergency vehicle pulled up and two EMTs jumped out. One of them wore a baseball cap with "Life is good" embroidered on it. Despite its irony, I found the phrase oddly comforting.

Triage wasn't necessary under the circumstances. The EMTs headed immediately for Freddy. The man wearing the ball cap felt Freddy's neck for a pulse, grunted,, and then slapped an oxygen mask on Freddy's face. Within seconds, he and the other EMT had transferred him to a gurney. "County hospital," the guy in the baseball hat shouted over his shoulder, as they slid the gurney into the back of their vehicle. Indicating me with a head jerk, he said to Bryan, "The guys behind us will see to her." He climbed into the back with Freddy, and I saw him attaching a heart monitor just before his partner slammed the door shut.

The truck left with its siren blaring and lights flashing. No more than five minutes had passed since the shooting. I guess that's the advantage of being shot next to the sheriff's office; the service is terrific.

A second emergency vehicle pulled up, and a man and a woman jumped out.

"I'm fine," I said, waving my hands in front of me in a never mind motion.

"Don't listen to her," said Bryan. "She needs to be checked out. Just look at her."

"Well, sir," said the female EMT. "We don't know what she looked like before, so it's hard for us to see what the problem is."

Bryan pulled out his wallet, extracted a photograph, and showed it to her. I looked too. It was a particularly flattering photo of me standing in front of my office-bungalow that Bryan had taken the day escrow closed. I had no idea he kept a copy of it in his wallet, and I felt flattered. The feeling passed quickly, though.

"This is what she usually looks like," he said.

The EMTs looked back and forth between the photo and me.

"We'll take her in and give her a thorough physical, sir," said the male half of the team, "but then we'll need to transfer her to another facility for a mental evaluation."

"For God's sake, I'm fine. A hairdresser accidentally dyed my hair red, and it turned pink when I tried to strip the color out. On top of that, my apartment was trashed last night, and I am wearing some of the few useable pieces of clothing I have left."

The woman EMT shook her head and tsk-tsked empathetically. "Yeah, red is really hard to get out." Her partner looked puzzled.

Bryan sighed and put the photo back in his billfold. "I guess you can go, guys," he said.

"Sorry for the confusion."

"No problem, sir."

The EMTs returned to their truck. No sirens or lights accompanied their departure.

"Let's go up to my office," said Bryan, scrubbing his face with his hands. "I need to get your statement, and this time you *will* tell me everything."

Bryan got a call while we were en route to his fifth-floor office. He listened for a while and then issued a series of brief orders to the caller. He ended the call and said, "We lost the car in a neighborhood just north of Buckeye and 59th Avenue. Our guys will go door-to-door and ask if the neighbors saw anything, but I don't expect much to come from it."

"How could you lose a red lowrider with a huge fluorescent orange tiger painted on the side, spinners, and chrome dual exhausts?" I asked incredulously.

"Easy. All he or she needs to do is pull into a garage and shut the door. The people in that part of town don't trust law enforcement, and while they'll shoot one another over a baggie of grass, they stick together when it comes to cops."

The elevator doors opened, and we stepped out into a small lobby presided over by Bryan's secretary, Carol, who sat behind a desk in front of the door to Bryan's office. Anyone wanting to see Bryan had to go through Carol first.

"By the way," continued Bryan, "we found your friend Michele and got her out of the port-a-potty. She's mad as hell and smelled like, well, like a port-a-potty, but otherwise she seemed okay. She told us she didn't see the face of the guy who pushed her in, but says to let her know when we find him because she wants to remove his body hair for free the old-fashioned way."

"The old-fashioned way?"

"Yeah. One by one ... with tweezers."

I guess beauticians' torture fantasies tended to be along professional lines.

Carol gave me a questioning look as we passed by her desk, but she said nothing. Bless her. The woman was the soul of discretion.

A mere decade ago, Bryan would have asked Carol to "hold all calls." But, this being the twenty-first century, he instead turned his cell to vibrate and shut his door.

"Take a seat," he said. I settled into one of the chairs facing his desk. Because he sat behind his desk instead of taking the chair next to mine, I could tell he was upset.

He's going to play this in official mode, I thought. *Fine. I can do that too.* Pulling off professionalism was a lot harder in kitty-cat tights, though.

Bryan pulled a legal pad out of his desk drawer and took a pen from the holder on his desk. I waited while he carefully wrote the time, the date, and my name at the top. When he was done, he did not look up, but kept hand and eyes on the paper and asked, "What happened?"

I revised the facts only slightly (at least that's what I told myself) to protect my clients. I told him how Freddy interrupted my appointment at Stranded, and Christopher walked in on us, and how he forced both Christopher and me to go with him. I explained that Tuwanda saw us leave Stranded and followed us, and Freddy made me drive to the same house he'd made me drive to the day before. After that, I detoured (slightly) from and facts and told him that Christopher and I overcame and subdued Freddy, and his partner ran off, and then Tuwanda arrived and drove us to the sheriff's department. I did not mention Larry at all, and I limited Tuwanda's involvement to her role as transportation provider.

Except for questioning Christopher's ability to physically overcome anyone—much less Freddy, who is at least a head taller and twenty pounds heavier than Christopher—Bryan did not interrupt me but continued to write furiously, only lifting his head to peer at me once in a while, probably to see if anything in my demeanor belied my words.

I left out anything that might incriminate my clients or disclose communications covered by the attorney-client privilege, but it occurred to me that I was representing entirely too many of the people involved in this mess: Tangerine, Larry, and, since Tangerine had retained me to represent the Care Bares, Tuwanda. I needed all of them to cooperate with the police and get me out of the middle, but until we found Tangerine, that wasn't going to happen. She was the key to everything, and without her and her willingness to explain about her customer list, Tuwanda, Larry, and I could only defend ourselves with hearsay and conjecture.

When I got to the description of the events immediately before and during the drive-by shooting, I started trembling as it sank in that Freddy had been shot, and I had come close to being shot as well. Then the tears started. Damn. I hate to cry. I feel like such a wimp when I cry. But I couldn't stop. Bryan stood and came around his desk. Pulling me out of the chair, he held me close and stroked my hair. We dropped all attempts to maintain professionalism.

"I'm sorry," he murmured into my hair. "You've been through a lot. I'll have one of my guys take you home. We can finish your statement later."

"What home?" I wailed. "My apartment is trashed; my office is trashed. I don't have anywhere to go."

"Yeah, I heard about your condo. We got a call from Cal this morning, and some of our guys went to check it out. I didn't know about your office, though. No one called that one in."

"I don't want police going through my office files. It's bad enough having them go through my clothes. They probably saw my underwear."

"Your underwear?" he asked, sounding startled.

"I mean the underwear on the floor of my condo, not the underwear I've got on."

"*That's* why Guilford has a stack of black undies on his desk. When I gave him a bad time about it, he defended himself by claiming it was evidence in a break and enter."

"You were right in giving him a bad time. I have lingerie in a wide range of colors, but apparently he thinks only the black stuff has evidentiary value."

Bryan laughed, and although I was still snuffling, I too smiled at the absurdity of Guilford and his pile of (my) panties.

Bryan pulled away slightly and looked at me, a smile still playing around his lips. "How about you stay at my place for a while?" he asked. "Maybe I can pry some of your underwear out of Guilford's hot, sweaty hands, and then we can stop off at Nordstrom and buy you some clothes before I drop you off. I mean, it's not that I don't like the psycho schoolgirl look you've got going now, but maybe you'd like something more comfortable to change into."

"Like jeans and a sweatshirt?" I asked with feigned innocence.

"That's not exactly what I had in mind, but okay. Nothing with cats, though."

"I think I'll pass on your offer to retrieve my black underwear. The thought of Guilford holding it in his 'hot, sweaty hands' grosses me out. I don't ever want to wear those things again. And I appreciate the offer of bed and board, and whatever else you have in mind, but I should get back and relieve Macy of her Ralph-watching duties. And I should probably sort through my clothes and take whatever is salvageable to the dry cleaner."

Also, I didn't want Bryan to be around in case Tuwanda or Tangerine called, but I left that part out. I was leaving a lot out lately.

"It doesn't sound like as much fun as what I had in mind, but if that's what you want to do, fine with me."

"Could you give me a lift to my car?" I asked.

"Sure. I need to take care of a few things first, but it shouldn't take long. Do you want something to drink or eat while you wait?"

"Yes to both."

"Let me see what we can scrounge up for you. It may not be much. I'm afraid our in-house chef is off duty today."

"You mean the guy who fills the vending machine didn't show up?"

"Right. So don't count on getting any nacho chips. The CSI guys on the first floor hit the machine early and hoard them, the bastards." Bryan pushed the intercom button and asked Carol to see what she could find for me to eat and to bring it to his office. Carol asked if I wanted anything to drink as well, and I mouthed, "Diet Coke." He added a Diet Coke to the order, and Carol signed off with a chipper "Will do."

God, I love that woman. Her attitude is consistently positive and can-do. She is a glass half-full person in a business dominated by the-glass-is-not-only-empty-but-it's-broken-and-I-just-stepped-on-the-shards-in-my-bare-feet kind of people.

I excused myself to go to the ladies' room, and then dialed Tuwanda as soon as I was in the hallway. She picked up right away, and I told her about the shooting.

"Freddy? Freddy got shot? That's a terrible thing to happen. Really terrible. Freddy's a prick, but he don't deserve that. I mean, he was wavin' a gun around at you an' Christopher, but it ain't likely he woulda shot you, 'cept maybe by mistake."

I wished I'd had the benefit of this character analysis before. It could have saved my getting a lot of gray—or pink—hairs.

"Do you mean to say that Tangerine was never in any danger from Freddy?"

"Nah, I ain't sayin' that. Freddy's capable of kidnappin' an' slappin' people around. I jus' never heard 'bout him shootin' no one."

But somebody out there didn't shy away from shooting to kill. Again, I wondered if Tom Fields could be as harmless as everyone thought he was, or if Freddy and Tom worked for someone with more dangerous capabilities—like Webber.

I told Tuwanda my plans for the rest of the day and promised to stay in touch with her. She confirmed that she'd called Margaret and left messages on Tangerine's office, home, and mobile phones, giving the all clear and asking that Tangerine contact me. If and when she did, I would have to tell her about the shooting, and that might send her right back into hiding again.

Tuwanda and I set eight o'clock that night as the outside limit on waiting time, agreeing that if we didn't hear from Tangerine by then, we would need to launch another search for her. I didn't mention it to Tuwanda, but if that happened, I intended to bring law enforcement in to help find her.

I visited the restroom, being careful to avoid my reflection in the mirror above the sink as I washed my hands and face. I'd been traumatized enough for one day.

When I returned to Bryan's office, I saw a thick turkey and cheese sandwich, chips, and a Diet Coke on the corner of his desk. It looked as if Carol had run out to the deli across the street to provide me with a repast a cut above—several cuts above—vending machine cuisine.

Bryan was on the phone, and I could tell from his side of the conversation that he was talking to Webber. Bryan hand gestured an invitation to me to dig into my food. I took my sandwich, chips, and drink to a small corner table and pulled up a chair. After I polished off half the sandwich, I called Beth to bring her up to date. My growing saga was sounding more and more like *The Perils of Pauline*. Beth told me that she, Sam, and M.J. had the office pretty much put back together, and they'd found nothing missing from the clients' files, although several items, most notably Sam's Brad Pitt photo collection and M.J.'s collection of china lemurs, had been damaged or destroyed. This last bit of information threw me. I had no idea M.J. collected china lemurs. I wasn't even sure what a lemur was. Some kind of big-eyed monkey-looking creature, I think.

I finished my food and skimmed through a current issue of *Menswear for the Modern Detective* (a magazine I was reasonably sure Detective Webber had never read) until Bryan was finished with his phone calls. I was dying to ask him what he and Webber were discussing, but I didn't want to open the door to further questions by him about what happened today. We took the back elevator to the parking lot at the rear of the building, where Bryan's official sheriff's vehicle was parked. The unmarked black Chevy Blazer was fully armored and outfitted with a stocked gun rack, and it was a geek's wet dream when it came to the amount and quality of its communication and computer equipment. The truck was Bryan's pride and joy.

As I got into the car, I avoided looking in the direction of where Freddy had lain.

We said very little to each other during the first few minutes of the drive. What we did say was limited to brief comments on the weather (from me) and the upcoming Cardinals game (from Bryan). I think he sensed that I was still shaken up and needed some Zen time. I probably did, but my brain would not cooperate; questions swirled around in an alphabet cyclone. I finally gave voice to the one that most bothered me.

Ignoring my previous resolve to stay away from subjects that would invite more questioning, I asked "Why was Freddy shot?". I didn't expect Bryan to provide the answer. I just wanted to talk through possibilities.

If Bryan was startled by the shift from sports and weather to Freddy, he didn't show it. "We won't know for sure until we catch the guys who did it, and you know how that works: if they lawyer up and refuse to talk, we may not even find out then."

He glanced at me. He could probably tell from the look on my face that I wasn't impressed by this feeble one-size-fits-all analysis.

"It could have been a random drive-by shooting," he offered, then added grimly, "Phoenix is known to have a few of them from time to time."

I knew he was thinking of the string of random shootings that occurred the year before. The shooter, whose victims included homeless people, middle-class working folks, pets, and even farm animals, terrorized the city for eight months before a task force of sheriff's deputies, police, and FBI agents were able to track him down and arrest him.

"You and I—as well as Tuwanda and Christopher (I omitted a reference to Larry)—were the only ones who knew Freddy would be at the sheriff's department. Except ..."

"Except what?" Bryan asked sharply when I didn't finish my sentence.

"Tuwanda thought she saw someone following us on the way to your office. She said it looked like a white Mercedes. That's the kind of car Freddy's friend Tom took off in after we beaned Freddy."

"Tom Fields, right? I've got my guys looking for him," said Bryan.

"If that *was* Tom following us, it wouldn't have taken him long to figure out where we were taking Freddy. He could have used a cell phone to contact the lowrider guys."

"Didn't you tell me that Tuwanda said Tom wouldn't make a move without Freddy? Ordering a hit involves a decisive—albeit sick—mind-set. Tom sounds more like a sidekick than a decision maker.

"By the way, Webber confirmed that a call did come in to the police about your, um, first kidnapping. The officer at the desk was new and forgot to record the call after she contacted dispatch. Webber said his guys lost the Mercedes somewhere in Scottsdale. I can see how that could happen. Trying to follow a white Mercedes in Scottsdale is like trying to keep track of a guy dressed like Darth Vader at a Star Wars convention."

"You sound like you've had experience with the latter," I commented.

"Two thousand six, at the San Diego Comic-Con. A friend of mine talked me into taking a three-day gig as security guard at the convention center. One of the Darths walked off with a vintage Batman comic valued at ten grand. I spent the next twenty-four hours asking people if they'd seen any Sith Lords acting suspiciously. Everyone had. Many of them were. I still have nightmares."

He didn't have a chance to get into the details of the Comic-Con episode, though, because we had arrived at Stranded. I would have to remember to ask him about it again when we had more time. It sounded interesting.

Bryan pulled into the parking lot and then, at my insistence, called the county hospital and checked on Freddy's status before we got out. The emergency room nurse said Freddy was in surgery, and she had no additional information on his condition.

Before I could get the passenger side door open, Bryan jumped out and opened it for me. This was a first. Maybe he was more concerned about me than he let on.

He poked his head through the driver's side window once I was in my car. "I'm going to follow you to your building to make sure you get there okay." He withdrew and started walking away, then hesitated and turned around, folding his arms across his chest in a defensive posture."I need to let you know that we're going to have to hand some of this stuff over to the police. The city has sole jurisdiction over your kidnappings. Although technically they have jurisdiction over the shooting as well, since it happened behind our headquarters and we were first on the scene, I think they won't have a problem with us sharing in the investigation. We'll stay in charge of the break-in at Tangerine's office since her office is in a county island. We can't find anything on Webber to tie him to Goldman or Tangerine, so we have no basis for insisting he be taken off the Goldman matter and kept away from the other investigations. The photo found on Goldman was clearly doctored, and, like I said: He wasn't lying to you about not finding anything on the system about your first kidnapping."

I should have been comforted by the news that Webber was cleared on all issues, but I wasn't. Maybe my personal dislike of him clouded my objectivity, but I still had a gut feeling that Webber was somehow involved in Goldman's murder and the assault on Tangerine. I kept my doubts to myself, however, because I knew it would take more than a gut feeling to persuade Bryan, and I'd played fast and loose with the facts enough for one day.

"As long as we get the bad guys, I don't care who's involved in the investigation," I said brightly.

I started my car but waited until Bryan had fired up the engine of the Blazer before I left. True to his word, he followed me back to my building, and even waited until I parked and got into the elevator before he left. I waved good-bye to him as the elevator doors closed.

When I got off on my floor, I was relieved to see that my apartment was not cordoned off with police tape. This meant the police were through with their investigation, and I was free to go inside without fear of being charged with disturbing evidence at a crime scene. I didn't want to add another charge to the pile I'd already incurred..

Not that there had probably been much of an investigation. Even though the victim was the sheriff's girlfriend, it was still just a run-of-the-mill breaking and entering, and nothing had been taken. The boys downtown had more important things to do, like track down drive-by shooters.

I knocked on Macy's door, but no one answered, and I didn't hear Ralph bark. I figured Macy was probably out taking Ralph for a walk. I reluctantly crossed the hall to my condo and unlocked the door. I wasn't looking forward to cleaning up the mess inside. Housekeeping is one of my least favorite things to do. Even pre-break-in, my apartment was on the messy side. Of course, it doesn't help when you have a dog like mine. Before I acquired Ralph, who was my first real pet (I don't count the goldfish my parents bought me when I was nine), I thought shedding was a biannual process tied to seasonal temperature changes, but Ralph is an overachiever. He rejects the biannual approach in favor of a full-out, full-time shedding schedule.

Bracing myself, I opened the door and walked in. I looked around the living room in disbelief. The furniture (meaning the couch and coffee table) was upright, and the broken lamp was gone. The slashes in the couch's upholstery had been duct-taped, and the room was spotlessly clean. I could still smell the wood polish. I explored further and found that the kitchen, bedroom, and bathrooms were in the same pristine condition. The best surprise was in my bedroom closet, where I found my suits and dresses hanging neatly, each of them covered with a dry cleaning bag. The clothes in my drawers were likewise clean and folded, although I noticed that all my black lingerie was missing..

I thought that, at the very least, Guilford should be forced to get therapy as punishment for confiscating my underwear.

Searching through the clothes in my closet, I saw that a couple of my suits were missing. Since one was gray and the other was navy blue, I assumed that Guilford did not have them, but that they were probably too stained or damaged to be rehabilitated by the dry cleaner. A pair of shoes was missing too.

I changed into jeans, a sweatshirt, and tennis shoes. I tossed the cat tights into the garbage so as render it impossible for me to wear them again, although I shuddered to think what circumstances would compel me to consider such an option. I transferred Tangerine's thumb drive into my jeans pocket and removed the Barbie necklace, yielding to the temptation to hit the button and hear "Barbie Loves You" before I put it back in the dresser. I found the message oddly life affirming; at least Barbie loved me.

I went into my bathroom, where new bottles of expensive department store shampoo, conditioner, body scrub, lotion and face wash sat on the shiny-clean tile counter. I usually buy generic stuff from the drugstore (or, as my friend Joyce refers to it, *generique*). I had a feeling the upscale products were courtesy of Cal. His taste in hair and skin products, like his taste in clothes, is expensive. He told me once that he uses only Sisley skin care products on his face, and his favorite brand of makeup is La Prairie. After commenting on the fine lines radiating from the corners of my eyes, he recommended an eye cream. Once I had recovered from a major self-pity session, during which I mourned my lost youth and considered various surgical options, I checked it out on the Internet. A half-ounce jar cost $250. I decided my lines gave me character and left it at that.

Thus far, I had done a good job of avoiding reflective surfaces, but prompted by a sliver of hope that the pink color had faded over time, I couldn't help sneaking a peak in the bathroom mirror as I washed my face. My hair still resembled cotton candy. I tried to remember where I'd put the knit cap.

I checked the time on my alarm clock, which, amazingly, had survived the ransacking. It was only four o'clock. It hardly seemed possible that so much could happen in such a short time. Considering the situation from a different perspective, almost an entire day had gone by, and I had accomplished very little. I needed to focus more on time management. Of course, it didn't help that I was kidnapped every time I went to get my hair done. Kidnapping is nonproductive from the point of view of the victim.

The doorbell rang, and I went to the door, being careful to look through the peephole to identify my visitor before opening it. I saw Macy and Ralph, their bodies fun house mirror distorted by the fish-eye lens, standing in the hallway.

I opened the door, and once I had dealt with Ralph's hysterical love-attack, hugged Macy. I swept my arm around the room. "Did you do all this?"

"Me and Cal, with a little help from Durmond's Dry Cleaners," she said, smiling proudly.

Guilt washed over me as I noticed the dark circles under her eyes. She and Cal had done a lot of work. They both had to be exhausted.

"Macy, thank you. I'm so grateful to you and Cal. You've already done so much, what with putting me up for the night and dog-sitting Ralph, and now this. Please come in and sit down. You must be ready to drop."

"It was nothin', sweetie. We had fun. Especially Cal with the bath and beauty products. He's dying to know if you like them. He told me to tell you to try the body lotion right away because it will help moisten your scaly, dry skin."

Cal sure knew how to suck the kindness out of a nice gesture.

Dodging Ralph, who was prancing excitedly around the room, stopping periodically to sniff something and reacquaint himself after his short absence, Macy came in and made herself comfortable on the couch, which is the only place in my living room to sit. I still hadn't gotten around to buying more furniture, but it was on my to-do list, along with buying groceries and more towels. (Owning only two towels requires a tight laundry rotation, and I hate doing laundry.)

"Can I get you something to drink?" I asked courteously.

"Probably not. You got next to nothing to drink *or* eat in this place. Cal and I checked. What do you live on? We noticed the doggy has lots of food. Do you maybe eat his food? Why is your hair pink? My granddaughter's Barbie room get to you?"

Actually, I had expected the pink hair question earlier, so Macy's inquiry did not take me by surprise, despite the total lack of segue. I was ready for it. Well, almost ready.

"Before I explain about the hair, do you mind if I get myself a Chardonnay? That is, unless my wine stash was destroyed too."

"There's a bottle in the back of the refrigerator," said Macy, "behind the half-empty carton of milk with the nineteen ninety-two expiration date. I would have tossed the milk, but I figured by this time it might be a collectible. Maybe you can sell it on eBay."

"You're exaggerating! I'm not *that* bad." But close to it. "Would you like some wine?"

"Well, maybe *a bisl*," she said. "And maybe some of those cookies I bought you. They're in a sack in the cupboard … under the counter to the left of the sink."

"I'm promoting you to the level of sainthood for buying cookies, Macy."

"I don't know if that works. I'm a Jew. I think ya gotta be Catholic to be a saint."

"Not as far as I'm concerned."

I trotted into the kitchen, poured a couple of Chardonnays, and grabbed the bag of cookies, not bothering to put them on a plate. I brought everything out and sat on the couch next to Macy. We each took a cookie and munched and sipped for a while. Cookies and Chardonnay are my idea of the perfect snack.

Ralph was lying on the floor next to me, his head resting on my foot. He gazed at me piteously, drooling on my shoe. I broke down and gave him a piece of my cookie. He downed it in one gulp, and then stared up at me as if to say, "Could I have some of your food? What? You say you just gave me some? Why, you must be mistaken. I recall no such thing. Please could you feed me?"

Macy swished a mouthful of wine around like mouthwash, then swallowed and said, "You were gonna explain the hair."

Ah, yes. The hair. "I'm just going to get another glass of Chardonnay before I take you through the saga. What the heck. I'll just bring in the bottle."

After I returned from the kitchen, poured each of us another glass of wine, and settled in on the couch again, I told Macy about the hair dye stripper, Freddy's interruption of the time-sensitive stripping process, Michele's imprisonment in the port-a-potty, Christopher's unhelpful intervention and our subsequent kidnapping, and our rescue by Tuwanda and a friend. I wrapped things up with a description of the shooting outside the sheriff's office.

Macy looked thoughtful and didn't say anything at first. She took a couple of sips of wine and then snagged the last cookie. When she finally spoke, she had a mouthful of cookie, so her words were distorted and accompanied by a light spray of crumbs. "Ooh shou' be marred."

"What?"

Macy swallowed and tried again. "You should be married."

I laughed. "I don't think getting married would solve anything. In fact, it would most likely cause more problems."

'Nah. You need balance. Marriage gives you that. And when you got someone else to worry about, you don't do such nutty things. Your life now is *meshuga.*"

"Marriage would make me crazier."

"How do you know? You ever tried it before?"

"Yes. It did not go well," I said, unable to keep the bitterness out of my voice. I'd married one of my college classmates two months after we graduated. We were both too young, and he, as it turned out, was an asshole. I hung in there for six months and then filed for divorce.

"This I didn't know. How do you keep something like that to yourself? Tell me about it, doll."

"No. I've done enough explaining today—first to Tuwanda, then to Bryan, and now to you. I want to talk about something other than my lousy life," I groaned.

Macy ignored my plea to change the subject to something other than me. "You never mentioned Tuwanda before today. She a new friend?"

I sighed. Macy was on a quest for personal information and would not be deterred by my show of self-pity. Macy put the *y* (or why) in yenta.

"Tuwanda is not exactly a friend. She works for a client of mine. She's been helping me out on a ... er ... case."

"Is she an attorney too?"

I emphatically shook my head no.

"That's good. So maybe you'll get to know each other better. I know you got that attorney-friend, Joyce, but a friend outside your field would be a good thing. You know, get your mind off of business and introduce you to a new crowd."

I had to bite the inside of my lip to keep from laughing. Hanging out with Tuwanda would certainly expose me to a different social circle.

"And don't get me wrong; Bryan is a nice guy. But he's a cop. Cops ain't good marriage material. They work crazy hours and the job's dangerous. You need someone stable who don't gotta run off every time his beeper goes off. There's a rule: only one nut per marriage, and you already got that base covered. Any chance this Tuwanda can fix you up with someone?"

It was more than I could take. "I'm sure she can," I gasped between giggles.

Macy looked at with concern. "Maybe I should let you rest," she said, patting my knee. "You've been under a lot of strain."

I nodded, unable to stop giggling long enough to give a verbal response.

"I'll let myself out," she said solicitously. "You get yourself to bed."

I managed to pull myself together long enough to thank her again for all she'd done. After the door closed behind her, I was seized by another paroxysm of giggles, but I eventually settled down. I closed my eyes and relaxed into the couch. The wine made me comfortably fuzzy and improved my outlook on life, but it also made me extremely sleepy. I decided to follow Macy's advice and get in bed for a nap before I fell asleep on the couch.

Ralph followed me into my bedroom and jumped up on the bed. I remembered to put my cell phone on the table next to me before I got under the covers in case Tangerine, Bryan, or Tuwanda called. I was asleep in seconds, with Ralph lying pressed up against my back, snoring loudly.

I'd figured out how to adjust the volume on my cell, and I turned it up as high as it would go so I wouldn't miss any calls. I hadn't bothered to change the factory installed ringtone, so I was awakened sometime later by a rap song playing full blast. The lyrics consisted of the repeated phrase *I got to get me some of that, that, that.* At first, my muddled brain didn't get the connection between the song and my phone. Searching for someone to blame, I ran a quick mental check of the likely suspects. M.J. topped the list since she had a habit of listening to loud music, mostly rap, while she worked. (After she ignored several colorfully worded requests by Beth to turn it down, I told her to cut it out or find a job where eardrum-splitting music was de rigueur, like an Abercrombie & Fitch store). When my brain cleared and I remembered I was at home and M.J. was nowhere around, I narrowed the possibilities and determined that the phone was the source of the racket. I grabbed it off the table and flipped it open. The cursed music stopped.

"Hello?"

"It's eight o'clock," said Tuwanda. "You hear from her?"

I checked my phone for missed calls to make sure I hadn't slept through anything, inconceivable though it might be. "No. Nothing."

"We gotta find her," said Tuwanda. "Let's get goin'. I'll pick you up. You be downstairs in fifteen minutes."

Tuwanda sounded determined and revved up. I hated to rein her in, but it was time we brought in law enforcement. We'd already waited too long as it was.

"Tuwanda, we need to turn this over to the police. Freddy's shooting may not have been a random drive-by, and it's possible that whoever did it is after Tangerine too. Someone else could have hired Freddy and Tom, and maybe that 'someone else' shot Freddy to keep him quiet. If that's the case, he or she is still after Tangerine"—*and me,* I thought—"or is keeping Tangerine against her will. We don't have time to mess around playing detective anymore. It's been too long since we've heard from Tangerine." Not one of my most persuasive arguments, but I was still a little fuzzy around the edges from sleep.

"Tangerine's got lotsa people mad at her—every pimp in town, to name a few dozen."

"Do you think Freddy might have been hired by one of them?"

"Sure. Tangerine's got a soft spot for Freddy, but everyone knows what a shit he is. If there's money involved, I don't think there's anythin' that ass wipe won't do. But if it's someone after

Tangerine's list, I don't figger pimps for it. It ain't like they can use it for direct marketing. You know, like where a competitor pays good money for your client lists so they can make phone calls and send out advertising to try and steal your business? That ain't done in my industry yet."

"But you've given direct marketing some thought?" I asked, bewildered.

"Tangerine ain't the only one who reads business magazines. I got dreams too, you know. I want to run my own ho operation someday."

I wondered if there was a business publication aimed at owners and operators of houses of prostitution. There probably was. There's a magazine or an e-zine for everything these days.

"Maybe one of Tangerine's competitors wants Tangerine's client list so they can blackmail the people named in it, and ruin Tangerine's business to boot. You said once before that lots of people tried to get the list to use it for blackmail."

"No ho services manager would use another manager's list for blackmail. It's against industry code. Someone in the industry breaks that code, next day he's floatin' face down in the canal."

I could hear Tuwanda suck in her breath as she realized the significance of what she'd just said.

I gave voice to the question hanging in the air between us. "Do you think that could be what happened to Goldman? Maybe he got greedy. It's possible Tangerine gave him the list for safekeeping and he kept a copy, and then decided to make some money off of it for himself."

"That's nonsensical. Why would Tangerine give out that list to an attorney? She got lots of places she could put such a thing and it'd be safe. Like a bank vault or somethin'. Keep on thinkin', girl. That don't make sense at all. Maybe ..."

Tuwanda fell silent. I was afraid of what she might be thinking. Her next sentence proved my concern was well-founded.

"You know somethin' 'bout Tangerine givin' lists to attorneys?" she asked suspiciously. "Like maybe you know 'cause that's what she did with you?"

I tried to avoid answering her question. "But Freddy couldn't have been working for Goldman because Goldman was already dead when Freddy came after me. Maybe Freddy killed Goldman, thinking Goldman had the file copy on him." God, I was an idiot. Why did I say that? I was bringing the focus right back into the danger zone.

"That's what I'm talkin' about. Why'd he think Goldman had a copy of the list? Same reason *you* surmise he did; Tangerine gave you the list, didn't she? That's why Freddy's been after you, ain't it? An' you just let ol' Tuwanda put her ass in the middle of this mess without tellin' her what's goin' on. That's jus' mean. Here I am thinkin' you tryin' to save Tangerine, when you jus' tryin' to save your own sorry ass."

Her unfair accusations hit a nerve. I wasn't about to take this lying down, literally or metaphorically. I threw off the covers and swung my feet to the floor. "Yes, Tangerine *did* give me an electronic file for safekeeping, and although I haven't looked at it, I think it may very well be the damned list. But, dammit, if I wasn't trying to protect Tangerine and her property, I would have handed the thing over to Freddy the minute he asked instead of hanging on to it through two kidnappings, a molestation, and the vandalism of both my apartment and office. Nor would I have put myself at risk of arrest by withholding information from the police about you, Tangerine, Larry, and Christopher. I've put *myself* in the middle of this mess. *I'm* the one whose butt is on the line. And, yes, if Tangerine would cooperate with the police, she could clear everything up and save my 'sorry ass.' But until that happens, I won't say or do anything that could prejudice her or your interests."

I heard Tuwanda suck in air and prayed she wasn't revving up for a nasty rebuttal.

"Whoa, girl. You made your point. I jumped to the wrong conclusion. I'm sorry. But goin' on the information I got, which was inadequate, my feelin's make sense. You didn't trust me enough to invite me into your circle of truth, an' that hurts."

Circle of truth? That sounded like something out of *The Lord of the Rings*. Tuwanda's vocabulary reflected extremely diverse interests.

"Okay. So we're both sorry," I said. "But that aside, I'm worried about Tangerine, and I don't know what to do except bring in the professionals. We haven't heard from her in almost twenty-four hours, and one person who worked for her is dead and another is close to it." *Or maybe dead too*, I thought. Freddy may not have survived his surgery. "I don't think we're going to be able to find Tangerine ourselves. The police have Freddy's address, so I'm sure they've already searched his house. Bryan would have called me by now if they found Tangerine there. We have no additional information about where she could be. But the police have resources we don't. I can let them know I have reason to believe she's in great danger and point to threats made by Freddy and Tom. Tom is still on the loose, remember. You and I may not think he's a threat to Tangerine, but the police don't know that. I promise I won't mention the list until I have a chance to talk to Tangerine."

"You speak for yourself, girl, 'cause *I* got a clue about where she is, an' I ain't sendin' no cops after her."

CHAPTER TEN

▼

"Wait!" I screamed into the phone, afraid Tuwanda would hang up.

"Dang, girl. You jus' about blew out my tympanum."

"Your tympanum?"

"Yeah. You know, my eardrum."

"Yes, I know what the tympanum is, but that's not exactly a term in normal usage."

"I took a course on human anatomy las' summer. I thought it might give me some new ideas for work. It didn't, though. The instructor talked 'bout people jus' like they was made up of car parts. Nothin' creative 'bout that. I'm more spiritual-like. Now, if you through wastin' my time, I gotta go."

I envisioned her telephone receiver speeding back to its cradle.

"No, wait!" I screamed again. Tell me where you think Tangerine is!"

"You did it again. Warn me before you scream into the damn phone so's I can pull outta harm's way. An' why should I tell you where she is? You jus' gonna tell your boyfriend."

"I won't. I promise." The next words were out of my mouth before reason had a chance to kick in. "I'll be downstairs in fifteen minutes. We'll find her together."

I ended the call and hurriedly put on my shoes. On impulse, I grabbed Ralph's leash, and, responding to the rattle,

Ralph leaped out of bed and rushed over to me. I clipped the leash onto his collar, and we left.

Macy stuck her head out of her door just as I was shutting mine. The woman had bat ears.

"You goin' out, sweetie?" she asked.

"Yes. I'm meeting Tuwanda."

"That's good. Like I said, get to know new people. Enjoy life a little."

"I will. Thanks," I said, smiling ruefully at the irony of her advice in light of what I was about to do.

Tuwanda pulled up in front of my building minutes after Ralph and I got to the lobby. Upon spotting Ralph, she lowered her window. "What you bringin' a horse for? You a Mountie or somethin'?"

"It's not a horse. It's my dog. I don't want to leave him alone again. He's had a rough day."

"Okay, but he's gotta empty himself first. I don't wan' him takin' a whiz in this here vehicle."

Ralph obliged by lifting his leg on the curb and shooting out a stream of pee that lasted a good fifteen seconds. When he was through, he looked at Tuwanda questioningly, as if waiting for his next order.

"Tha's impressive," she said. "I never seen a dog pee on command like that. Does he got special trainin'?"

"No. I guess he's just gifted," I opened the back door for Ralph. Once he was settled inside, I slammed the door shut and got into the front passenger seat.

Tuwanda made no move to put the car in gear. "Buckle!" she ordered.

"Oh, sorry, I forgot. Does he need to buckle-up too?" I asked, indicating Ralph with a jerk of my head.

"I don't think the seat belt back there will fit him, which is too bad. I ain't thrilled with the idea of two hundred pounds of hairy dog flyin' forward if I gotta stop hard."

Tuwanda pulled into traffic, heading east. "Where are we going?" I asked. Noticing her stiffen, I added, "I'm not going to call the police and tell them. I promised, remember?"

She seemed to relax, but she still eyed my cell phone distrustfully. I sighed and handed it to her. "Here. Take it if it makes you feel better."

"I trus' you. I wouldn't be lettin' you and your damn dog come with if I didn't," she said. But she still took my phone and put it in her pocket.

"I got busy callin' the other Care Bares this afternoon to see what they knew. I got a couple more leads on where Tangerine could be. Seems she owns a house over in Tempe; she leases it out to university students. She's also got a rental property in Mesa. We can check both places."

"Will you let me bring the police in if she isn't at either of these places?" I asked.

Tuwanda rubbed her forehead. "I jus' don't know what to do. In our business, the las' thing you ever want is to get police involved. Police don't help folks like us. They ignore us or arrest us. Tha's all. I could be lyin' in front of the police station bleedin' an' the cops would step over me on their way to save the people that count. Or maybe they'd arrest me for obstructin' justice."

I didn't argue the point with her. I knew that all too often a community's police ignored 911 calls from certain neighborhoods and types of people. The only reason law enforcement would help us is that I would be the one doing the asking, and I was white, middle class, and had connections.

"So which house are we going to first?" I asked.

"The one in Tempe's closest. It's right off of Mill Avenue, near the university."

I glanced at my watch. It was a little before nine. Mill Avenue is lined with bars and a sprinkling of restaurants and boutiques, and, as far as the students at the university are concerned, is party central. In an hour, the street would be filled with young scholars in various stages of inebriation. The Tempe police had long ago given up any hope of crowd control, so drivers were on their own when it came to negotiating a path through the dense, largely irrational, pedestrian traffic.

"Perfect timing. Mill Avenue should still be manageable at this hour," I said.

"Yeah. I know what you mean. I went to see *Aida* at Gammage Auditorium a couple weeks ago. It lasted until about ten thirty. The singin' was amazin', but that's a sad story, *Aida* is.What I never could figger out is why, when she's in that tomb at the end, with hardly no oxygen left, she uses all the air that's left, and then some, to belt out a tune. Makes no sense.

"Anyways, I was drivin' down Mill on my way home an' once I got north of the university, it was like that movie *Night of the Living Dead*, where everyone walks around bumping into things, 'cept in the movie they was quiet 'cept for a little moanin; these people was noisy as hell. I kept it under five miles an hour for four blocks, flashin' my lights and honkin' my horn. A couple of 'em still didn't put two and two together and walked straight into my car. They wasn't hurt, but one of 'em threw up all over the hood. He said 'Thank you' when he was through and patted the top of the car like it was a dog. I don' know what he thought it was."

I'd had a similar experience on my way home from a concert at Gammage Auditorium. "Maybe it would be better if we detoured around Mill."

"Nah. Like you said, we got time. The zombies don't come out 'til after ten."

We drove along in silence until my cell phone went off with another ear-splitting performance of *I Got to Get Me Some of That*—at least I assumed, I think logically, that that was the name of the song.

Ralph started to howl.

"Damn!" screamed Tuwanda, throwing the phone at me like it was a live grenade. "Make it stop!"

I sighed and flipped the phone open. Peace was restored. "Hello?"

"Where are you?" Bryan demanded.

"I'm out with Ralph." At least half true.

"I just got a call from one of the police detectives working on your kidnapping."

"Which one?"

"Kidnapping number two."

I must be one of a handful of people in the world whose kidnappings were assigned numbers. Lucky me.

"Remember the keys your guy found on Goldman?" Bryan continued.

"He's not my guy. I told you, he—"

"Okay, okay. I'll refer to him as the perv—is that better? Anyway, it turns out the key the perv found fits the front door lock on the house your kidnappers took you to."

I quickly analyzed this information. It was possible Goldman had a key to Tangerine's house. He was her attorney, after all. Maybe he was keeping it for emergency access. Although never in my career had a client given me his or her house key for any reason, I figured it could happen; after all, no one had given me a list of johns for safekeeping before either.

"Have you figured out who the house belongs to yet?" I asked, feeling guilty that I already knew, and half hoping Bryan and his people had not figured it out. This whole evasion bit was getting on my nerves, but I was stuck with a Hobson's choice. Bryan was a good sheriff and a good man. Nevertheless, the duty of a lawyer to a client overrides all other considerations, and I needed to continue to act in the best interests of my client, no matter how decent or blue-eyed the law enforcement guy was.

"The owner of record is a corporation. We're trying to track down some information about it now," said Bryan, completely unaware of the legal-ethical debate raging in my mind.

"Have your guys or the police searched Freddy's house yet?"

"Yes. Nada. The house is empty … and I mean empty. Toilets, cabinets, lighting fixtures, floor tile—all gone. A foreclosure notice was taped to the door."

A lot of them had cropped up around Phoenix lately. They were more popular than holiday wreaths. Merry Christmas.

"Are you going to be at this number for a while?" asked Bryan.

"Yes, barring the sudden destruction or disappearance of my new cell phone, which, if history is any indication, are real possibilities," I said. "I appreciate your calling me and keeping me up to date, Bryan. Thanks."

"Just take care of yourself, Kate. It's getting crazy out there."

Tell me about it.

I snapped the phone shut, cutting off the connection.

"Was that your boyfriend?" asked Tuwanda.

"Yup." I told her what Bryan had said.

"Goldman and Tangerine were pretty close," said Tuwanda. "We was all sort of surprised when he retired and then jus' sort of disappeared. Tangerine was real stoic about it, though, and didn't show no emotion. But then again, she never does. She keeps everythin' way deep inside. I don' think that's healthy. Her insides must be a real mess. Eventually, you gotta run outta space for all that bad stuff so ya gotta throw out some of the good, useful stuff to make room. Pretty soon, you're just like one big ol' garbage can packed full of old smelly, rotten shit with that slimy crap at the bottom that you don't know what's made of."

"Your imagery is very vivid, Tuwanda," I said, grimacing.

"Yeah. I took a night course in creative writing at the community college, an' that's what the teacher told me too. In fact, he tol' the class to not eat anythin' before my presentations 'cause my work was just that provokin'.

"Hey, I think that may be the street we lookin' for up there. Take a look at the sign. I can't see real well without my glasses."

I squinted at a small sign about a block ahead of us. "I think it says Rosemont. Is that the street you're looking for?"

"That'd be it." Tuwanda swung the big car into the left lane and turned onto the road. "It's number 405."

She slowed the car to a crawl, and we searched the addresses on either side of the street.

"That's it up there," she said, pointing to a two-story house that looked like it used to be white but was now mostly gray, with occasional patches of peeling white paint. The landscaping was "nouveau junkyard." The expanse of packed dirt was littered with red plastic beer cups, empty liquor bottles, and cigarette butts. Every light inside the house seemed to be on. Shadowy figures moved back and forth behind the curtains.

"Looks like somebody's home," I said.

"Looks like a lot of bodies are at home."

Sensing that we might be stopping soon, Ralph had gotten up and was standing with his head thrust forward between me and Tuwanda. He eyed the lighted house with interest. Ralph was always up for a party.

Tuwanda pulled over to the curb, parked, and turned off the engine. Neither of us made a move to get. With the motor off, we could hear loud music and singing: *I got to get me some of that ...* A window on the second floor opened, and the music got louder. A man stood at the open window.

Tuwanda gasped. "Oh, shit. Is he doin' what I think he doin'? Look at that. He's peein' out the window. That's jus' nasty. I ain't gonna walk on that. That pee hits the dirt, and it's gonna make mud ... pee-mud. I don't want no pee-mud on my shoes."

Ralph was riveted. In his dog mind, I was sure excretory functions prevailed over all else as the most fascinating occurrences on earth. He'd never seen this approach before. I hoped he wasn't getting any ideas. I'm guessing my condominium association wouldn't be too thrilled at the idea of intermittent showers of dog pee coming out of a seventh-floor window.

"I think it's highly doubtful that Tangerine is in that house," I said. "They wouldn't hold a party if she was being held against her will, and she wouldn't be at a party if she was hiding out. I'll try to get in and do a quick once-over to make sure. You stay here and keep Ralph company."

"That's fine with me. Jus' wipe your feet before you get in this car when you come back. An' I suggest you don't shake no one's hand in there. People who pee out of windows don't seem like the type to wash their hands after."

Good point.

"Hold Ralph's collar while I get out, so he doesn't try to follow me."

I got out of the car and walked to the front door of the house, careful to skirt what I estimated to be the urine-affected area. The doorbell was hanging from the wall on a frayed wire, so I knocked rather than risk electrocution. No one answered, so I knocked again, louder this time. Still no answer. I tried the knob, and the door swung open. Not one of the fifty or so people packed into the small living room looked in my direction. A thick fog of cigarette and marijuana smoke hung in the air. I tapped the shoulder of the nearest person, a bearded young man wearing a T-shirt with REALITY SUCKS printed on the back.

"Do you know where the owner of this house is?" I asked, raising my voice to be heard above the music.

"You with the police?" he responded. A stream of smoke shot out of his mouth, and he ineffectually tried to wave it away with one hand while hiding a joint behind his back with the other. I briefly considered giving him one of my business cards. I had a feeling this boy was going to need an attorney on speed dial.

"No. I'm just trying to find a friend."

The young man looked relieved and took a long hit to celebrate the good news. He held the smoke in his lungs for a few seconds, and then responded in the midst of a massive exhalation. "Man, aren't we all. Aren't we all."

Great. I was in a hurry, and this jerk was waxing philosophical.

"I need to talk to the owner of the house. Now!" I said in my courtroom voice, pinning him down with a glare I usually reserved for opposing counsel. The voice and glare had the desired effect.

"The owner is some ol' lady that comes around once a month to pick up her check. The guy who gives her the check is over there." He pointed unsteadily at a short, stocky young man wearing an oversized football jersey over Bermuda shorts. "His name's Chad."

Chad was holding a huge red plastic cup filled with a foamy liquid I assumed was beer. He was talking with great intensity to a cute blonde in a dress shorter than most of my shirts. His free hand moved around wildly, and beer slopped out of his cup with each emphatic gesture. Obviously, this was not his first drink of the night. The blonde did not appear to be enjoying his lecture, and she glanced around furtively, as though looking for a break in the wall of bodies through which she could bolt.

I excused myself as I made my way through the crowd toward Chad. The floor's surface was alternatively slippery wet, then crunchy. By the time I got across the room, my jeans and sweatshirt were pretty much saturated with spilled beer and more creative concoctions. Somewhere along the way, someone had placed an ASU Sun Devils cap on my head. Trying to look on the positive side, I rationalized that, except for the twenty-year age difference, I blended in well with the crowd.

I grabbed Chad's arm when it was in mid-gesture to avoid being hit in the face.

"You don't mind if I interrupt to ask this nice young man some questions, do you?" I asked the cute blonde.

"No. Go ahead." Her face reflected the same mixture of hope and relief as that of my clients when they were released without bail. She immediately began to work her way through the crowd toward the front door.

"I'll call you, Sharon!" Chad shouted at her rapidly retreating back. I'd bet money that the first thing Sharon did tomorrow was change her phone number.

"What can I do for you, Pink Lady?" he slurred, turning to me and placing his arm around my shoulders. To do this, he had to balance on the balls of his feet because I had about six inches on him.

I shook his arm off. "I am looking for Katherine Paar. Is she here?"

He gave it some thought. "She owns this place," he said slowly.

Ours would not be a snappy dialogue.

"Yes. You rent from her, right?"

"I do indeed. But she's not here. Hell, if she was here, I'd be in deep shit. I don't think she'd be too happy with me having so many guests over. It's a great party, though. Man, it's a *great* party." Chad's focus shifted to a young woman, another blonde, standing less than a foot away. I could tell he was suffering from AAD (as in "alcohol attention disorder").

"Would you mind if I took a quick look around to make sure she's not here?" I asked.

"No problem," he said, without taking his eyes off the new blonde.

The kitchen, downstairs bedroom, and upstairs bedrooms were as packed with people as the living room. I didn't spot

Tangerine anywhere. A long line of guests evidencing varying degrees of desperation waited outside the only bathroom, which gave me a better understanding of the Window Guy's reasoning. I waited in the line for a while but then convinced myself that it was probably no big deal if I didn't search the bathroom. I'd caught glimpses of the bathroom's interior when the door opened and closed briefly between visitors, and it looked impossibly small. It was highly improbable that anyone using the bathroom would let the presence of a middle-aged woman go unremarked, regardless of that person's level of desperation or inebriation.

I went back downstairs and checked around for a door that might lead to a cellar. Most houses in the Phoenix area don't have cellars, so I wasn't too concerned when the only doors I found led to closets, which were also fully occupied. Hanging clothes and mothballs are no deterrent to young love and raging hormones.

I spotted Chad as I was leaving. He had cornered blonde number two and was once again holding forth on a subject about which he appeared to have a great deal of emotion. I worked my way over to him and interrupted his pontificating long enough to tell him I was leaving, give him my business card, and ask that he call me should his landlady show up. As an afterthought, I asked him for his last name and his number in case I needed to contact him. He cooperatively wrote his name and number on the back of another one of my business cards and handed it to me.

"You can call me anytime, sweetie. Maybe we can get together and find out if *all* your hair is pink," he said suggestively.

I shuddered. "Sorry, but we can never be more than friends." (If that). "I have a height requirement." Not one of my better comebacks, but I was stressed, and the polluted air and loud music had given me one heck of a headache.

I exited the house and walked to Tuwanda's car, taking deep breaths of air along the way. I figured I had inhaled enough Marlboro smoke inside to make me a good candidate for lung cancer. Ralph had taken over the passenger seat during my absence, and was spread out comfortably, with his head in Tuwanda's lap. I waited for Tuwanda to get him into the backseat before I got in.

"No Tangerine?" she asked.

"Nope. She appears to be the only one in town *not* there, however. That place is packed. I tracked down the tenant, who confirmed that Tangerine is his landlady. I left my card with him and asked him to call if she showed up."

"Who is this guy? This place reminds me of that movie *Animal House*."

I pulled out the card Chad had written his name and number on. "Chad Fields," I read.

"You think he's any relation to Tom Fields?"

"Maybe. I mean, Fields is a common name, but still … it's a weird coincidence. Maybe Tom knew Tangerine rented this place out and told his son or nephew about it."

"Wouldn't be nothin' strange 'bout that. Fact that this Chad found out about the house from a relative who knows Freddy don't mean Tangerine's there. The one fact don't necessarily lead to the other."

"Plus, I saw no sign of Tangerine anywhere inside, and I checked pretty much every room."

"There's that." Tuwanda fell quiet while she negotiated a particularly tricky route between several groups of students who appeared to have mistaken the middle of the street for a cocktail lounge.

"I jus' don' get it. You gotta be damned drunk not to respect five thousand pounds of metal comin' straight at you. These kids mus' jus' trust drivers not to hit 'em. But what happens if the driver's had a few too? That's when their system don't work."

We both sat forward on our seats, nervously scanning our surroundings for the oblivious or unconscious. We didn't relax until we were well clear of Mill Avenue.

"So where are we headed now?" I asked.

"Mesa. Like I said before, that's where Tangerine's other rental house is."

"I mean, what is the address we're going to in Mesa. Mesa is a big city."

Originally a small, closely knit community largely made up of Mormons, Mesa had grown over the past decade into the state's second largest metropolitan area. As with most Arizona towns, the development theme had been "malls and sprawl."

"It's out by Falcon Field."

"Where?"

"I forgot you're kinda new to town. Falcon Field's an airport 'bout six miles from the old downtown part of Mesa. The whole area used to be orange groves. There's still some left, but it's mostly houses and businesses now. I was out there a couple times, when I was takin' flyin' lessons."

"You took flying lessons?" Tuwanda was indeed a Renaissance woman.

"Yeah. I didn't get my flyin' license, though 'cause the guy teachin' me quit to become a chef, and I never did get around to findin' 'nother instructor. I think it's a good thing he found 'nother line of work, though. I never seen anybody so nervous, an' he screamed jus' like a woman at ev'ry little thing. And the cryin' was terrible. I finally tol' him to get some Valium 'cause I couldn't take his cryin' no more."

"It certainly sounds as if he didn't have the temperament necessary to be a flight instructor," I said sympathetically.

"You got that right. I'm a naturally curious person. You tell me to do somethin', I wanna know why and how everythin' works before I do it. I want information, not some guy screamin', 'Dear God, we're gonna die!'"

I reversed my opinion of the instructor, but didn't say anything. I wanted to stay on Tuwanda's good side.

Tuwanda pointed out the Mormon temple in downtown Mesa, and as we drove by, I admired the beautiful building and surrounding gardens lit with Christmas lights and luminaries. A concert was taking place on the rolling front lawn of the temple, and the sound of Christmas carols filled the air. It struck me that Christmas was just a few weeks away.

With all that had happened in the last couple of days, I had completely forgotten about Christmas, which is normally my favorite time of year. I hadn't done any Christmas shopping, and my fake tree was still lying in a storage locker in the basement of my condo building. I made a mental note to see to the tree this weekend. Once the tree was up and decorated, the empty space beneath its lowest branches would inspire me to do my Christmas shopping. Not that I had many presents to buy. I would give Beth, Sam, and M.J. bonuses, so I only needed to buy presents for Ralph, Joyce, Bryan, Macy, and Cal.

I was still creating a Christmas list in my head when Tuwanda pulled onto a dirt road leading through neat rows of mature orange trees. The road ended in a small clearing occupied by an old farmhouse in a condition similar to that of the Tempe animal house. The bleached wood of the front door was devoid of paint or varnish, and a broken window on the second floor was covered with cardboard. The roof had few remaining shingles, and the yard was mostly bare, packed earth, with a scattering of dispirited patches of yellowing grass. Unlike the previous house, though, no lights were on, no loud music pierced the air, and no parked cars blocked the driveway. In fact, there were no cars at all, and the only sounds were crickets chirping and the occasional distant roar of a plane.

"Don't look like no one's lived here for a good while," said Tuwanda.

After the car came to a stop, Ralph stood up and gave a short bark.

"He seems to be interested, though," commented Tuwanda.

"That's his 'I have to go to the bathroom—now!' bark. I'd better take him out and let him do his thing."

"It ain't been that long since he peed, an' he peed so much then that I bet the city had to put out a flash flood warnin'. An' he ain't had nothin' to drink since he been in this car. He got a kidney condition or somethin'?"

"Or something." The source of Ralph's never-ending supply of urine was a mystery to me, but, mystery or not, it was reality.

I clipped Ralph's leash to his collar, a process made difficult by the fact that Ralph was wiggling and hopping around the backseat. I couldn't tell if he was ecstatic about going for a walk or frantically trying to avoid a premature discharge. It was probably a combination of both. Once I got him outside, he started sniffing around like a narcotics search dog hot on the trail of a stash of heroin. He pulled me after him as he searched for the perfect spot, a determination he made pursuant to private criteria to which he strictly adhered despite the level of urgency. The ground around the car apparently lacked the necessary piquancy. Ralph expanded the search area to include the front steps of the house, where he stopped, inhaled deeply, and then lifted his leg and let loose before I could stop him. A voice called out in midstream.

"Git that dog away from my house. How'd you like it if I peed on one of your car tires? Or maybe I'll follow you home and take a dump on your lawn."

Unfortunately, Ralph was already too committed to the process to stop, so the best I could do was pull him away from the steps, forcing him to hop on three legs while still maintaining an uninterrupted flow. I peered at the front door, but it was too dark to see anything. Then a porch light came on, and the front door opened. Margaret emerged, arms akimbo. She stood on the porch and glared down at us.

"Margaret!" I exclaimed. I was surprised to see her in what felt like the middle of nowhere. I was even more surprised at her colorful vocabulary and the vehemence of her warning. During our previous meetings, Margaret had come across as a sweet, harmless, somewhat vague-minded elderly woman. But then, I hadn't committed a breach of lawn etiquette before now.

I heard the car door open, and I turned as Tuwanda got out and walked over. I looked back at Margaret.

"It's me, Kate." Gesturing toward Tuwanda, I added, "And this is Tuwanda. She was with me the other night at your house. Do you remember us?"

Margaret squinted her eyes and studied us carefully, but said nothing.

"I'm so surprised to see you out here," I continued, in what I hoped was a calming voice.

"It's my house," she said. A look of recognition appeared on her face, and she seemed to relax.

"I thought you lived in Glendale," I said.

"Tangerine bought me that house because she didn't want me living alone out here. But I like it here. I grew up in this house, and this is where I raised Tangerine. She wanted to rent it to some of the orchard workers, but I told her I didn't want anyone else living here."

"How did you get out here?" I asked. Except for Tuwanda's car, there were no other vehicles parked in the yard.

"Car's in the garage," said Margaret, her head jerking toward a freestanding garage partially hidden from view by a stand of orange trees. "Why're *you* out here? Are you still looking for Katherine?"

"Yes, ma'am, we are," said Tuwanda. "Do you know where she is?"

"I do. I also know she doesn't want to see anyone."

"I have certain files Katherine gave me for safekeeping, and I need to know what she wants me to do with them. Several people are after these files and are willing to kidnap and kill to get them," I explained, hoping to convey the seriousness and the urgency of the situation without disclosing too many of the facts. There was no reason to involve Margaret in this mess any more than necessary.

Margaret stared at us blankly. Maybe I had stated things too strongly, and she was in shock.

Tuwanda tried next. "Please, ma'am. We think Tangerine … I mean, Katherine … might be in danger. We need to talk to her to find out what she knows so's the police can catch who's after her, and after Kate here too. Kate's a real good attorney, and she's not tellin' the police anythin' about the files or Katherine's private affairs without Katherine's say so, but Kate's in trouble from tryin' to protect your daughter, an' it's time Katherine came out and took some responsibility and helped find the bad guys."

I looked at Tuwanda with a mixture of disbelief and gratitude. I had no idea she felt that way about me. I'd assumed all along that she was out to protect her boss and her livelihood at all costs, and thought I was just doing my job when I stuck my neck out to help her. I appreciated that she realized how truly far above and beyond the call of duty I'd gone.

"Of course, Kate here's gettin' paid a bundle a money for all she doin', and Tuwanda ain't gettin' shit—jus' a lot of pissed-off clients likely lookin' elsewhere for services, though I don' know where they think they gonna find 'nother Tuwanda."

This was more like it. Tuwanda had not been taken over by the Pod People after all.

Margaret appeared unmoved by our pleas. The only response she'd given was to cross her arms tightly across her chest. Not a good sign.

"Do you have any idea where Katherine is?" I repeated in a nonthreatening voice tinged with what I hoped was the right level of desperation.

An uncomfortable silence ensued while Margaret continued to stare at us with an unreadable expression. At least she didn't go back inside the house and slam the door in our faces. Finally, her look softened, and she uncrossed her arms.

"To be honest, I don't know exactly where Katherine is right now. I do know she's okay, though. I've spoken to her several times. She may come by later. She likes to check up on me when I'm out here.

"Why don't you two come inside and wait a bit. I'll make you some tea. You'll need to leave the dog outside, though. You can tie him to the porch." Margaret was once again the sweet, soft-spoken elderly woman I'd met at the Glendale house. I attributed her previous, uncharacteristic lack of hospitality to fear, which was, after all, a natural response for an elderly woman confronted alone at night by unexpected visitors.

I tied Ralph to the railing and then followed behind Tuwanda as Margaret led us inside. To my surprise, the house's interior was comfortably furnished and well kept. Margaret pointed to a couch and invited us to be seated.

"I'll get some water for the dog, and then we'll have our tea."

"What a kind gesture," I said gratefully, although I was having serious guilt pangs about leaving Ralph outside. He seemed to take his fate in stride at first, but he'd started whimpering as soon as we disappeared inside the house.

Margaret went through a swinging door, and I caught a glimpse of a well-appointed kitchen that was in marked contrast to the outdated version at the Glendale house. I thought it was odd that Margaret went to the bother of updating a run-down shack while ignoring the much nicer Glendale home, but maybe it could be explained by her greater emotional attachment to the old homestead. Also, Margaret was Tangerine's mother, so eccentricity was probably a genetic trait.

I heard the refrigerator door open and the sound of pots and pans rattling. Margaret emerged a few minutes later with a cake pan filled with water and a plate of roast beef. "Is it okay if the dog has a snack?" she asked.

"It's more than okay," I said, jumping up to open the door for her. "He'll love you for it and forgive me for leaving him outside." I smiled apologetically. "He's kind of insecure. He's had a rough life. I think it's a form of attachment disorder."

Margaret clucked sympathetically as she went outside and put the water and food in front of Ralph, who, after politely sniffing the roast, inhaled it. The beef was gone before Margaret made it back into the house.

"Let me help you with the tea," I said. Tuwanda made the same offer.

"No, no. You two relax. I'll be back in a jiff. Would either of you like cookies?"

We responded with an enthusiastic chorus of yeses.

"Man," said Tuwanda in a low voice after Margaret disappeared into the kitchen, "I liked the look of that roast beef. You can tie me to the porch anytime if I get some meat like that. I'm starvin'. All this dectectin' an' searchin' is makin' me hungry."

Breathing makes you hungry, I thought. Once again, I stared enviously at Tuwanda's trim figure.

We heard a crash and the sound of glass breaking. Tuwanda and I jumped up and ran to the kitchen. I was the first to push through the door. And that's where my memory starts to get fuzzy.

CHAPTER ELEVEN

▼

I remember a flash of pain. That part was indelible. The next thing I remembered after that was waking up and wondering why I was on the floor, who the floor belonged to, and whose shoe was in my face. The room I was lying in was small, cold, and musty smelling, and the only source of light was a single, flickering bulb hanging from the ceiling by a frayed wire. I raised myself on one elbow and immediately went down again. My head hurt like a son of a gun, and the room spun. I knew the feeling only too well. Something or someone had hit me on the head. This was not the first time I'd received a hard knock to the skull. I closed my eyes and contemplated the possible long-term effects of multiple concussions. I'd read somewhere that they could result in personality changes. Who knows; maybe that would be good. I didn't seem to be winning too many people over with my current personality.

I reached up and felt the shoe in my face to see if it was attached to a foot. It was. And the foot was attached to a leg.

"What the fuck you doin'?" demanded Tuwanda loudly. The sudden noise of her voice made us both groan.

"What the fuck you doin'?" she repeated in a whisper, not letting go of the subject but compromising on the issue of volume.

"I saw a shoe in my face and wanted to know if it was attached to anything. Obviously, it is attached to you."

I heard Tuwanda moving around. The shoe disappeared and was replaced by her face. "I never hurt so much in my life," she whispered.

"Unfortunately, I have," I answered ruefully.

"You been smacked on the head before? Damn, you got some nasty karma: kidnappin' and concussions. You must've been Judas or Hitler or somethin' in a former life."

"You're not helping," I groaned. "Where are we?"

Tuwanda looked around without sitting up. "Looks like we're in someone's cellar."

"Do you know what happened? The last thing I remember is hearing a crash and going into the kitchen to see if Margaret was okay."

"The las' thing I remember is seeing the back of your head gettin' hit with a long black metal thing. I guess I was next."

"Did you see who did it?"

"Uh-uh. I was lookin' at you, and then I was lookin' at nothin'."

I searched my pockets for my cell phone, with no luck. Whoever hit us probably took it. Counting M.J.'s and Goldman's, that was the fourth cell phone I'd gone through this week.

I raised my head and propped myself up on my elbow again. The pain was just as bad, but this time I knew what to expect and braced myself for it. One look around told me Tuwanda had likely guessed right. The room we were in looked a lot like a cellar. Either that or one of those bunkers built in the sixties in anticipation of the Big Bomb, when the government advised a nervous population that either an underground shelter or placing our heads between our knees were the only things that could protect us against radiation. When I was growing up, a neighborhood friend had a bomb shelter in her backyard. We used it for a playhouse. The protection it purportedly afforded against irradiation was a side benefit we never considered. The room Tuwanda and I were in now, like my friend's bomb shelter, had no windows, and the cement block walls were lined with shelves full of canned goods, which, from the look of the layer of dust covering them, were far past their expiration dates. A rusty metal door in the far wall appeared to be the only means of ingress and egress.

"I'm going to see if it's open," I said determinedly, pointing at the door.

"I'm gonna wait here for you," replied Tuwanda. "Ain't no reason both of us need to drag our asses over there."

That was a rather apt description of how I managed to get across the room. Standing was out of the question. I was too dizzy and in too much pain to go for full vertical. Once I made it to the door, I reached up, grabbed the handle, and not so much pulled as hung on and let gravity take care of the rest. The handle didn't budge.

There was a gap of about an inch between the bottom of the door and the floor. I rolled over on my stomach and tried to peer through the narrow opening. The area on the other side of the door was lighted, but I could not identify the source of light. I wasn't sure if what I was seeing was electric light or sunlight. I remembered that we had arrived at the orchard house at about ten thirty pm, though, and it didn't feel to me as if we'd been in our small prison all night. My head hurt, but my limbs didn't have the stiffness associated with lying in the same position for a long time. So, more likely than not, I was looking into another room. "Help!" I cried out through the crack.

"Ouch. Damn," said Tuwanda. "Warn me before you yell like that so I can cover my ears."

"Cover them," I whispered, then waited a few beats before I yelled for help again.

"You been to law school an' that's all you come up with? I took a self-defense course once, an' the instructor tol' us that you gotta scream somethin' like 'Fire!' ... 'cause' folks don't pay no attention to people screamin' for plain ol' help."

"Do *you* want to come over here and give it a try?" I shot back, offended at her lack of appreciation for my effort.

"I trus' you to handle it. Jus' yell 'Fire.'"

Rather than waste my limited energy on further debate, I pushed my mouth as close to the crack as I could and yelled, "Fire!"

A shadow moved across the opening. I yelled again. "Fire!" This time, the light under the door was blotted out completely, and I heard frantic snuffling. "Ralph?" I asked tentatively. Scratching accompanied the snuffling.

"What's goin' on?"

"I think Ralph's outside."

"Does Ralph have any experience openin' locked doors? Too bad it ain't Lassie. There ain't nothin' that dog couldn't do. She hauled Timmy's ass outta more shit. Must've gotten tiresome for her after a while. I bet plenty of times she thought it might be better to jus' let it go."

Tuwanda was beginning to slur her words, and if her side trip into Lassie Land was any indication, she was having a hard time focusing. It occurred to me that her injuries might be more extensive than mine were, and bleeding or swelling of the brain required immediate medical attention. I began to panic.

The snuffling and scratching was replaced by loud, rhythmic thumping. Ralph was throwing his body against the door! I appreciated the gesture, but I didn't see how it would do any good. The door was old and rusted, but it still looked sturdy.

The thumping continued as I considered what to do. Ralph definitely got an A for energy, if not for efficiency. Then something amazing happened. The hinges on the door started to give. Small chunks of plaster and rusted metal fell to the floor as the topmost hinge broke. Then the middle one split. Only the bottom hinge remained.

The top of the door lurched inward, and I scrambled out of the way. I'd been "doored" before, and it wasn't a pleasant experience. Ralph hesitated, and I could hear him panting loudly.

"Come on, Ralph, you can do it!" I called out.

"Yeah, Ralph. Put your shoulder into it, or whatever other dog part works best!" Tuwanda yelled out encouragingly.

Ralph obliged and the thumping began again. On the fifth thump, the door came crashing down, and Ralph leaped through the opening. He joyously licked my face, hands, and ankles, and then flopped down on the floor beside me, breathing heavily.

"Good boy," I murmured, patting his head.

"Damn right. He's a damned saint," contributed Tuwanda. Her voice sounded weak.

The warm air that rushed in from outside when the door gave in felt good at first, but now it was becoming uncomfortably hot. There was something else too; a thin haze of smoke now covered the room.

"Fire!" I screamed.

"Give it a rest, dammit. The dog already saved us. Let's just nap a bit before we get outta here," said Tuwanda, her voice now reduced to a soft whisper.

"No, I mean there's a fire. A *real* fire. We need to get out of here *now*." I saw flashes of flame spear through the air at the top of the stairway in the next room.

No energy drink on the market can compete with a good dose of adrenalin. I sat up, fought through the whirlies, and crawled to Tuwanda. "Come on," I said, tugging at her arm. "Stay close to me and keep as low to the floor as possible."

"I'm already stayin' as low to the ground as I can. Can't get no lower than layin' on it." Tuwanda was not noticing my sense of urgency. She was in bad shape.

I hooked my arm under her shoulder and dragged her to the room's entrance in a series of short jerks. The door, a solid barrier now reduced to a low hurdle, but a hurdle nevertheless, lay across the opening. Dragging Tuwanda over a smooth floor was a piece of cake compared to hefting her over an obstacle all of three inches high, and I had a hard enough time with the piece of cake part. I tried to shove the door out of the way with my foot and only succeeded in jamming it more tightly into the opening. Ralph, who had been running back and forth between us and the bottom of the stairs, as if torn between loyalty and survival, seemed to have figured out the problem and was nudging Tuwanda with his nose. I got an idea.

"Tuwanda, put your arms around Ralph's neck and pull yourself up enough to clear the door."

"That's just sick. I ain't gonna be found all crispy and dead down here with my arms aroun' a dog. I wanna die with some dignity."

"Ralph can help pull you out of here. I can't do it on my own. If things start to look really bad, just let go of him and assume whatever position you feel is most dignified."

Tuwanda appeared to consider her options. "Okay," she said, after what seemed to me to be an unnecessarily long period of deliberation.

Ralph sat patiently while I helped Tuwanda raise herself up to where she could get her arms around his neck and scoot along on one foot beside him. Her other foot seemed to be strangely uncooperative, refusing to support any part of her weight. We moved slowly across the flattened door to the bottom of the stairs. By this time, the top two wood steps were engulfed in flames, which had grown from tentative shoots searching for a hold into a solid wall. Thankfully, most of the smoke rose up into the house, so the basement was relatively smoke free.

I looked around for another escape route and spotted a narrow window at the top of the wall behind the stairs.

"We can't use the steps. We'll have to go for the window!" I shouted over the growing noise of the fire.

"Shit. Ev'ry hotel I ever been in says to take the stairs in the event of a fire. That's jus' 'nother lie tol' by the Man."

At least she's still alive, I reasoned.

Our little trio worked its way over to the window I'd spotted. The obvious problem was how to reach the window, which was set into the wall about seven feet above us. I considered whether I could jump high enough to grasp the sill, pull myself up, open the window, and then push Tuwanda and Ralph through. Yeah, right. And after that, I could leap over a tall building and tip over a locomotive.

I leaned my back against the wall and searched the room for something to stand on. A washer and drier in the corner met the height requirement, but I dismissed the possibility of moving either one to the window. A stack of boxes next to the washer was a better candidate. I crawled over, praying the boxes were light enough to move but sturdy enough to hold up under our weight. I dragged the highest box to the floor. The top was open, revealing a pile of what Cal refers to as "girlie magazines," and what I refer to as porn. I gave the box a shove toward the window and grabbed the next box, which, upon brief inspection, contained more such magazines. Shoving first one box and then the other, I made it back to the window in six-inch increments. I positioned both boxes under the window and then, with supreme effort accompanied by shooting pains in my head, lifted one on top of the other.

"I'm going to open the window, and then you're going to get on the boxes, and I'll push you through," I explained to Tuwanda. She grunted in response. I wasn't sure if that was a yes or a "Like hell you are," but it's not as if we had a lot of options.

I climbed on top of the boxes, and then hand walked into a standing position beneath the window. It was operated by a crank, but apparently not often. The handle was stiff with rust and difficult to move. The heat from the fire was getting fierce. Energized by a spurt of adrenalin, I managed to open the window a crack, then shove it the rest of the way open. I scrambled, but mostly fell, down the boxes, grabbed Tuwanda under her arms, and hauled her up. "Get on the boxes," I ordered.

"This'll cost extra," Tuwanda mumbled.

"What?! Snap out of it, Tuwanda. We have to get out of here."

I'm not sure, but I think she called me a cheap bastard. Thankfully, though, she seemed to get the point and the urgency of my request because she managed to get her good foot on top of the boxes and allowed me to butt shove her up until she was standing on the boxes. "Try to pull yourself through the window!" I screamed.

"Try to shove your head up your own ass!" she countered. I took this as an encouraging sign that she was coming around a bit more. Tuwanda grabbed the sides of the window frame and indeed hauled herself up a few inches. I continued to shove from the other end, until, miraculously, her head popped through to the other side, and then , the rest of her disappeared over the sill.

"Come on, Ralphie ol' boy. You're next," I called. Ralph got the plan immediately. He jumped on top of the boxes and put his paws on the windowsill. As with Tuwanda, I shoved from behind, and Ralph, with a great deal more energy than Tuwanda had exhibited, scrambled out the window, slapping me in the face with his tail in a final farewell.

I was next. My exit was more problematic in that no one was available to give me a boost. I grabbed the windowsill and tried to pull myself up, but I couldn't do it. I lacked both the strength and the necessary muscle groups. I needed more height. I glanced over at the washer, where the remaining boxes had begun to smolder. If I was going to get one of them, I had to hurry. I got back down on the floor and crawled toward the washer. Smoke from the stair fire was filling the room. I held my breath and pulled on the side of the topmost of the two remaining boxes. It fell apart upon impact with the floor. Magazines spilled out and spread across the floor. The ones closest to the stairs ignited immediately. The heat and smoke were already unbearable, and I had just contributed some excellent kindling to the growing conflagration.

Grabbing as many of the untouched magazines as I could, I stuffed them into my pockets and jacket front, and scrambled back to the window. By stacking them on top of the boxes, I gained me a few more inches. I climbed on top of the slippery magazines and again tried to pull myself through the window. The smoke had discovered the window as well and was billowing around me as if too were trying to get away from the fire. This time, I succeeded in pushing my head through, but I could feel my arms giving out, and worse, my brain. The smoke had become too much for me.

Just as I was about to slide back in, someone or something grabbed the sleeves of my jacket and pulled. A primitive section of my brain got the message to my limbs, and I pushed up against the wall with my feet like a mountain climber, grabbing and pulling at anything that felt solid. Once my torso cleared the window, I pulled my legs through and rolled away from the building. I didn't stop rolling until the air around me started to clear. I heard the distant sound of sirens, then nothing.

CHAPTER TWELVE

▼

I came to briefly in the ambulance. A mask covered my mouth, and I sucked the pure oxygen in hungrily. When I came to again, I was lying in a hospital bed. Bryan was sitting in a chair at the foot of the bed, reading a magazine titled *Banzongas and Butts.*

"Nice," I said, or, more correctly, croaked. My throat was dry and sore.

"Welcome back," he said, looking up from the magazine, "and thanks."

"I didn't mean 'nice' as in a compliment. I intended a sarcasm-laden delivery, but my voice wouldn't cooperate. I was referring to your choice of reading material."

"Oh, weren't you done reading it yet?" he asked innocently. "I thought since you were asleep you wouldn't mind if I borrowed your magazine."

"*My* magazine?"

"Well, I assume it's yours since it fell out of your pocket when you were being carried to the ambulance. One of the EMTs gave it to me for safekeeping. After he'd read it, of course. In fact, all the guys in the break room read it. They were impressed. Apparently, it's some sort of classic."

"It's not mine!" I croaked indignantly. "I found boxes of magazines in the basement of the house. I piled them on top of each other so we could reach the window. I ..." The memory of the fire stopped me in mid-rant.

"Are Tuwanda and Ralph all right?" I asked, afraid of the answer.

"Tuwanda is still in ICU, but things are looking up. She must have been cracked on the head pretty hard. She had some bleeding into her brain. They've put in a shunt, though, and she should be fine. You were luckier. No bleeding. But you got smacked good too. Ralph is downstairs in the lobby, in violation of several provisions of the state health code, but since he's a hero, they're letting it slide."

"He *is* a hero. So is Tuwanda. She must be the one who pulled me out the window. But how did you know all this? Did Tuwanda tell you?"

"Tuwanda was out of it. You, on the other hand, were quite chatty. You told the EMT quite a bit during your ambulance ride. Apparently, you were a font of useful information, none of which you previously shared with me."

"I couldn't, Bryan. Please understand that I'm bound by the attorney-client privilege."

"Well, at least now I know how to get around it in the future: just bash you over the head and start asking questions."

Another disturbing thought occurred to me. "Margaret! Margaret was in the house when we got there. Is she all right?"

"She must have gotten out before the fire started. We're still trying to track her down. We did find a body on the first floor, but it was male. The medical examiner just called in the ID. It was Tom Fields. Had to use dental records. Wasn't much else left for an ID."

Yet another thought occurred to me, and I reached for my waist. All I felt was the flimsy cloth of my hospital gown.

"You looking for this?" asked Bryan, holding the thumb drive up by its cord and swinging it like a pendulum.

"That belongs to my client," I said, sitting up and holding my hand out. Bryan obligingly reached over and placed it on my palm. I closed my fingers around it and then looped the cord around my neck.

"Sheesh. If I ever decide to turn to a life of crime, I want you as my attorney. I'm guessing your obsession with protecting this little device caused all the trouble you've gotten yourself into?"

I glared at Bryan, or at least I gave it my best shot. My face hurt from a million cuts and scrapes, so expressions were difficult to manage.

"Do you think Tom was the one who hit me and Tuwanda? Both he and Freddy were after the information stored on the thumb drive. He could have come to the house thinking maybe Tangerine had stashed it there, but found us instead and panicked."

"That's one theory, but we're still pulling the evidence together."

"Do you know what started the fire?"

"Not yet. They're still putting out hot spots. The boys from arson are on standby and will move in as soon as the fire department gives them the all clear. By the way, on a related subject, we found the kid who shot Freddy."

"The *kid*?"

"Yeah. He's all of seventeen. Says some guy hired him to kill Freddy, but swears he doesn't know who he was. He only talked to him over the phone. He's pissed because he never got paid, so he's as interested in finding the guy as we are."

"I thought it was standard hit man procedure to get half the hit money up front."

"Like I said, he's a kid, and I didn't feel like giving him a lecture on Business 101 for assassins."

"How is Freddy, by the way?"

"Dead. Died in surgery."

This bit of news hit me harder than I would have expected. Even though Freddy and I were far from friends, we had spent a lot of time together and had bonded at least on the issue of hair care.

"With Freddy and Tom gone, there's a good chance this whole thing is over, Kate," Bryan said softly.

I closed my eyes and nodded weakly. I let my head fall back against the pillow.

"Why don't you rest awhile? I'll come back later to check on you. I'll take *Bazongas and Butts* with me and donate it to the staff lounge, if it's okay with you."

I opened one eye. "Thanks, Bryan," I whispered hoarsely.

He saluted before leaving. Seconds later, a nurse bustled in and handed me a small paper cup containing two capsules. "Pain meds," she offered by way of explanation. It sounded like a good idea to me. I dumped the pills into my mouth, and she handed me a glass of water as a chaser. Within a short time, the pills did their job and I fell into a deep, dreamless sleep.

I have no idea how long I was asleep, but it didn't seem like much time had passed when I was rudely awakened.

"Shit! This here ain't nobody's idea of a nightie. I'd just as well tape a couple Kleenexes on me. It'd be better coverage. Not that I'm shy, mind you. I'm proud of my body. Jus' that I'm off the clock, you know?"

"Tuwanda?"

"Damned right, Tuwanda. I'm layin' in the damned bed next to you. They probably put us in the same room 'cause both of us got cheap-ass insurance."

I rolled my head to the right and slowly opened my eyes. I had a roaring headache, and the bright fluorescent lights in the room didn't help.

Tuwanda's head and shoulders were propped up on a pile of pillows. She bore no evidence of injury except for a white turban of bandages covering her head, which on Tuwanda looked more like an elegant fashion statement than medical dressing.

"I been tryin' to get someone to bring me some coffee for the last half hour, but all they do is come in and take more blood an' shove a thermometer up my ass. I don' think they need to be doing that. I know they can take a temperature at the other end. It's 'cause I'm black, I jus' know it. Say, you're a nice white girl, Katie. Why don' you try an' get us some coffee."

I blinked slowly. "How can you be so energetic? Aren't you in pain?"

"Uh-uh. Mr. Vicodin and I got a thing goin'. Works just fine. I'd get up and walk outta here if I didn't get so damned dizzy ev'ry time I move my head."

I understood the dizziness part. I got the whirlies when I so much as repositioned my head slightly.

Tuwanda's mention of coffee triggered my own craving. I reached down and pushed the call button hanging from the side of my bed.

"They come rushin' in with coffee and doughnuts for the white girl, I'm gonna go all Malcolm X on their ass," muttered Tuwanda.

A tired-looking nurse's aide poked her head through the door opening. "Do you need something?" she asked politely.

"Yes," I said, matching her polite tone. "I was hoping my roommate and I could get some coffee."

"Let me check your chart to see if you're permitted to have coffee." She took a file out of a holder hanging on the door and opened it. "It shouldn't be a problem," she announced after serious consideration of the file's contents. "But we'll need to take your temp and do some blood work first. I'll be right back."

My request had evoked the same response as Tuwanda's.

Tuwanda snorted. "They still ain't gettin no Martin Luther King award 'til I see which end they put that thermometer in."

In a few minutes, the hospital staff proved to Tuwanda's satisfaction that they were not guilty of any civil rights violations, at least with respect to their medical procedures.

Tuwanda was not ready to give up her theory, though. She just expanded her definition of "minority status" to include white women with pink hair.

A few minutes after the nurse left, a young blond woman wearing a pink smock came in and placed a small carafe and two ceramic cups on the table between our beds. "Would you like cream or sugar?" she asked, pouring coffee into the cups.

I answered no.

"I like it black. I like all things black," said Tuwanda.

If Pink Smock got the double meaning, she didn't let on. She merely smiled, chirped "Have a nice day," and left.

"Have a nice day. How we gonna have a nice day? We layin' here havin' sticks shoved up our asses every five goddamned minutes."

I silently seconded Tuwanda's sentiments.

The coffee's effect on Tuwanda seemed opposite to that experienced by most of the population. She immediately fell asleep, still holding her half-full cup. Rather than buzz the nurse and risk more tests, I gingerly got out of bed, gently removed the cup from her hand, and placed in on the bedside table. I still had my back to the door when I heard "Hellooo," followed by a wolf whistle. I turned quickly, too quickly, and started to fall sideways. Bryan caught me before I hit the floor and helped me get back in bed.

"Most people don't look good in hospital gowns, but this one frames your best feature."

I took a swipe at him, but it's hard to land a blow when you have double vision.

"Shhh. Keep your voice down. Tuwanda's asleep," I whispered.

"Tuwanda's zonked out on Vicodin. She wouldn't wake up if the Black Watch stood next to her and played 'Scotland the Brave.'" I noticed, however, that Bryan reduced his voice to a whisper too.

"When can I get out of here?"

"The nurse at the desk said you can leave as soon as the doctor gives you the okay."

"What doctor? I haven't seen a doctor all the time I've been here."

"One *has* seen you. You were out of it at the time. Do you want me to see if I can track her down for a consult?"

"Yes. Please. Thank you." I threw the please and thank-you in as afterthoughts. I was still annoyed by Bryan's opportunistic voyeurism.

Bryan left, reappearing a few minutes later with a striking young woman in a white lab coat. She extended her hand and introduced herself as Dr. Simon. Her handshake was firm, and her gaze was open and direct.

"You are looking better than the last time I saw you," she said, with a slight Spanish accent. "How are you feeling?"

"Not bad, although I'm a bit dizzy and have a headache, and for some reason, my hair hurts."

"Ah, yes. That last symptom is unfortunate. One of the emergency room techs was convinced you were wearing a wig and tried to remove it before your CAT scan. In his defense, pink is an unusual color, no?"

We all chuckled. Mine was forced.

"The headache will go away in a short time. We will send you home with some pain medication that should help. The dizziness, or what we call posttraumatic vertigo, will take longer to completely disappear. At first, any movement will seem to trigger it. Over time, you will notice that only certain movements or positions will bring it about, so it becomes easier to manage. I recommend that you stay at home and rest a couple of days until the worst of it passes." She opened the file she'd taken off the door when she first came in, quickly scanning the pages. "You've been taking Vicodin every six hours. Does that seem to work for the pain?"

I nodded, thinking, *Every six hours? How long have I been in here?* I wanted to ask what day it was, but I was afraid Dr. Simon would consider such a question evidence of a relapse and hold me in the hospital longer.

"What the fuck. Ev'ry six hours? What the hell time is it?" The thin privacy curtain the doctor had pulled around my bed was not an effective sound barrier, its function being primarily symbolic in nature. Symbolism was lost on Tuwanda.

"Ten o'clock in the morning. Friday," provided Bryan. We had gone to the orchard house Wednesday evening.

Doctor Simon looked questioningly at Bryan. "That's Tuwanda," he said, indicating the other bed with a jerk of his head. "She's the lady who was brought in with Kate."

"She's the lady who *saved* Kate's ass," clarified Tuwanda.

"Oh, yes. Tuwanda is Dr. Sanjin's patient. I've heard about her."

"Don' be talkin' 'bout me like I ain't here. Open the damned curtain."

"May I?" Bryan asked. Dr. Simon and I both nodded. Bryan slid the curtain back. Tuwanda peered angrily at each of us in turn.

"Am I goin' home too?" she demanded.

"You will have to speak to your doctor about that," said Dr. Simon smoothly. "Would you like me to find him for you?"

"Damn right. I don' wanna stay here if Kate goes home." I thought that was kind of sweet until she added, "Ain't no white girl gonna get outta here before I do."

Dr. Simon took Tuwanda's chart off the door and flipped it open. "I can't speak for Dr. Sanjin, but it looks like you have a shunt, so release is unlikely, at least until the shunt is removed."

247 Becky A. Bartness

"You get this Dr. Whatsis in here, and we'll see 'bout that," said Tuwanda.

I think everyone in the room except Tuwanda said a silent prayer for Dr. Sanjin. As was the case with me and Dr. Simon, he probably hadn't seen his patient conscious yet. I doubt he was prepared for what was about to befall him.

Turning back to me, Dr. Simon asked, "Do you have a ride home?"

"Yes," Bryan answered for me.

"Then you can leave whenever you wish. I will sign the release forms at the front desk. Just buzz when you are all set to go. Hospital rules require that you ride in a wheelchair and be escorted by a staff member to the front door."

Dr. Simon shook my hand and wished me luck. I wasn't encouraged by a doctor deferring to luck over expertise, but I was too overjoyed at the prospect of going home to comment.

"Don't forget to track down that Dr. Sandwich for me," Tuwanda called out to Dr. Simon as he left.

A nurse showed up a short while later and handed me a white plastic bag containing my clothes. An acrid smell drifted out of the open bag.

"I bet I could talk them into letting you wear your hospital gown home if you want," said Bryan. "I kind of like it."

"Wait outside," I ordered.

Within an hour, I was back in my condo. Just before I left the hospital, Dr. Sanjin had come into the room and told Tuwanda that she would be staying another couple of days. Needless to say, she did not handle this news well. Dr. Sanjin—a small, polite man who had come over from China on a work-exchange program—was probably tearing up his visa and checking flight schedules for Beijing.

Bryan filled a couple of vases and some drinking glasses with water for the many flowers sent by Beth, Sam, M.J., Macy and Cal, and my friend Joyce. Their offerings had been so generous that my wheelchair looked like a float in the rose parade when I left the hospital. Each bunch of flowers had been accompanied by a get-well card, except for M.J.'s, which came with a birthday card in an envelope that had the name Chelsea crossed out and my name inserted.

I dismissed Bryan after he finished his florist duties, but before he left, he made me promise to stay in bed and rest. He said he would return with takeout from Paco's Mexican Restaurant around seven that night. I have no doubt that he also stopped by Macy's on his way out and told her to keep an eye on my condo to make sure I didn't leave. I had no intention of leaving, though.

My first priority was a shower. After my shower, I inspected the clothes I had been wearing. They were torn, singed, blackened, and reeked of smoke. Deciding they were beyond rehabilitation, I tossed them into the garbage can. It's just as well. I didn't need any more reminders of the fire. Of course, Ralph was a different matter. His coat smelled like smoke and charred hair, as well it should, but I wasn't about to toss him out, and I was too tired to give him a bath, the latter endeavor requiring a level of optimism and strength I could barely manage on a good day. I would have to tolerate his *odeur de chien* until I could get him to a groomer. Considering he was a hero, enduring his smell was a small price to pay.

I made some tea and fed Ralph a couple slices of ham from the fridge, which Bryan had been kind enough to stock in my absence. I took my cup to the bedroom and placed it on a side table. Then I got in bed and snuggled under the covers, emerging only to take an occasional sip of tea. Ralph jumped up on the bed and lay next to me. I added "Wash the sheets" to my mental to-do list.

While my body was desperate for sleep, my brain insisted on reviewing the events of the past few days. The danger to me may have passed with the deaths of Tom and Freddy, but I was still worried about Margaret and Tangerine. Since they had no way of getting hold of me, I wasn't surprised that I hadn't heard from them, but Bryan mentioned on the drive back to my apartment that neither the police nor the sheriff's office had been able to locate them. Unless Tuwanda had a few more possibilities up her sleeve, they had run out of places to look. At least I could take some comfort in the fact that I had fulfilled my duty to protect my client's property and confidences, even though I had several damn good reasons over the last couple of days to take that duty and shove it. I glanced over at the little black plastic rectangle lying on my bedside table and marveled at how this innocent-looking little thing could cause so much trouble. Its contents must be damaging to lots of important people in this town for it to garner such fame and attention.

Suddenly, I was seized with curiosity. I had never looked at the disk's contents. Everyone else seemed to know what was on there, and I had a good idea what it was, but it occurred to me that Tangerine had never actually come out and told me, and I, the protector of the holy grail of ho-dom, had never actually opened the file. This hardly seemed fair or reasonable.

I reached over, grabbed the thumb drive, and got out of bed to go to my laptop in the living room. I had to endure a couple bouts of the whirlies in the process, but I was learning to wait a few seconds for each bout to pass before making another move, so movement was manageable, just slower. Bryan had told me the techs from his office were reasonably sure whoever had tossed my office had tried to search my computer files, the laptop's mechanism was unharmed and functional. I found it sitting on top of a moving box that comprised one-half of a matched set of end tables (I really need to get some furniture). Taking it into the kitchen, I made myself another cup of tea before sitting at the kitchen table and turning it on.

It took a few minutes to power it up, after which I inserted the thumb drive into a little slot on the side. A window popped up, telling me that the drive contained one file. I selected OPEN on the menu and waited expectantly. A message popped up:

FILE EMPTY. I tried again. Same message. I had expected the file to be encrypted, but if that were the case, I would either see a message that read CANNOT OPEN FILE, or an indecipherable mishmash of symbols. I sat back and stared at the computer screen. I'd risked my life for a blank disk. Had Tangerine set me up as a decoy? She knew people were after her list of clients, and she'd used me to throw them off the scent.

I heard a tentative knock at my front door. It was probably Macy coming over to check on me. I was surprised it took her so long. Macy loved taking care of people, so, with the many opportunities for ministrations that I'd provided since I'd moved into the building, I was the ideal neighbor. I got up to let her in. Ralph, who was still zonked out on my bed, hadn't even bothered to bark. I should have recognized this as a warning because Ralph only barked greetings to his owner and her friends; he let burglars and vandals slide.

I opened the door and froze. Margaret was standing in the hall. She held out a small brown paper bag and said, "I heard you were indisposed, so I brought some cookies over for you."

"Margaret!" Her name burst from my lips. "I'm so happy to see you. I was afraid you'd been injured in the fire. Please come in."

Margaret walked into my small living room and turned to me. "May I sit down?" she asked politely.

"Of course," I said. Margaret looked doubtfully at the duct tape but then, probably realizing there was no other options, sat on the couch. I shut the door and joined her.

"What happened to you the other night? We heard a loud crash in the kitchen and ran in to see if you were all right. Then someone hit us hard. Real hard."

"Oh dear. I'm so sorry. One of my daughter's friends— Tom, I think his name is—showed up at the back door. I invited him to stay for coffee too and then realized I was running low, so I went out to the storage area in the barn to get another can. It took me a while to pull one off the shelf because the deliveryman put the peach can cases on top of the coffee cans. When I got back to the house, I realized I'd been locked out. I tried calling out to you, Tuwanda, and Tom, but no one answered. I thought maybe you all left for some reason, so I sat on the steps and waited until one of you came back or Tangerine came by. I kind of dozed off, and when I woke up, I could smell the fire. I ran to the nearest neighbor's house, and they called the fire department. Then I got hold of Tangerine, and she picked me up at the neighbor's. I assumed you, Tom, and Tuwanda had left before the fire started.

"Tangerine dropped me off at a hotel and then went back to check on the house. She called said the firemen were there, but it didn't look good. She didn't mention anything about there being people inside. Maybe you and your friend had already been taken to the hospital by the time she got there.

"We read about what happened in the newspaper the next morning, and I felt just terrible. Tangerine was afraid to leave the hotel, and she didn't want me going out either. But I had to do something. When I called the hospital and found out you'd been released, I convinced Tangerine to let me come over here and make sure you were okay. Tangerine knows where you live, so she gave me the address and lent me her car, and here I am. She's the one who suggested I bring the cookies. She knows you love them."

Margaret seemed nervous, and she kept looking around the room throughout her recitation. I attributed it to conditioning; experience had likely taught her that bad things happened whenever I was around.

"How is Tangerine?" I asked.

"Fit as a fiddle," Margaret responded brightly. "But she feels terrible about what happened to you and Tuwanda." Margaret nervously traced her finger around the flower pattern on her skirt. "She asked me to find out if you still have the thing she gave you."

I had a suspicion that maybe Margaret's visit had not been her own idea, but was prompted by Tangerine so she could check on her thumb drive. I stood, wobbling a bit, and retrieved it from my computer. Out of the corner of my eye, I saw Margaret watching me. She would know I had opened the file and looked at it, but I didn't care. Whatever game Tangerine was playing was no longer of interest to me.

"Is this what Tangerine was asking about?" I asked, holding the thumb drive out to her. Margaret took it and, without taking her eyes off me, placed it in the pocket of her cardigan.

"You looked at the file," she said in an atypically brusque voice about two octaves lower than her normal speaking tone.

"Not much to see," I said, shrugging.

"I'd like you to take a drive with me so I can show you something." Her tone was again light and sweet.

"It'll have to wait. I'm under orders to rest."

"It's a matter of great importance. A matter of life and death, in fact." Margaret raised a trembling hand and covered her face.

"Tangerine is in trouble?" I was worried now. Margaret's emotion seemed real enough. I didn't like the trick Tangerine played on me with the blank thumb drive, but I was still her attorney. One of my sane brain cells, of which I have very few of late, piped in and suggested that I call Bryan.

"Is it something we should tell the police?" I asked, just to humor the sane cell.

"God, no," said Margaret. "We just need help. And guidance."

"For what?" The sane brain cell had gathered quite a group now.

Margaret leaned over and rustled through the large handbag she carried. When she sat up again, she had a gun pointed at me.

She motioned for me to stand and then moved around behind me and pushed the barrel of the gun in my back. I had a feeling of déjà vu.

"We're going to go for a ride."

I almost laughed. She sounded like a character in *The Sopranos*.

I heard Ralph moving on the bed, and then heard the click of his nails on the floor.

"Keep your dog at bay, or I will shoot him," Margaret said calmly.

Ralph ambled into the room. "Sit, Ralph. Stay," I ordered.

Ralph had never obeyed any of my commands before, but miraculously did so this time. He plopped his butt on the floor and looked at me expectantly. I think he may have remembered Margaret from the orchard house and recognized her as someone who, although a good provider, did not appreciate dogs.

Margaret shoved me to the door and out into the hallway. I hoped Macy heard our departure, but prayed she did not come out into the hall to check. Margaret was edgy, and I did not want Macy to get shot.

Margaret had parked her car near the building entrance under a large mesquite tree with low-hanging branches. I had to duck and deal with prickly foliage before I could get in. As always, I was ordered to drive. The car was the familiar white Mercedes, so I had no learning curve. Margaret, who, because of her height, had escaped unscathed by the mesquite branches, ordered me to head east and turn left on Fortieth Street. This route took us to the canal.

A path used by joggers and cyclists borders much of the canal. At this time of day, there were bound to be a few of them out. But Margaret took me to where the path detoured around a Salt River Project pumping station, where a grassy berm blocked us from view. Steps led from the pumping station down to the water. Goldman's body had been found caught in a grate by the first bridge downstream from where we stood.

"Please … why are you doing this?" I asked, partly because I wanted to stall for time, and partly because I sincerely wanted to know. Dying sucks. Not knowing why you died adds insult to, well, death.

"Money," replied Margaret.

I wanted more than a statement of a nearly universal motive.

"Money?" I asked. It wasn't a brilliant cross-examination, but I was under a great deal of pressure.

"Freddy and Tom were supposed to steal the thumb drive from you and then go to Hawaii. I already gave them a copy of my client list. If the fake file was stolen from you, though, we could blame the theft for the release of the information and throw suspicion off me. Then Freddy and Tom were free to blackmail my clients. They were to retain a small fee for themselves and pay the balance of the blackmail proceeds to me. But you kept tracking me down, and I couldn't be around when the information was stolen from you. I had to appear completely uninvolved so I could continue my business with my remaining clients."

"Your remaining clients?"

"Yes. The blackmail list I gave Freddy and Tom only had the names of people no longer using my company's services. I could make money off both former and current clients. It was a brilliant business plan."

"Why do you keep referring to *your* clients and *your* services? Isn't Katherine the president of Pole Polishers, Inc. and its subsidiaries?"

"Yes. I often make that mistake. You must understand, though—Katherine and I are close, and she relies a great deal on my business advice."

The sweet old lady was a psychopath, and her daughter apparently inherited the psycho chromosome.

"Did you kill Goldman?" I was on a blurt-it-all-out roll.

"Yes. He found out about the blackmail scheme and wanted in on it. He threatened to tell the police if I didn't pay him fifty percent of the proceeds."

"The blackmailer gets blackmailed," I commented. Margaret didn't seem to appreciate the irony.

"What about Freddy and Tom? Are you responsible for their deaths too?"

"I am. As I see it, it's all part of the cost of doing business. Freddy and Tom failed to get the thumb drive from you … and, worse, you and Tuwanda kept tracking Katherine down. I finally decided to pull the plug on the whole operation. I killed Tom and Freddy because they were idiots, and I couldn't be sure they wouldn't tattle on me and Katherine once I cancelled their profit-sharing agreement. As for you getting caught in the fire, though, I was telling the truth about going out to the shed to look for a can of coffee. When I got back, Tom must have already put you and Tuwanda in the cellar. I had no idea you were down there when I locked Tom in and started the fire.

"But now you've looked at the file I gave you and know it's empty. I knew you would eventually figure out what Katherine and I were up to. So, rather than take that risk, I chose to dispose of you. Getting rid of people gets easier the more you do it, you know. I barely think about it anymore."

"You were in my condo. You must have lefts prints somewhere. The police will figure out you killed me."

Margaret peeled a thin latex glove off her hand.

So much for fingerprints.

"I learn as I go along," she said. "I also don't plan to make the same mistake I made with Goldman. You're not going to float. It will be a while before your body is found." She gestured with her free hand to a cinder block lying next to the pump station. It looked like it was used as a step to reach the lock on the fence latch.

Margaret held up a piece of twine. "Loop this through the cement block and tie it around your wrist."

I saw a slight movement at the top of the berm and looked up hopefully. Katherine turned her head to see what had caught my attention. A startled bird rose into the air, and Katherine snickered. "No superman is coming to save you," she said, returning her gaze to me.

I continued to watch the berm as Larry's head and then the rest of him appeared. Without hesitating, he hurled himself into the air, landing on Katherine, who then fell forward on me. All three of us went into the water. I surfaced at the same time as the other two and thought I spotted some sort of water mammal swimming toward me—as if I didn't have enough problems. I slapped the water frantically, hoping it would turn away, but it followed the current and came closer. I took another thwack at it and ended up with a fistful of hair. Margaret tried to grab it from me. Her face was peeling like a Minnesotan's after a day in the Phoenix sun.

I did a mental head slap. A trick of posture could make her seem shorter, a latex mask could modify her facial features, eye color could be changed by contacts, hair could be covered with a wig, and the extra pounds could either be stuffing or an illusion created by loose clothing

Furiously treading water, I stared at Margaret/Tangerine for a second, and then sputtered out between gulps of air, "Tuwanda was right when she didn't believe you could have a mother."

In the meantime, while I was battling the aquatic wig and discovering Margaret's true identity, Tangerine and I were quickly being carried downstream. Larry, who had swum against the fast-moving current, gained a foothold on a submerged step next to the pump house. He lifted himself out of the water and then pushed off in another flying lunge at Tangerine. Tangerine lifted her gun out of the water and fired wildly just before Larry took her under. The bullet pinged harmlessly against the security fence. Larry resurfaced seconds later, waving the gun triumphantly over his head. Larry and I swam for the pump house stairs, while Tangerine continued downstream toward the bridge. I fought as hard as I could against the fast-moving, foamy water, but I seemed to lose a foot for every six inches I gained. Larry made it to the steps and then, just as I went under, reached out, grabbed my arm, and hauled me in. I popped out of the water like a pajama-clad trout.

We climbed out of the canal and sloshed around the berm to the recreation path. A group of bicyclists came toward us, but sped up and passed us by. I told Larry to stow the gun so we'd have a better chance of flagging down a Good Samaritan. He did, and the next cyclist to come along stopped and kindly called the number I gave him—Bryan's office number—on his cell. He reported our location and condition to the person who answered. I heard a loud response and recognized Bryan's voice, although I couldn't understand what he was saying. The cyclist looked and me and asked, "Is your name Kate?"

I nodded yes, and he passed this information on to Bryan. More emphatic noises from Bryan's end. "He wants to talk to you," he said, handing me the phone and looking like he was damned glad to get rid of it. I heard Bryan ordering a car out to our location. His voice was muffled, so I gathered he'd covered the mouthpiece with his hand, probably so I couldn't hear his final remark to the dispatcher, which alluded to my lack of mental stability. When he came back on the line he got right to the point. "What the hell is going on?"

He seemed to be asking that question a lot lately.

I gave him the short version, emphasizing that Tangerine was still in the canal and heading downstream the last time I saw her.

"I have a couple of deputies on the way. Do not move this time. Hear me? Stay put."

I started to protest that it was hardly my fault if people kept kidnapping me at gunpoint, but he cut the connection. I handed the phone back to the cyclist and thanked him for his help. He peddled off, and Larry and I sat down on the grass to wait.

"Larry, how did you know where I was?" I asked.

Larry, who was pawing through the grass in search of something, replied, "I didn't. I was lookin' for more stuff. I had good luck the last time I was around here, remember? I found a jacket, a cell phone, a billfold ..."

Yeah. And a dead body, I thought.

"... so I added this part of the canal to my regular route. I saw the white Mercedes and remembered I'd seen it here before when I found all those other things. I thought maybe I got lucky again. Then I saw you with that lady. She had a gun on you, and that looked unnatural. I was still mad at you for not giving me an allowance and for being such a cruddy mom, but kin is kin, so I helped you out."

"Thank you, Larry. I really appreciate what you did," I said, patting his arm.

"Hey! Look at this," he said, holding up a quarter. "I thought I saw somethin' shiny in the grass, and here it is. This place *is* lucky."

I heard sirens in the distance. Larry looked apprehensive. "I'm not going to jail, am I?"

"No, Larry. What you did is good. The officers may want to ask you some questions, but no more than that."

"Uh-uh," he said shaking his head ferociously. "I don't want to talk to any more police. I'm sorry, but I have to go." Larry was on his feet and disappearing down the path within seconds.

Two sheriff's cars came down the path from the other direction, raising a cloud of dust behind them. The lead car continued toward the bridge, presumably to find Tangerine. The second car pulled up next to me. Deputy Guilford, a.k.a.

Mr. Panty-man, jumped out of the driver's side. I glanced down and noticed that because of my dunk in the canal, my pajamas were translucent. Mr. Panty-man would be thrilled—no more fantasizing for him. This time he'd get to see the real deal.

Another deputy, one I didn't recognize, emerged from the passenger side, offered me a thick wool blanket, and introduced himself as Deputy Sheriff Haselton. I introduced myself in return and gratefully wrapped the blanket around me before Guilford could get much of a thrill.

"I thought the sheriff said someone else was with you," Guilford said.

"Nope," I answered. "You or he must be mistaken. There's just me." Pointing to the white Mercedes, I added, "That's the car belonging to the woman who tried to kill me."

Haselton went over to it and briefly inspected its exterior. He then inspected the interior of the vehicle to the extent he could without opening its doors. He did not touch the car at any point during his investigation. He wrote the license number in a small notebook and then called in the car's location and license number.

I remained seated on the ground while this was going on. I could feel ants investigating my crotch, but I was too cold and too tired to brush them off, much less relocate to a pest-free area.

I watched as Haselton placed crime scene tape around the vehicle. When he finished, he walked back to where I was sitting, and then both deputies helped me up and put me into the backseat of their car. Just as they were closing the door, Guilford's cell rang. His part of the ensuing conversation was brief and consisted mainly of "Yes, sir." After he signed off with a final "Yes, sir," he motioned for me to lower the car window, and then bent down so his face was even with mine. He needed a Tic Tac.

"Sheriff's down by the bridge. He says they found Tangerine, and she's still alive, but barely. They're taking her to the hospital. We're supposed to take you there too."

"No, please, I'm all right. If you could just drop me off at my condo, that would be terrific."

"Boss says to take you to the emergency room at county," he said, as he straightened up.

"May I use your phone?" I asked in my sweet, "nice" voice, the one I use to cajole Ralph and also on older judges with a reputation for paternalism. I think I may have even batted my eyelashes.

Guilford did not answer right away. I figured he was probably engaged in a worst-possible-outcome analysis. Apparently, he decided that lending me his phone was unlikely to result in dire consequences. He took it from his pocket but did not hand it to me. "Why don't you give me the number, and I'll dial it for you."

I smiled demurely and said, "That would be kind. Just hit redial."

He looked surprised but did as I requested and handed me the phone. Rather than step away to give me privacy, he stayed put and listened to my conversation with undisguised curiosity.

Bryan picked up after the first ring. "Guilford?" he asked. "What's she done now?"

"It is I, Kate. Deputy Guilford lent me his phone. He tells me his orders are to take me to the emergency room. I feel fine, and I want to go home."

"You may *feel* fine, but you're probably either still in shock or in the midst an adrenalin rush and wouldn't notice if you had a knife sticking out of your ear."

"Believe me, the adrenalin rush has passed, if in fact I ever had one. I think I used up all my adrenalin trying to escape from the fire. I can't seem to muster much up in the way of shock either. I'm getting a 'Whatever' message from my nerves.

Please. I promise I won't leave my condo, and there's no one left who would make me leave. Tom, Freddy, and Tangerine are all out of commission."

Bryan sighed. "Put Guilford back on the line. I'll tell him to take you back to your condo, but he and his partner are going to take turns standing guard outside your door until we get everything sorted out here."

I was about to protest the necessity of a guard, but something in Bryan's voice told me I shouldn't push the issue. I handed the phone back to Guilford.

There was a short discussion between Guilford and Bryan, then a whispered conversation between Guilford and Haselton. The deputies got into the car, with Guilford at the wheel and Haselton on the passenger side. As we pulled onto the blacktop at Fortieth Street, I saw Larry walking with his back to us toward Camelback Road. He was wearing a bulky nylon ski jacket. I didn't want to think about where he might have found it.

Guilford and Haselton escorted me to my apartment, and Guilford took the first watch. Haselton was kind enough to take Ralph outside for a walk before he left. Ralph is a wonder dog in all respects, except for his bladder capacity, which is equivalent to that of a Chihuahua.

I changed into dry pajamas, after which I fell asleep. Bryan came by at seven and dropped off a couple of bags of food from Paco's—one for Guilford and one for me—but did not stay. I ate one of the black bean burritos and fed the other to Ralph. Macy came over to walk him later, an act for which I was extremely grateful; the burrito had made Ralph incredibly gaseous.

I tried to read a novel I had been intending to get to for weeks, but I gave up because reading hurt my head (breathing hurt my head for that matter), and my vision was still blurry. After I brushed my teeth, washed my face, and brushed my hair—the last of which did absolutely no good, but was more a matter of habit than a serious attempt at rehabilitation—I got back in bed and fell asleep again.

When I woke, it was daylight, and I could hear the murmur of voices outside my room. I got out of bed slowly, mindful of Dr. Simon's advice, and found Bryan, Guilford, and Haselton in the living room, sitting together on the couch and eating bagels with cream cheese and drinking coffee. I cleared my throat.

"Good morning," they chorused. All of them looked tired, and I immediately felt guilty. They had probably been up all night working while I slept.

"Good morning. Got anymore of those?" I asked, pointing to the bagel in Bryan's hand.

"Of course," said Bryan. "Let me get you a chair. We were just discussing the status of the investigation." He placed his bagel on the coffee table and jumped up to get me a chair from the kitchen. Once again, I promised myself that as soon as I was well enough, I was going to go furniture shopping.

After I was seated, Bryan returned to the couch, rummaged around in a white bakery bag, and pulled out a bagel. "Sesame seed okay?" he asked. I nodded yes, and he slathered a thick layer of cream cheese on both slices, placed them on a napkin, and handed it over. In the meantime, Haselton filled a Styrofoam cup with coffee and placed it near me on the coffee table.

"Tangerine's still in ICU. The padding she was wearing took on a lot of water and weighed her down, so she'd been under a little over a minute before we could fish her out. The ER docs removed what was left of the latex mask she had on, and we bagged it as evidence. Also, some homeless guy fished a gray wig out of the canal this morning and dropped it off at our reception desk this morning. He wouldn't leave his name or address, saying something about needing his mom to be there before he could talk to us. He said she was with the CIA. I doubt that. The guy looked to be in his thirties or forties, so his mom's got to be up there in age."

Not necessarily, I thought.

"Deputy Haselton here was telling us about the results of the search of Tangerine's office when you walked in. Go ahead, Terry. Finish what you were saying."

Terry finished chewing and swallowed before speaking. "We got a warrant to search Tangerine's office and other properties. We started on her office first. When we got there, some of the employees were standing outside the building. No one had unlocked the door that morning. The first shift had already left, but the second shift was waiting to see if anyone showed up. No one had seen Tangerine for three or four days. Tom had been opening up for business in the morning and telling them that Tangerine was on vacation. Everyone thought that was odd since Tangerine had never taken a vacation and professed not to believe in them. But apparently, Tangerine is a tough taskmaster, so no one was going to complain if she was gone for a couple days.

"I got their names and addresses and sent all of them home, except for a lady named Marge Pierson, who identified herself as Tangerine's secretary.

"Tuwanda had given us her key card, so we had no trouble getting in. We removed all the computers and took them downtown to be analyzed by the tech guys. The janitorial company had been there recently, according to Marge, but we were still able to pull some blood specimens off the floor near the toilet. It's the same type as Goldman's, but we have to wait on a full analysis to confirm the match. We found a gun in Tangerine's desk drawer that's the same caliber as the one used to kill Goldman, but, once again, we need Ballistics to do their thing before we can conclude anything about whether it's the same gun that was used to murder Goldman. We also found a message similar to the 'tag' message found written on Goldman. We didn't find anything else of interest. Tangerine's secretary said Tangerine kept a day planner, but we couldn't find it anywhere."

That's because it's still under the passenger seat of Tuwanda's car, where I left it the night I took it from Tangerine's office. I decided not to mention it yet. I would wait until Bryan and I were alone. Besides, the information we got from the appointment book added nothing new to that which I had already given Bryan.

Guilford piped in at that point. "We ran a records check and located all the properties owned or leased by Tangerine, Pole Polishers, or one of its subsidiaries, including the old church now being operated as a men's house of prostitution."

"Aren't *all* houses of prostitution for men?" asked Bryan.

A slow blush crept up Guilford's neck and face. "It's a guy-on-guy place, so to speak."

Bryan looked at me with an unreadable expression. "Did you know about this, Kate?"

I opened my mouth to speak, but he filled in the blank himself. "Attorney-client privilege, right?"

I nodded yes.

"Tangerine's real name is Katherine Norwood. We located her mother. Her name is Janice Norwood. Janice lives in a small town about forty miles northwest of Minneapolis and hasn't spoken to her daughter in years," continued Guilford. "Mrs. Norwood describes herself as a 'God-fearing Christian woman.' She and her daughter had a falling out when Tangerine started a fundraising club at the local Lutheran church's youth group and called it 'The Coming.' It turned out to be an early version of Pole Polishers. The Coming raised enough money to build a new youth annex before the local constabulary caught on to nature of the club's activities. Within a year, the town's mayor, the Lutheran minister, and most of the church elders had resigned, and Tangerine had enough money to go out on her own. Blackmail was suspected but never proven because the alleged victims refused to cooperate with the police.

"It seems Tangerine traveled around over the next few years and landed in Phoenix in the early eighties. Except for a minor setback when Rantwist was in office, her business has been growing ever since."

"If her business is so successful, why did she feel it was necessary to branch out into blackmail?" I asked.

"Could be simple greed," said Bryan.

"Or it could be the lousy real estate market," offered Guilford. "Tangerine owns a lot of properties in Phoenix, most of which are mortgaged. With the plunge in values over the last two years, her lenders are close to pulling the plug, and it's not as if she can pledge her businesses' receivables to the bank as additional security."

"Oh, I forgot to mention," added Bryan. "We think we solved another minor mystery: remember you told us you heard Margaret call from her bedroom when you were talking with Tangerine at the Glendale house?"

I nodded. That little detail had been bothering me.

"We found a remote control tape recorder in the desk of the master bedroom," he continued. "A bunch of phrases were recorded on it in Margaret's voice, including the one you heard. All Tangerine had to do was hit the right number on the remote, and the tape recorder would play the appropriate phrase. She probably used it when Freddy and Goldman were around, or whenever else she needed someone to buy into her deception—like you.

"In any event, everything we've found out so far supports what Tangerine told Kate about her blackmail scheme. We'll just have to wait for the evidence guys and the lab to fill in the blanks."

Terry, Guilford, and I nodded in agreement. At least, Guilford and I did. I think Terry was just nodding off. He had relieved Guilford sometime during the night and was probably exhausted.

Terry did that involuntary body jerk thing people do when they start to fall asleep in a place they shouldn't.

"I need a nap," he said. "I'd better head out before I fall asleep on your couch."

"And I'd better get back to guard duty," said Guilford. He said it like it was the last thing in the world he wanted to do.

"No need, Percy. I'll take this shift," said Bryan.

Percy? Guilford's first name is Percy?

Guilford must have read my mind. "My mother was English," he explained defensively.

Bryan shooed his colleagues out of the apartment while I cleared up the remains of our breakfast. I toyed with the idea of trying to get in to see Michele for a hair color correction, but Bryan convinced me it could wait, that there were better things to do. We spent the day reading the paper, watching television, and doing what Bryan considered, and I agreed, were "better things." Bryan had to go back on duty at seven, so Guilford showed up to take night guard duty. Beth, M.J., and Sam called and offered to come over and spend time with me to break the boredom of recovery. I thanked them, but told them please not to bother, in that all I needed was rest. I didn't mention that Bryan had been there all day, so I wasn't suffering from a dearth of socializing.

The next morning, I felt almost back to normal. So much so that I decided to go to church services. I'd slept too late for the nine o'clock service, but I could easily make the one at eleven o'clock.

I found Percy still sitting outside my door when I left. Apparently, Haselton had been held up on another case, so Guilford was working overtime. I told him where I was going, and since he was still on guard duty, he trailed along with me.

No one in church mentioned my pink hair because that's the way Presbyterians are. We of the "frozen chosen" are incredibly polite and nonintrusive. I felt bad about clashing with all the festive red sweaters and jackets, though. Pink is more of an Easter color.

Only two weeks remained until Christmas, and today was the annual Christmas pageant performed by the Sunday school preschool and elementary school children. This was one of my favorite services. The children were adorable, and invariably screwed up, which made them even more adorable. This year's performance turned out to be a pip.

First to come down the aisle were Mary and Joseph, two nine-year-olds. I recognized them from the fourth grade Sunday school class, which, about a month before, during a momentary fit of insanity, I'd agreed to teach when the regular teacher went home with the flu (or so she said). Joseph was wearing a large terry robe, probably provided by one of the dads, and Mary was draped in a long blue shift that looked like it was made out of, well, drapes. The two seemed to have unresolved issues, maybe from the earlier service, because each surreptitiously shoved the other several times during their trip down the aisle. Their smiles were tight, and distrustful side-glances abounded. The towel-wrapped doll Mary carried was obviously intended to represent our Lord Jesus Christ. As a result of the shoving, the towel cum blanket slipped and dragged on the floor behind them, and our Lord was revealed to be wearing a lacy pink dress. Mary and Joseph made it to the stage, hit their marks, and stood eying each other warily.

The three wise men came down next, wisely giving Mary and Joseph a wide berth on the stage.

Next came the Star of Bethlehem, a large, lopsided asterisk made of yellow construction paper. The star was glued to the end of a yardstick that was held aloft by a serious six-year-old. Twenty or so angels, clouds and lesser stars wandered amiably behind the star, stopping every so often to wave to family and friends in the audience. The angels wore sheets with construction paper wings pinned on the back. The wings had been colored and covered with sparkle. The élan with which the children must have applied the sparkle was evident from the huge amount of the stuff in their hair. The clouds were represented by poster paper cutouts covered by glued on cotton balls. Some of the children had been less diligent than others, and their clouds were mangy-looking affairs with randomly placed cotton balls. One of the children had bagged the cotton balls completely and drawn a picture of Batman.

Midway down the aisle, the Star of Bethlehem came crashing down when the star bearer tripped over what I suspected was the foot of one of his classmates sitting in the audience. A pileup came next as clouds, angels, and stars fell on top of each other with much wailing and gnashing of teeth. Parents and Sunday school teachers leaped into the fray to upright fallen celestial bodies and comfort hysterical nimbi. A level of order was reestablished, and the children proceeded to the front, where, due to the confusion, no one stood where he or she was supposed to, but grouped around Mary and Joseph according to faction. Those who blamed the star bearer stood in one huddle, those who blamed the tripper stood in another, and yet another consisted of a few emotional wrecks too distraught to commit. Meanwhile, the tension between Mary and Joseph had grown, and they were now openly scowling at each other.

The animals came next, played by the preschoolers, the result of typecasting, no doubt. No attempt was made at historical accuracy; rather, the children were simply told to dress as their favorite animal. So while donkeys, sheep, and possibly camels had been in attendance at the original nativity, we had lions, bears, bunnies, dogs, cats, elephants—you name it.

Preschoolers are notoriously distractible and incapable of holding more than one thought in their heads at a time, if that, so the group had been drilled repeatedly to walk to the number they were assigned, which was taped to the floor of the stage. In other words, all they had to do was hit their mark. Period. Unfortunately, the group already on stage was in disarray due to the falling star incident, so when the little tykes got to the front they variously broke into tears, shoved, or told on the trespassers as they attempted to claim their territory. Mary finally snapped and took a swing at Joseph with the baby Jesus and all hell broke loose as parents and teachers again intervened to rescue offspring and students.

The rest of the service was fairly mundane. Guilford, who had enjoyed the Christmas pageant immensely and even recorded part of it on his cell phone, fell asleep during the sermon. I felt sorry for him so I didn't wake him up until it was time for the benediction and the final hymn.

Haselton was waiting when we got back to my apartment, so Guilford dropped me off and headed home. I spent the rest of the day reading the paper and watching television. Bryan came by at seven again with dinner. He dropped off the food and then went into the hall to talk to Haselton. When he came back in he said, "I told Haselton not to show up tomorrow. I dismissed both him and Guilford from guard duty. I think we have enough information to safely conclude that we've got our man—or woman, rather. You should be okay."

"Should?"

"You have a tendency to get into unusual situations. We can't protect you from yourself, or your karma, or whatever it is you've got going on."

I couldn't argue. "How is Tangerine?" I asked.

"Tangerine is out of ICU, but she's still pretty weak. To be on the safe side, we've got guards posted outside her room and on the hospital grounds twenty-four seven. She says she won't answer any questions without her counsel present. With her history, I wish her luck finding someone willing to represent her."

I was relieved to hear Tangerine was under heavy guard. I knew that even with her physical condition compromised, she would avail herself of any opportunity to slip away before she was transferred to a jail facility. She had a bad habit of disappearing and an even worse habit of holding a grudge, against lawyers in particular.

"I tried to call Tuwanda at the hospital, but the floor nurse said she wasn't taking calls. What gives?" I asked Bryan.

"She told the nurse she didn't want to be bothered by clients, and when the switchboard operator refused to screen her calls, she told them to just take messages. Tuwanda views her hospital stay as a vacation. The hospital staff views it as a test.

"Her doctor removed the shunt and anticipates she can go home tomorrow. Now that she has a private room, though, I don't think she's in any hurry to leave."

I raised an eyebrow. Whatever else could be said of her, Tangerine must have a dynamite insurance plan in place for her employees.

"Don't be impressed," said Bryan. "She has a private room not by design but by default. The staff gave up trying to place another patient in bed one."

"What did she do?"

"The woman transferred into the room after you left had just had her gallbladder removed. Tuwanda told her about an article she read on how gallbladders were real popular snack-food in Asia, and then she put forth the theory that hospitals harvested gallbladders not for valid medical reasons, but so they could sell them overseas. By the time Tuwanda was through with her, the woman insisted the doctors either put her gallbladder back in or pay her top dollar for it."

"I think maybe Tuwanda was thinking of the harvesting and sale of bear gallbladders. According to traditional Chinese medicine, bile from bear gallbladders has curative properties," I offered in an attempt to defend Tuwanda's rationale.

"Yeah, well, she didn't mention the bear part to her roomie. Speaking of Chinese," Bryan held up a plastic grocery bag. "Chinese food. We need plates."

All Chinese food smells more or less the same, but I guessed it was our usual assortment of egg rolls, sweet and sour pork, Mongolian beef, and fried tofu. Whatever it was, my mouth was watering.

He followed me into the kitchen and removed white cardboard containers of food and cellophane packages of chopsticks, soy sauce, and hot mustard from the bag and placed them on the table while I got plates, napkins, serving spoons and drinks: two bottles of water, a beer for Bryan, and a Chardonnay for me. We sat down and dumped rice on our plates before passing cartons back and forth and spooning out food until we each had a mini-Matterhorn in front of us.

"What have you found out that convinces you I no longer need to be under house arrest?" I asked through a mouthful of egg roll.

Unlike me, Bryan had the manners to wait until he swallowed his food before answering.

"Things have moved quickly. Between Webber's men and mine, we've managed to cover a lot of ground. The guys in the labs put in some overtime this weekend too. They confirmed that the bullet in Goldman came from the gun we found in Tangerine's office. They also matched the blood in her bathroom to Goldman's ... and to blood found in the trunk of the Mercedes she was driving."

Bryan shoved a mound of Mongolian beef into his mouth. I took advantage of the temporary lull to ask more questions.

"What about Freddy and Tom's deaths?"

"We can't tie Tangerine to their murders yet. But give it time. The investigation isn't over."

"So Tom was murdered too?"

"Yep. The arson team found three empty gas cans in what was left of the kitchen. The cans plus the ignition pattern makes it clear that the fire was started intentionally. You and Tuwanda can place Margaret/Tangerine at the scene, so it's a simple matter of connecting the dots. Webber is in charge of the police investigations of all the murders."

We chewed for a while in silence.

"How does the picture found on Goldman fit into all of this?" I asked.

"You mean the photo of Webber and Chris?"

"Christopher," I corrected automatically.

"Chris*topher*. We found Tangerine's laptop in her car. The computer techs from the police department located a deleted folder of photos, including the one of Christopher and Webber. She'd apparently taken a publicity head shot of Webber she probably found in the newspaper and pasted it on a picture of Christopher taken at the opening of As You Like It. Webber thinks Tangerine planted it to both throw off the murder investigation and get back at him. About a month ago, Webber started to suspect that Tangerine was expanding her business and had been watching her office building to see who was going in and out. She wasn't happy with his surveillance activities and raised a racket with his supervisor. I think I already told you that Tangerine has cooperated in police investigations in the past, so she has—or rather had—some pull in the police department." Bryan must have seen something in my face, because he added, "I know you're not particularly fond of Webber. He's a bit of a jerk, but he is a good cop."

I pushed a grain of rice around on my plate with a chopstick. My next question was difficult to ask. I took a deep breath and plunged in. "Do you think Tuwanda knew anything about Tangerine's blackmail scheme?"

"We haven't told Tuwanda about Tangerine's attack on you and her connection with the murders of Goldman, Tom, and Freddy. The police want to wait until she is out of the hospital before they talk to her. We haven't found anything to tie her into Tangerine's activities, though. Tuwanda is one of Tangerine's top employees and has been with her the longest. But the office staff said Tangerine maintains a certain distance from all her employees, Tuwanda included, and Tuwanda was never invited into meetings among Tangerine and Goldman , and her business associates." Bryan stared at me thoughtfully for a while. "You like her, don't you?"

I nodded. "Tuwanda is, um, different. She's a good person, though, and she's very loyal to Tangerine. It's going to kill her to hear the truth about her boss. I want to be there when they tell her."

"I'll talk to Webber. There shouldn't be a problem. You are, after all, her lawyer, aren't you?"

"As well as the lawyer for just about everyone else involved in this mess."

"Except Tangerine. She practically foams at the mouth whenever your name is mentioned. She wants to sue you for malpractice"

"*Malpractice?* I came close to being killed because I was trying to protect her and her stupid files, when she was using me the whole time. Also, I'm not sure the case has ever come up, but I bet attempted murder is a defense to a malpractice claim." I was sputtering by this time.

"By the way," said Bryan, "do you know anyone by the name of Chad Fields?"

Bryan's question took me by surprise. I'd forgotten all about the party-crashing episode the other night.

I nodded. "He's a college kid in Tempe. How do you know about Chad?"

"Our guys did a search of all properties Tangerine or one of her subsidiaries holds an interest in. One of the deputies, Deputy Thomas, told me they went to the Tempe house yesterday afternoon. No one answered the door, so they tried the handle and it was open. Thomas described the inside of the house as 'post-apocalyptic.' They found Chad sleeping under the coffee table. As soon as they woke him up, he protested his innocence to everything, even though they hadn't accused him of anything, and went on to name names and corresponding violations, including minor in possession, illegal use of regulated substances, use of illegal substances, and pissing on private property. Then he whipped your card out of his pocket and told the deputies you represent him."

I told Bryan how Tuwanda and I had gone to the Tempe house to look for Tangerine before we went to the orchard house on Friday night, and how I had given my business card to Chad and asked that he call me if Tangerine showed up later. "I thought he might be related to Tom Fields," I said after I finished.

"Not that we could find," said Bryan. "Their last names are a coincidence."

"Are you going to press any charges against Chad?"

Bryan snorted. "Nah. I figure he has enough problems. Thomas told me he had an impressive shiner. When he asked Chad how he got it, he said some blond chick decked him for no reason. He'd been telling her about his theory of sexual selection, which according to him is complex and requires careful listening to comprehend, when she punched him."

"Theory of sexual selection?"

"Thomas said Chad started to go into it, and he had to stop him because he was afraid he would hit him too. Apparently, the theory is offensive and intensely Chad-centered."

I put my chopsticks down, comfortably sated. The food and wine had made me sleepy. Bryan suggested I watch some television while he cleaned up. I fell asleep watching a *CSI* rerun before he was through.

When I woke up, I was in my bed. Bryan was already gone, but he'd left a note on the pillow: *I walked Ralph; coffee is in the kitchen; you snore. Love, Bryan.*

"I do not snore," I muttered to myself. I looked over at Ralph, who had been asleep on the floor but lifted his head when he heard my voice. "*You* snore," I accused.

Ralph wagged his tail at me as if to say, "Yes, I do. Isn't that cool?"

I had a slight attack of the dizzies when I got out of bed, but I figured it was nothing I couldn't manage. I'd been lying around long enough. It was time to get back to work, not that there was a lot to do now that my biggest client had fired me. Oh well. There was always Chad. I had great hopes for him as a future source of business.

It was amazing how quickly things seemed to get back to normal. By the end of the week my hair was, though not its previous blond, a presentable brunette. I'd been with Webber and Bryan when they told Tuwanda about Tangerine, and at her request, served as her counsel during the following question-and-answer period. She appeared genuinely shocked to hear what Tangerine had been up to, and her answers to Bryan and Webber's questions made it obvious that she had no idea what was going on. I stayed to talk with her after Webber and Bryan left, and she confided her sense of betrayal and uncertainty about her future. Tangerine and the company were the only family she'd had after her mother died.

Christmas came and went. I had a party at my condo New Year's Eve and bought two armchairs for the living room in honor of the occasion. (I was having a hard time letting go of the couch, even though it looked particularly alarming with all the duct tape. It had become a sentimental favorite with Bryan and me). I invited my friend Joyce and her husband; M.J. and her boyfriend, Mitchie; Sam; Beth; Bryan; Macy; Cal, Larry; and Tuwanda. Bryan raised an eyebrow when Larry arrived, and I explained only that Larry was a client and a friend. I left out the part about him saving my life, because Larry still didn't want anything to do with the police investigation of Tangerine. Thankfully, Tangerine didn't remember much about her dunk in the canal.

We toasted to the New Year together, with Larry standing outside on my small balcony and toasting with an acai berry smoothie instead of Champagne since he'd sworn off all empty calories, Ding Dongs in particular, and was back on a health food kick. At my invitation, Tuwanda had brought her dog, Walter, to keep Ralph company, and despite their size difference, the two seemed to get along quite well. After completing the butt-sniffing formalities, Ralph showed Walter his chew toys and food bowl, and the two of them flopped down and took turns chewing and eating, stopping every so often to enjoy belly rubs and pats on the head bestowed upon them by the human guests.

A week after New Year's Eve, Tuwanda came to my office and announced that she'd taken over management of Pole Polishers, and she would continue to retain our firm to represent the company and its employees. As You Like It was being purchased by Christopher, with the financial backing of an undisclosed investor. I thought this was just as well because Christopher had no future as a hair stylist.

Tangerine went to trial in March for the murders of Goldman, Tom, and Freddy. Because no private attorney would take her case, she was represented by a nervous young public defender who flinched every time she leaned over the defense table to speak with him. The judge ordered the guard to escort Tangerine out of the courtroom during my testimony because she would not stop throwing books, papers, and pens at me. Even after her attorney moved all portable objects outside her reach, she hocked a couple of loogies at me, one of which sliced to the right and hit the judge on the forehead. Tuwanda held up well during her testimony, but the hurt and sense of betrayal she felt were evident from her answers. I noticed Tangerine at least had the decency to look ashamed.

The jurors convicted tangerine in less time than it took to read the charges. She avoided the death penalty, but she was sentenced to three consecutive life sentences.

Stu still hadn't completed the work on my office building. I still needed to find more clients.